Eden's D

By

Terry Pellman

Also By Terry Pellman

Looking Toward Eden
Weston Road
Averton
When I Was Young

Progression of Chapters

Day one of the CSA
Day two of the CSA
Day three of the CSA
Day four of the CSA
Day five of the CSA
Day six of the CSA
Day seven of the CSA
Day eight of the CSA
Day nine of the CSA
Day ten of the CSA
Day eleven of the CSA
Day twelve of the CSA
Day thirteen of the CSA
Day two hundred eleven of the CSA – Eden's Dawn
Day three hundred of the CSA
Remembrance in Eden – November 30, 2023

Day one of the CSA

"This is Cynthia Warren, in Omaha, Nebraska, and we continue our coverage here on NewsNet, of the first full day of the existence of the Constitutional States of America. I am standing just outside the room where the fledgling government of the CSA is undertaking the monumental task of establishing a new nation of sixty-seven million people.

"As you may remember, this historic event is taking place here in Omaha at the Army National Guard Armory for security reasons, a factor that must be frustrating to the leaders of this movement. A large building in downtown Omaha has been designated to be the operational headquarters, the capital if you will, of the CSA. In light of the violent demonstrations that took place yesterday, it was decided to temporarily conduct business here. It is hoped that in a few days the new government will move to the easily protected and brand new Great Plains Convention Center on Interstate Highway 680 on the south side of the city. It is expected that operations will continue there until the permanent headquarters is readied, a project that is expected to take no more than two months.

"Last night, in downtown Omaha, former Nebraska Senator Bryce Hamilton was chosen to serve as Interim President of the CSA. Although it is now only 8:45 AM, the delegates, serving as an inaugural legislature, chose Oklahoma Senator Franklin Chiles to serve as the interim Vice President. It is expected that elections will be held late next summer.

"While no other official appointments have been made by President Hamilton, something very unusual took place at 7:00 A.M. this morning. At a meeting at which myself and six other representatives of the media were allowed to be in attendance, President Hamilton and a group of his advisers met in an open session to discuss various candidates for important positions in the new government. A video of the entire meeting is now available to you on the NewsNet website.

"Once again, in open session, Present Hamilton decided to ask Texas Attorney General James Carlisle to assume the same post for the new nation. Advisor Tom Edelstein, an economist who became familiar to our viewers over the past several days, is being asked to be the new Secretary of the Treasury. Former Congressman Patrick Bridger, who along with Bryce Hamilton orchestrated much of what has happened during the past two weeks, will be the new Secretary of Commerce. However, his duties will be primarily devoted to promoting business ventures.

"Although the status of military matters seems to be in a state of flux, Hamilton has asked General Monte Crief, Commander of the Texas National Guard, to serve as Secretary of Defense, and to serve as the overall commander of CSA military forces.

"There's another interesting development in terms of appointments, and illustrates just how much preparation work was being done in advance, either under the radar of the media, or perhaps all this was just ignored... but in any case, a list of probable appointees to the Supreme Court of the CSA was made available just a moment before I went on the air, and I was able to get a little more information about these individuals.

"For the position of Chief Justice, President Hamilton has tabbed Emory Langley, currently a justice on the Tennessee Supreme Court. He will be joined by James Wingfield, a professor of law at the University of Idaho.

"Also on the court will be Thomas Musgrove, a veteran constitutional attorney from Charleston West Virginia, and Loretta Alvarez, a member of the law faculty of the University of Texas. Another Texan on the court will be Wilson Harrington, a member of the Texas Supreme Court.

"There is one member of the new court from Kansas. That is Avery Hermann, a distinguished Appellate Court Judge from Wichita, Kansas. He will serve alongside Nadine Lawrence of North Dakota, noted to be an expert in the field of contract law.

"The last two appointments are of individuals who are serving as state Supreme Court justices, Lawrence Richmond of Idaho and Stephen Richter of Nebraska.

"The appointments to the CSA Supreme Court will also be notable for the demographic makeup of the justices. Chief Justice – designee Langley from Tennessee is black, as is Justice Richter from Nebraska. Justice Hermann is of the Hebrew faith, and, of course Nadine Lawrence will join Loretta Alvarez in the female contingent on the court, with Justice Alvarez also being Hispanic.

"One thing that President Hamilton emphasized when he released these names, was that all are known for being what are called strict constructionists on the bench, meaning that they will take a more literal interpretation of the Constitution into the courtroom. President Hamilton said that a committee within the Council for a Free America had spent several months screening the judicial philosophies, not necessarily the rulings, of various judges for inclusion on a list of recommendations for appointment. He also pointed out that…".

Suddenly the viewers were seeing an attractive dark-haired woman sitting at a desk. "This is NewsNet correspondent Marsha Bentley in Washington, and we are interrupting this morning's broadcast of American Morning to bring you a special report. We now go to Gwen Munro on the scene in St. Louis. Gwen…?"

The camera was focused on a petite blonde woman in a black overcoat standing next to a yellow police tape barrier. "Cynthia… St. Louis is burning. Right after the Missouri state legislature in Jefferson City voted in a late-night session to secede from the United States of America and ask for membership in the Constitutional States of America, much of the city of St. Louis descended into chaos.

"Legally, as of this moment Missouri is still not a member of the CSA, but the secession was effective at midnight. Throughout the night, rioters and looters have been roaming the streets battling police, and now the city is swarming with National Guard troops, and the entire city has been placed under martial law. At the last count we received from law enforcement officials, more than fifty-two buildings were reported to be on fire.

"You may recall that there have already been incidents in which some St. Louis residents have been moving into East St. Louis, across the river in Illinois out of concern for a possible secession by the state. Unfortunately, there have been isolated incidents reported of signs appearing on the Illinois side of a racially – charged nature. A white supremacist group that is said to be operating in southern Illinois has claimed responsibility.

"There are anecdotal reports filtering out of East St. Louis, that nearly all rental housing is now full, and there have been some unconfirmed but frightening reports of car loads of white supremacist gang members following and attempting to intimidate black people with Missouri license plates driving through East St. Louis. There is also a credible report that an off – duty East St. Louis police officer was witness to a car load of young white men shooting at several young black men who appeared to be wearing gang paraphernalia. Preliminary reports were that three of the alleged gang members were wounded, one critically.

"I have also been told that the East St. Louis Police Department is in possession of a video captured with a cellular phone that shows several white men wearing khaki shirts and pants attempting to set up a roadblock in the middle of the night at an intersection that serves as an unofficial border between low income black and white neighborhoods. There are reports that an altercation broke out around 3:30 AM, resulting in some minor injuries and property damage, but no exchanges of gunfire. This is Gwen Munro, reporting from St. Louis for NewsNet."

"This is Marsha Bentley, back at our Washington NewsNet studio, and we are going to stay right here to discuss this morning's developments in St. Louis. And I'm being joined by Mike Silver, host of News In Depth on NewsNet, and Joshua Simmons, a columnist for the Potomac Review and a NewsNet contributor.

"Mike, let me start off with you… some were predicting that this entire secessionist movement was tinged with racial overtones. Do the developments in St. Louis bear this out?"

"To a certain degree, considering the rhetoric in our nation over the past several years, the incidents related to race are going to quickly go to the front of the line in terms of media coverage, and rightly so. To think that a racist organization would attempt to block people from moving away from a political environment they do not want to live in, is abhorrent. I want to point out that, it appears that the members of this racist group reside within the United States of America, and I will assume that the United States Department of Justice will make it a priority to come down hard on these individuals, as they should."

"And Joshua, since the CSA is in its first day of existence, what resources can they summon to come to the aid of those whose freedom of movement is being denied by intimidation and threats of violence?"

"This entire situation is drenched in illogic. We have members of minority groups wanting to leave a place where they fear they're not welcome, because so many people have been telling them they're not going to be wanted, running into violent, racist fools who absolutely and without question don't want them. And the only people they can turn to for protection, are the people they had been told they needed to fear. I don't know who's going to figure this one out."

Marsha Bentley turned once again to Mike Silver "Let me ask you this…". Marsha suddenly pressed her ear piece closer and looked down as she listened. She shook her head, and then looked up. "This is not going to be a slow news day. We are now going to switch over to Simone Dickerson at the NewsNet Business Network desk. Simone…".

The scene was now one of a slender blonde woman standing in front of several television monitors showing business correspondents from around the globe. "We are sometime away from the opening of the New York Stock Exchange, but as of this moment the Dow Futures are down nearly 3400 points on rumors coming out of the Hong Kong Exchange in the middle of the night. Global bond investors are speculating that the U.S. bond market is facing an immediate crisis in the aftermath of the secession, and that stocks worldwide are going to be badly destabilized in the process.

"The trigger in the bond crisis appears to be that the secession of so many of the more fiscally responsible states decimated the confidence of foreign investors holding U.S. corporate and Treasury bonds, or any others backed by the federal government.

"When a corporation issues a bond, it is to borrow money for things such as a plant expansion, a new facility or to buy new technology or equipment. Should a company go bankrupt, the bondholders are at the top of the line in being reimbursed for the loan they made to the company by buying the bond. In the case of a government bond, the collateral, so to speak, is a full faith and credit of the treasury of that government. Because of our debt in comparison to our revenues, that full faith and credit has for some time been wobbly. The secession was the proverbial straw breaking the camel's back.

"This has been especially destabilizing to China, the biggest holder of our government – backed debt obligations. It also brings a specter of territorial tensions between China and the United States and its allies. '

"China has for some time coveted some of the energy – rich areas of the Pacific off the coast of Southeast Asia. However, the financial entanglement with the United States has always served as a tempering factor in regard to any saber rattling by China over such resources. There is a concern that, should China come to believe that their bond investments in the United States are of dubious value, they may decide to cut their losses and go for the underwater energy fields in the South China Sea as a way for making up for lost revenue. If China views the United States as having its defenses in disarray due to the secession, they could decide to move on those energy regions during a period of national distraction.

"If all this were not enough, domestic bond investors are likely to take a hit from an announcement planned for later today by several major cities in the United States that they will be defaulting on their own debt interest payments. This could deliver a crushing, if not fatal blow to the municipal bond market. And considering the hunger for tax revenue at all levels, it is doubtful that any investment instruments that are tax-advantaged will be resurrected. This is Simone Dickerson for NewsNet Business... Marsha, back to you."

Marsha turned toward Mike Silver: "So if cities are defaulting on their municipal bond interest payments, who is going to bail them out?"

The veteran correspondent shook his head: "Consider this: the states cannot bail them out. Out of seven major cities expected to be involved in the default announcement today, all are located in three states that have hearings scheduled for this week on proposals to severely scale back welfare programs.

"States have to put up a percentage of the cost of welfare benefits, even the Medicaid Program. But just for the moment, we are looking at states not having the revenue to pay their matching portions of the monthly welfare benefits. That means that either the amount of the monthly benefits will have to be reduced, or the federal government would have to step in with more money to keep the monthly welfare payments at the same level.

"Now if the federal government has no means to do so, there is no alternative but for the states to reduce those benefits each month. Now mix that in with cities where the welfare recipients are concentrated not having enough revenue because no one will now buy the bonds they issue, coupled with a reduction in revenue sharing from the state... I think you see where I'm going with this."

Marsha turned to Joshua Simmons: "But, Joshua, do the states have the authority to take the steps that Mike just outlined?"

"With all due respect to my friend Mike, I see a different scenario playing out. In the aftermath of the secession, the Democrats now have sweeping majorities in the House and Senate, in addition to holding the Presidency. They will have no choice but to enact very dramatic tax increases on the very wealthy, and on an emergency basis."

Mike Silver raised his hands as if he were pleading. "Joshua... I ask you this... If that happens, do you doubt that even the most liberal, wealthy business owners will move to the CSA? If the Democrats do as you suggest, the business owners remaining in the United States are not going to have to scramble over a wall to move to Texas or Idaho.

"I always felt that people on both sides of this tragic divide had stars in their eyes. I think that first up it will be the liberals reaping major disappointment the first time they try to pass more taxes while under the illusion that the job creators remaining in the United States will stand and applaud their efforts. If they drive out more businesses than have already announced their move to CSA states, the revenue to the states and cities shrinks even more, and we all get to watch the death spiral."

Joshua Simmons shook his head theatrically. "I predict that most businesses are going to stay right where they are. Not everyone wants to move to a place where people are probably going to be walking around with six – guns in holsters while grocery shopping, and oil rigs replace school playgrounds."

Marsha Bentley smiled at the camera: "And that will be the last word in this segment, and when we return, we will take a look at some of the potential candidates looming out there for the first Presidential election in the Constitutional States of America."

President of the United States Calista Meyers glared at Elaine Ford, the junior Senator from Pennsylvania. She slowly turned her gaze to the other woman at the table: "And Senator Howard... I trust you did not know about this in advance?" Senator Marie Howard took off her glasses and rubbed her face, and she shook her head back and forth, her silver hair falling into her eyes.

"I was not the President for twenty-four hours, and I was dealing with a major mouth in my own party... proposing we do away with the Constitution of the United States of America. How grand is that?"

Senator Ford sat upright and rigid. "It is not my intention to make your accidental Presidency more difficult. I just said what a lot of us have been thinking for some time."

The President turned to the Senate President: "Senator Howard... I take you at your word that you did not have advance warning of this little speech. But I want your thoughts... I want to hear your opinion from your own mouth, not through a report on the evening news."

"Madam President... Elaine is just putting it out there. Personally, I would have preferred to have this controversy surface after President Malcolm's funeral, but her point is well taken. We are in a state of transition, and we all know that nothing will ever be the same again. So, perhaps it is indeed time that we nailed down our legacy... we are the party of the future. We can draw a stark contrast with that pathetic remaining cadre of milquetoasts and scattered right – wing zealots across the aisle.

"Even taking into account that there are some solidly conservative southern states still in the union, and Ohio, Indiana and Wisconsin will still send some sycophants to Washington, this place is ours. They are so outnumbered now, they're going to feel like odd specimens in a zoo. Then you take away the Constitution and replace it with the United States Code with a revised role for the Supreme Court, it is all over for them. Every Democratic primary in most states will determine the next Senator... the next Member of Congress."

President Meyers looked at the ceiling and rolled her eyes. "So Mr. Pryor... as Attorney General, what do you foresee happening with this?"

The seasoned attorney felt as if he had aged ten years in the course of two days. "If I had been asked this question several weeks ago, I would have gone off on my predictable speech about how a majority of the state legislatures have to vote to make even a minor change in the Constitution, let alone dissolve it. I can't imagine the

14

few remaining Southern states or Ohio and Indiana going along with this in any kind of a quiet fashion.

"I see no possibility of Ohio seceding, although it may turn into a seething cauldron. However, I would expect to lose at least two more Southern states and Indiana over this. And although the matter of the Upper Peninsula is a matter for the State of Michigan to settle, a move like this would likely bring that issue to a head."

The President rose and began to pace the floor. "But Elaine... that impromptu speech of yours may have just needlessly stiffened the opposition. Your words fit into every fantasy of every conservative talk show host in America. You propose to do away with the Constitution... all that they hear is a way of getting rid of the Second Amendment."

The President walked to the side of her desk and sat down. "Elaine... I want to know something. Do you care that you may have already driven other states to want to secede?"

No, Madam President... considering which states are the most likely to leave, I don't care about that at all."

"This is Cynthia Warren for NewsNet, here at the Army National Guard Armory in Omaha, Nebraska, the capital of the Constitutional States of America. I would like to give you a recap of some of the business that has been conducted by the fledgling government here this morning.

"In response to the crisis taking place in Missouri overnight and this morning, the delegates serving as the temporary legislature of the CSA, voted unanimously to admit that state, effective immediately. So now, Missouri is no longer part of the United States of America. President Hamilton issued a statement a few minutes ago to the effect that he is expecting other member states of the CSA to provide whatever support necessary to assist Missouri in keeping order and protecting its citizens.

"President Hamilton also called upon President Meyers to ensure that CSA citizens wishing to leave and move to another state within the United States of America, will be protected. A member of

President Meyers' staff who insisted on speaking off the record, was furious at the implication by Hamilton that minorities moving from CSA states to the United States, had to be protected from acts of racial bigotry. Another Meyers aide, also speaking off the record, brushed the Hamilton comment aside as nothing more than a cynical attempt to strike back at those who had correctly and justifiably predicted that the CSA will not provide an environment of equality to minorities and women.

"President Hamilton also heard a report from Tom Edelstein, his pick to serve as the CSA Secretary of the Treasury. Edelstein reported that there have been no reported glitches in the handling of Social Security benefits, although the true test will come at the first mass benefit distribution. Edelstein also reported that there have not been any reports of businesses in the CSA refusing to accept United States currency. Edelstein is in charge of the effort to establish a separate currency for the new nation. He is also in charge of coordinating the process of withheld income taxes being forwarded to a large Omaha bank under contract with the CSA. It is expected that one of the first orders of business of the new Congress of the CSA will be to establish new income tax rates, rates that are expected to be considerably lower than were being paid to the Treasury of the United States.

"One of the task forces of the Council for a Free America prepared a suggested simple tax code to be put into place after secession. Edelstein said that if the new Congress accepts that program, the new lower rates and simplified tax regulations should go into effect by January 1. Edelstein adds that once the new codes and rates are made official, and the public becomes more aware of the details, the result could be a mass of inquiries from businesses and individuals living in the United States.

"President Hamilton also received a personal briefing from the Governor of Texas who arrived early this morning, and spoke of some of the discontent being expressed by residents unhappy about the secession. He noted that most of the opposition is found in the larger cities, and told President Hamilton that he expected for there to be some lingering issues.

"And now, we would like to welcome Gwen Munro as the chief of the brand-new NewsNet Omaha Bureau. Gwen… congratulations."

"Thank you, Cynthia, and as we get our new Bureau organized here in Omaha, we're going to be finding ourselves quite busy right out of the gate as we cover the initial stages of operation of the Constitutional States of America.

"Earlier you were given a rundown of some of the appointments being made by President Hamilton. But already, the new government has encountered its first philosophical deadlock. The speed with which the CSA was established resulted in some matters not being fully discussed and agreed upon by the various states.

"For example, there had been much speculation that the CSA may have a House of Representatives, but no Senate. That possibility seemed to go down in flames just about a half hour ago, when delegates from states such as Montana, Wyoming and North Dakota objected to the proposal, noting that states such as Texas and Missouri with their much larger populations would dominate legislation with their larger Congressional delegations. Therefore, there will be a Senate, and each state will have two senators regardless of their population.

"An unofficial delegation of observers from the Upper Peninsula of Michigan has been assured, that should that section of the state break away, they will also be entitled to send two Senators to Omaha. Scholars of history may be quick to note that it has not taken long for this new government, barely into its infancy, to have encountered the same type of issues as arose in the late 1700's when the United States of America was being formed.

"A subsequent resolution was passed to establish that each state will be entitled to send the same Congressional delegation to Omaha, as was sent to Washington. It will be up to each state legislature to certify the membership of its delegation, and should any former members of the U.S. Congress not wish to serve in that capacity in the CSA, the states will appoint replacements until they hold their own rounds of elections, and that will certainly happen next year.

"During a recess at mid – morning, President Hamilton was asked to comment again on the unrest in St. Louis, and to a lesser degree in some Texas cities and Tulsa, Oklahoma. President Hamilton expressed his concerns for those who had been injured, and called upon residents of the new nation to take some time to evaluate for themselves what life will be like in the CSA. He reiterated that those wishing to have the chance for a brighter and more prosperous future will find more job opportunities developing then they could reasonably expect to find in the remaining United States.

"When asked about comments made by liberal and progressive politicians predicting that low – income residents of the CSA are being pressured to leave through promised reductions in government benefits, the president noted that states still within the umbrella of the United States will be facing no choice but to cut back the generosity of benefits to the poor, if they have not done so already. Hamilton went on to say that the difference is, in the CSA there is a reasonable prospect for an improving economy.

"We may be grateful that the secession of the CSA states did not result in an armed conflict, but one thing is certain – the war of words is well underway. And when we return, we will have more coverage of the effects of this secession on the rest of America."

"One more question, Gwen. I understand that the CSA is in its first day of existence, but I'm curious as to whether anything is being said about the election process that is expected to be some months away."

"There are rumors... I think that it is safe to say that the CSA will hold elections early in 2020 so as not to interfere with elections in the United States. But the most interesting tidbits I am hearing are the suggestions that Senatorial and Presidential elections may not be held in the same manner in which we are accustomed to seeing."

"Thank you Gwen… and when we return, we are going to have to report on how the new lead – established nation may affect businesses currently operating in the United States."

When NewsNet returned from a commercial break, viewers were greeted by the sight of a tall blonde woman standing in an overcoat outside a factory. "Thanks for joining us today on NewsNet. My name is Monica Samuelsson, and we're going to be taking a look now at some of the ramifications the secession will have on the remainder of the United States.

"Behind me is the main production facility for Liberty Firearms. Over the past several years, Liberty has grown to be the largest manufacturer of firearms and ammunition in North America, surpassing Colt, Smith & Wesson and other gun makers with whom you may be familiar. In fact, nearly all firearms manufacturers in North America have seen their business flourish over the past several years, driven by the concerns of private citizens that guns would either be seized, or their production halted by government edict. But Liberty also found its own special niche in the firearms market by producing its own line of holsters, custom-made for its handguns.

"Liberty also manufactures several increasingly popular models of rifles and muzzleloaders to be marketed in those states where one will find some very complex hunting regulations regarding weapons. As Liberty has expanded its product line to meet nearly every conceivable corner of the firearms market, not only has its market share flourished, but it has also become one of the larger industrial employers in the New England region.

"However, Liberty executives have found their company under increasing pressure by the progressive elected officials who dominate this part of the nation. And Liberty, with its main manufacturing facility here in Rhode Island, and subsidiary plants in other New England states and Pennsylvania has observed elected officials from those states expressing a desire to pass laws that would effectively restrict Liberty's sales and profits.

"Therefore, it came as no surprise last night when Liberty CEO Benjamin Hamaker announced that the company's board of directors had voted to give him the authority to relocate all of Liberty's manufacturing processes to Oklahoma City. Apparently, Hamaker had already been in quiet negotiations for the purchase of an empty factory on the outskirts of the city. Now Liberty, and its thousands of well – paying manufacturing positions will be taking up residence in Oklahoma.

"Hamaker stresses that the company will assist with moving costs for employees wishing to move to Oklahoma. But for new England, it means that a large employer who had always been willing to hire employees without technical skills, but provide on-the-job training, will only find local government even more badly strained.

"The CSA has only been in existence for three days, but already some of the predictions of job movement are coming to pass. The states in the East, the Midwest and far West that have already been unable to avoid red ink while imposing some of the highest tax rates in the nation, could find themselves reaching a breaking point more rapidly than had been previously projected. Throughout the day, and over the coming days, we will be exploring other ways in which the secession of now sixteen states, may greatly change life in the remaining United States of America. This is Monica Samuelsson, reporting for NewsNet."

President Calista Meyers sat behind a desk in the White House Library, sipping at a cup of coffee while sitting across from the new Speaker of the House Angela Hostettler from New York and Attorney General Mitchell Pryor. "Mister Attorney General... I feel for the incredible position that has been thrust upon you... not that I cannot relate. But I need for you to help me think through this most unusual concept that Elaine Ford so unceremoniously tossed out on the Senate floor."

The veteran attorney felt his blood turning cold. "Madam President... I think it can happen. We adhere to the Constitution basically because we want to. In this entanglement of illogic we could be facing, we could see the Senate and House vote to remove the authority of the Supreme Court to preserve its authority. In other words, could the Supreme Court tell Congress that it cannot do away with the document that establishes the Court and provides its entire meaning for existence?" Pryor lowered his head and began to rub his temples. "I have always had a difficult time answering questions that were never supposed to be asked. But here we are.

"What we are talking about here is, in essence, a form of a legislative coup. Congress would simply vote to establish that the Constitution of the United States of America as it stands today is no longer valid or legitimate. The Supreme Court could not logically be appealed to, and the Court cannot seize power...".

The President moved her gaze to the Speaker. "Will the people in our party in your chamber take the same attitude as the Senate?"

"It will pass. It won't be by such a stark percentage as will happen in the Senate, but it will pass. To a large degree, it will pass because of the Second Amendment. There is such a grudge match between our party and all the various gun rights advocates and organizations... I think you understand where I'm going with this.

"Not only that, Madam President. Without the Constitution, what we have known as the First Amendment is open for negotiations. Perhaps you would be appalled if you would hear some of the conversations that take place over cocktails... comments about talk radio... certain television talking heads... websites. Please, Madam President... don't underestimate how much hunger there is out there among more than a few people elected to office to turn down the volume on selected individuals and organizations.

"Think back to the uproar in 2013 when IRS staff was found to be targeting conservative groups. You would not want to know how much nostalgia there is for those days."

The President turned once again to the Attorney General. "Realistically... is there anything that can be done?"

The Attorney General began to drum his fingers on the desk. "Here is the paradox... I can give you only one answer. And that answer, is to say that such an action would be unconstitutional. So if an action was filed with the Supreme Court, and the Court struck down such a motion by Congress, what real difference would it make? As was said earlier, and as will be said frequently over the next couple of weeks, the only reason the Constitution is in effect, is because of our mutual belief in it and our collective agreement to follow its tenants. Take that away... the Constitution is done."

The President looked down at the desk. "In the immediate fallout... Indiana... Kentucky... Georgia...". She closed her eyes and leaned her head back. "I will have to sit on this for a couple of days."

"The Speaker leaned forward in her chair: "And what about the Chairman of the Joint Chiefs?"

The President shook her head. The Speaker leaned her head forward as she nodded and raised her eyebrows. "Madam President... I was just told before I came in here that the General has announced his retirement effective immediately."

The President slammed her hand on the desk and stood up to pace the floor. "He must really be pissed at me to not even call me first."

The Speaker pressed the issue. "He announced that he is moving home to live in his mountain cabin and hunt elk. There is press speculation that a rift developed, possibly over a desire for him to halt the secession by force. That has been reinforced... I will let it go to say that in a meeting with John Malcolm, you allegedly expressed that desire. Obviously, someone in that room is not your best buddy."

The President regained her composure and sat back down. "And what do you see as the fallout from this?"

The Speaker clasped her hands together and looked down. "First thing that comes to my mind... it will alienate the members of our party and those sympathetic to us in the media who bought into the good riddance concept. There's nothing wrong with being compared to Abraham Lincoln, but this may take that comparison a little further than you would really care for.

"After that settles into everyone's brains, the reality of what that move would have meant starts looking rather bloody. Then, whether you care about this or not, it takes down the trust level with the Hamilton Administration and the CSA several notches. And forgive me, Madam President, but it will look like you were playing both sides against the middle."

The President pursed her lips and looked aside for a moment. "All of that stings... but I'm a big girl. So after John's funeral tomorrow, everyone is going to expect us to get down to business. As for the funeral itself, it's going to be a rather odd event considering the circumstances of his death."

The Attorney General exhaled a deep sigh. "Mrs. Malcolm did not change her mind? Just a televised service at the Cathedral, then a private burial at Arlington?"

The President nodded. "Under the circumstances... a suicide... the secession... the family felt it would be best for them and the country. I can't say that I disagree with them. And from a personal and selfish standpoint... I have to say that since it will only take me out of the office for a couple of hours, well... you both understand I hope. We have lots to deal with."

The Speaker opened a folder. "Those hearings on benefit reductions start tomorrow in Illinois, Massachusetts and New Jersey. How are you going to respond to pleas for federal funds to hold the states harmless?"

The President looked down and rested her forehead on her fingertips. "I got a phone call from the Fed Chairman at 6:00 A.M. this morning. He explained that within twenty-four hours of the secession, our debt capacity took on the characteristics of a rubber band about to snap. He said that within two weeks, we have to stop incurring any additional debt. It seems that the circumstances took away any of our flexibility to keep us from going into default.

"So, in answer to your question, there is nothing the federal government can do to bail any of the states or cities out of their situations. In fact, the two of you will be the first to know that a federal hiring freeze is going into effect at midnight tonight. That will be announced at a press conference this evening. In addition, not only are we not going to be able to help out states and cities, I am also going to be proposing that Congress enact a general ten percent reduction in funding to them, retroactive back to October 1 when the federal fiscal year started. That includes funding for the transfer programs and Medicaid.

"We are also going to have to put a freeze on any increases in Social Security payments, and reduce payment levels for a lot of Medicare services."

The Speaker began to rise slowly, and leaned partway across the desk. "You can't be serious. This is impossible. I will favor any level of tax increases instead of this."

"This is the very conversation I had with Bob this morning. And it was not at all comfortable. He was very squeamish about telling me this, but Bob had been warning President Malcolm for several months that this could happen, well before there was any real belief that a secession would take place.

"Of course, we will have to raise taxes... and quite steeply. And we still have to do what I just said we have to do. And Bob is ready to appear before Congress as early as the day after tomorrow to emphasize those realities."

The Speaker slowly lowered herself back into her chair. "All because of this damned secession...?"

The President shook her head. "It's a cascading effect. Our debt situation was already precarious at best, and our bond market had become quite fragile. It didn't take much of a shock for it to collapse."

The Speaker could be heard to moan quietly. "So is that why you asked Eli Skinner to come out of retirement and be the Vice President? Or am I wrong? Are you not assigning him the task of informing all these governors and mayors that the tap has been turned off?"

The President smiled for the first time during the meeting. "A former governor... a former mayor... no one can soothe an angry soul like the golden – tongued Eli Skinner. In fact, he is working the phone as we speak." The President looked at the Speaker and held up her hands as if to ask for patience: "... and he is making it clear, this is my proposal, and you knew nothing about it."

"This is NewsNet correspondent Megan Howard here at the Great Plains Conference Center on the outskirts of Omaha, Nebraska, the capital of the Constitutional States of America. In just a few moments, President Bryce Hamilton will be holding his first press conference as a head of state.

"This convention center is slated to become a temporary headquarters for CSA government operations until a permanent location is readied in downtown Omaha. There are no regular guests or other activities taking place at this facility, as it is now under exclusive contract for use by the government of the CSA. It was expected that CSA officials would be operating out of this convention center by now, but due to security concerns business is being conducted at the Omaha Army National Guard Armory.

"Needless to say, security here at the convention center is tight for those reporters filtering in to cover the press conference. As I drove in, my car was thoroughly searched and checked out by specially trained dogs. In addition, security personnel even used mirrors on long handles to inspect the undercarriage of the car.

"The large meeting room behind me is where the press conference will begin in just a minute, and our own Carol Rogers will be among the assembled press corps. I am being told that either later today or sometime tomorrow, NewsNet will provide some coverage of the dilemma now being proposed to media executives, who must now decide how to cover two separate capitals in the collective land of America. We are now going to be switching over to coverage of the press conference."

Bryce Hamilton strolled into the room and toward the podium. Among the cadre of reporters present, some stood as they always had when the President of the United States would arrive for such an event, while others stayed seated. The President adjusted the microphone slightly and nodded to the reporters. "Thank you for being here today. Before I take any questions, I just want to express my sympathy, most of all to the family and closest friends of President John Malcolm, and to all of the American people.

"When President John Malcolm died, all Americans suffered the loss of a good and sincere man who only wanted what was best for the people he served. I also want to wish the best to President Meyers, and express my willingness to work with her whenever possible. I will now take some questions."

Hamilton pointed toward a correspondent from NBC: "President Hamilton, how do you plan to react to the dilemma of some of the Missouri residents facing difficulties in trying to move to Illinois?"

"First of all, let me once again condemn the actions of those who have taken the course of such cruel bigotry. Next, I have spoken to both the governor of Missouri and the mayor of St. Louis, and both have assured me that additional law enforcement personnel are being stationed nearby, but it will be up to the authorities in Illinois to address what is happening when people cross into that state. We are also preparing fliers and getting ready to employ social media to invite any citizens of the Constitutional States of America to contact us regarding any of their concerns."

A reporter from CBS stood up to shout a question: "President Hamilton... the announcement by Liberty Firearms of their intention to move to Oklahoma will mean the loss of jobs to thousands in the New England region. Were there some kind of incentives... some type of deal offered to bring them there?"

Hamilton slowly nodded. "I am not insensitive to the situations that are going to be faced by current employees of that company. I hope that all of them will entertain the offer of the company to assist them with moving costs to work at the planned Oklahoma facility. We will welcome them with open arms.

"As for any deals or incentives... I will say that indeed there were. There was the deal offered at the founding of the United States that a nation had been established where freedom would reign. We offer that same deal. As for incentives, we offer businesses the prospect of being able to operate in an environment of logic and freedom from unnecessary government regulation and meddling in their enterprises. As for Liberty Firearms in particular, we offered by our very nature, a place for them to operate where their products are valued, desired and respected."

A Fox reporter stood: "Mister President... as we speak, the bond market is nearing a crisis, and many economists are blaming that on the secession of the states and the establishment of the CSA. Would you comment on that please?"

"You left out an important part of that. The economists are also noting that the bond market is now in peril because so many of the states who withdrew from the United States and formed the CSA were among the states operating in a more fiscally responsible manner. The recklessness of spending and borrowing that weakened our fiscal solvency and the stability of the bond market was set into motion long ago, and while those of us in the leadership of the CSA are greatly concerned, we certainly do not accept responsibility for what could easily and simply been headed off long ago by making some difficult and unpopular decisions. Unfortunately, political expediency won out over the future economic stability of the nation."

The same reporter shouted out: "A follow – up question if I may... at this moment two states are conducting hearings on reducing public assistance benefit levels, and another is scheduled to begin early this evening. You and other members of the Council for a Free America were roundly criticized for proposing that welfare – type benefits needed to be targeted for scaling back. Do you find any irony in these latest developments?"

"I take little solace in irony. I think it is nothing but a tragedy that so many residents of a nation that has offered such unprecedented opportunity for success and self – sufficiency have found themselves dependent upon the government – mandated generosity of their neighbors. I speak not of those who are disabled, injured or suffering some type of temporary setback. It is nothing but tragic that people living in America have turned to living on money taken from their neighbors by the force of law for extended periods of time.

"I was a math major at Creighton University before I changed my mind and decided to study law. But even before I went off to college, I understood that numbers had to add up, and even in high school when I studied basic bookkeeping, I would do my homework with my father's old adding machine... the kind with a roll of tape for you youngsters sitting out there... and when a number came up printed in red ink, it meant something. Somehow, feeling a sense of alarm at seeing numbers printed in red lost its sense of significance along the way. At least, for those who live and work in Washington, and too many state capitals and city halls.

"I guess this is just a long-winded way of saying that money does not grow on trees. For a government to have money of any actual value it must be taken away from someone who earned it, then used wisely without entering into an extreme level of deficit. For some reason that I cannot explain, it became difficult to understand that only so much money could be taken away from the successful before there was no longer money left to buy things to create jobs, or to start businesses that would create jobs, and in turn, result in money going to the government in income taxes.

"Everyone started to buy into this concept that it was best just to go straight to the wealthy and take their money, because it was declared to be the fair thing to do. However, doing so took away the inherent pressure on others to be more productive and self-sufficient.

"Of course, when a government abandons the concept of having money based upon a solid currency and prints more money and goes into extensive debt, you end up with the same effect. You have a government that is bloated, trying to maintain operations and programs that are underfunded, if not counterproductive to a capitalist society. And that is why we're at the point we are today."

Hamilton pointed toward a CNN correspondent: "Mister Hamilton... there are unverified reports that within hours of being sworn into office, President Meyers attempted to have the military of the United States stop the formation of the CSA. Do you have any comments on that?"

"All that I know is what you have reported. I have no verification of anything of that nature. As I said earlier, I plan to work in as cooperative a manner as possible with President Meyers. It is important that we begin this new configuration of America with a relationship based in trust."

Hamilton called upon a reporter from ABC: "President Hamilton... there have been reports that work will soon be under way to open up energy exploration in the CSA in areas where the government of the United States had prohibited such activities. Is that correct?"

"Indeed it is. First of all, refineries that had been collecting dust for several years are likely to be active within the next two months. It is also expected that individual states will soon be issuing exploration permits for oil and natural gas, and several companies are already pursuing new leases for the surface mining of coal. One thing that we want to take a look at is the potential establishment of more electrical power plants fueled by both coal and nuclear energy. It is quite possible that we will establish a more modern and reliable power grid within the CSA, one that could benefit all of North America. It is expected that such an undertaking would create over 300,000 jobs. Already, several community colleges and technical schools within the CSA have expressed an interest in offering additional courses of study in these fields."

The same reporter shouted out another question: "But what about the pollution from the use of coal?"

"That is an excellent question. Any power plants constructed in the CSA will use the latest but cost-effective technology to hold air pollution to a minimum. I remind everyone, we all live in one world. If we want to really express our concerns over pollution from the use of coal, we need to take a look at other nations with rapidly expanding economies and populations, and ask that they take the same care of our planet as will be the case in the CSA."

A reporter from the Associated Press stood up: "Just this morning, the United Nations issued a statement expressing concerns over new energy exploration in the CSA. How do you intend to respond to that?"

Hamilton pursed his lips and looked down before answering. "First of all, please refer back to my previous comment. In the totality for the planet Earth, pollution generated by plants in the CSA will not be a drop in the bucket in terms of overall global pollution.

"In addition, the CSA will have to decide at some point in the future whether we will request admission to the United Nations. While I personally would favor doing so, I certainly understand the point of view of those who feel there would be no benefit in seeking admission. But as for the United Nations in any way influencing any internal policy of the CSA... I would not bet a steak dinner on that. A middle ground I may propose would be for us to simply apply for observer status, so that we could at least enhance our lines of communications with other nations.

"The CSA has been in existence now for three days, and any effort and energy to be spent debating an actual membership in the United Nations is likely to be far in the future. However, based upon conversations with others involved in the activities that resulted in the establishment of the CSA, I feel confident in stating that no one should expect the CSA to sign onto any agreements or treaties that would give the United Nations any right of interference in our economy or domestic policies, especially those regarding the ownership of firearms."

A reporter from the New York Times stood up. "Mr. Hamilton... why do you and the leadership of the CSA, and previously in the role of leadership of the Council for a Free America... speak so frequently about the right of gun ownership?"

Hamilton shrugged at first. "Because people in the press keep asking us why gun ownership is important to us."

The same reporter shouted out another question: "But Mister Hamilton, if the CSA becomes the gun – friendly haven everyone expects, and you would embrace so many gun manufacturers, do you fear for the safety of your citizens?"

"There are some cities that are now part of the CSA that have a history of too much violence. But none of them measure up to places like Chicago... Detroit... Washington. I think it is safe to say that none of our states are going to tolerate the use of firearms to commit crimes. States will determine their own laws, as they largely have for generations. But I think that it is a safe bet, that within the CSA, once an individual commits a crime with a gun, that person is unlikely to spend much more of his or her life out in society."

A Los Angeles Times reporter asked a related question. "Are you hinting that those who commit crimes in the CSA are going to face harsher sentences than those in the United States?"

"Yes."

Hamilton pointed to a Boston Globe reporter. "Mr. President... how will the matter of public education be addressed? Do you have concerns that public schools in the CSA may suffer in comparison to those in the United States through a lack of funding and resources?"

Hamilton nodded. "An excellent question. I have been involved in many of the preliminary discussions and seminars held by the Council for a Free America regarding the subject of public schools. Our overall attitude is this: the states will individually decide how public schools will be operated. Personally, I believe that if a person is dedicated to teaching youngsters, and is given the basic tools and resources needed to do so, the children will be well educated.

"We all know that teaching is not for the faint of heart. We do not need to make it unnecessarily more burdensome for those already willing to do what may be a society's most important work. There will not likely be any type of department or bureau overseeing education across our new nation. Once again, educational oversight will be a state responsibility."

Hamilton pointed to a reporter from the Wall Street Journal. "Aside from Liberty Firearms, are you aware of any other companies indicating a desire to relocate to the CSA?"

"It is likely that next week there will be a major briefing conducted by our Secretary of Commerce, but I will say a few things about this. Out of consideration for those companies, I will not mention their identities. However, there are numerous companies and industries who have been in informal contact with us. We are also aware of much preliminary discussion going on regarding purchases and leases of land and available industrial sites.

"Of course, there is much excitement being generated within the energy industry. Many of the states in the CSA either have an established history in the field of energy production, or are known to have energy sources that are either untapped or ripe for expansion of production efforts. I do not have a crystal ball, but many analysts are telling us that the CSA will come to rival, if not exceed, the Middle East as a source of oil.

"In addition, the resources of natural gas in the CSA states may end up providing not only an economic boom here, but could benefit all of North America through lower energy prices. And for people concerned about the side effects of electricity being generated by coal – fired plants, they need to understand that homes can be converted from electric heat to natural gas."

Another question came from the ABC reporter. "As a follow-up to a previous question regarding education... what about the role of unions in the CSA... I mean, for teachers and workers in other fields as well?"

"If an employer has a contract signed with a labor organization, I am assuming that the agreement will have to be honored, but I suppose there could be some possible exceptions for clauses in labor agreements that reference laws of the United States, which of course, would no longer apply. I would expect that states will quickly make determinations as to whether they will or will not be what we refer to as right to work states. That may be necessary, as there is no longer any jurisdiction from the United States Department of Labor.

"That very well could mean that when current labor agreements expire, and a state has become a right to work state, an employer would have the right to refuse to collectively bargain unless a previous, existing contract contained a provision that somehow provided for perpetuity of the agreement."

"A follow-up question please… what is to keep an auto manufacturer from moving all of its jobs from places like Michigan and Ohio?"

Hamilton shook his head. "Absolutely nothing. Perhaps an automaker may want to move jobs to the CSA, rather than shutting down a plant in the United States and sending those jobs to someplace like Mexico.

"Our domestic automakers have to compete with foreign competitors who pay much less. For those of you over the age of sixty, think back to the days when that cute little German Volkswagen was such a popular item. Would you have foreseen the day they would be manufactured in Mexico of all places?

"I also wish it were still possible for a young person to graduate from high school and go straight to a good paying job in the automotive industry, look forward to a lifetime of employment and a nice pension, and enjoy good benefits all the way through. In fact, I wish for a lot of things that no longer are."

President Calista Meyers and her new Vice President Eli Skinner sat on opposite sides of the desk in the Oval Office. The President looked around and shook her head. "I still find it difficult to sit in here, knowing what…".

The Vice President nodded in sympathy. "I would expect that within a day or so you're going to be finding yourself so burdened with issues that you won't even have a chance to think about it."

President Meyers gestured toward the still – silent speakerphone on her desk. "So what are we to expect from Governor Gibraltar… a rewind of what she said to you earlier?"

Skinner shook his head. "She's too creative. I expect she will have something new to throw at us by now. But oh, is she ever pissed."

Suddenly the phone buzzed, and the President pushed a button. "Governor… thank you for agreeing to do this over the phone. I understand your House is holding the hearing as we speak."

"President Meyers… I cannot believe you are taking such a stand. We are being cut off at the knees, and there is no way we can avoid cutting assistance benefits without an immediate infusion of federal cash."

The President took a deep breath and glanced toward her new second-in-command. "Governor… I am sure you know all about the debt and bond developments over the past several hours. We are suddenly in danger of a national default as an aftermath of this secession. What you're asking is simply not possible."

"And what the hell am I supposed to do with hundreds of thousands of welfare recipients finding out their payments are being cut? They don't make enough as it is."

The Vice President held up his hand and took a deep breath. "Governor… a morsel of advice to you. When speaking to the public, don't use the words… 'They don't make enough'… Please don't inadvertently equate receiving welfare funds with earnings. You don't need that extra problem."

The Governor nearly screamed in response. "Eli… you damned well know what I meant."

"Just a friendly word of caution, Helen. I sympathize with your situation. We just can't fix it."

"My God… the word is already getting out. Can the two of you imagine the scene in front of the state administration building tomorrow morning? I have the state police coming in tonight… the mayor is already throwing a fit and demanding more state money to help cover the overtime his police department will incur. Then, when the word leaked out that we were calling in more police, I started getting phone calls asking if I was making unfair and stereotypical… even racist… assumptions about the behavior of poor people."

The President hesitated before she spoke. "Governor… I think that you understand… there are two other states facing virtually the same immediate problem."

"I know… you can't help them either."

"That's not my point. Right now, you're the flashpoint because your hearing process progressed more rapidly. Perhaps you want to make sure that media coverage gets diluted. Perhaps some of your friends in the local press, could encourage some of their contacts in those other state capitals to ramp up the volume there. Then, you won't be facing this all alone, and it becomes a national problem, rather than just local."

There was silence for a moment. "I can't tell you how much I appreciate that."

Even through the speaker, the Governor could hear the President sigh. "Well, when we make it a national problem, it's easier for me to deflect some of the blame onto Bryce Hamilton and his new little kingdom. Heaven help me if I should not confess my selfish reasons for anything that I do. But doing this in this manner, will serve both our purposes."

The Governor could be heard chuckling. "So the Council for a Free America brings about a secession to help the rich. Then, as a result of their treason, we face a fiscal emergency, and the first to suffer are the poor. Sounds like a winning scenario to me."

President Bryce Hamilton sat at the head of a small conference table in a meeting room of the Great Plains Conference Center. At the same table were Vice President Franklin Chiles, Treasury Secretary Tom Edelstein and Commerce Secretary Patrick Bridger, the latter two having just been approved for their positions by the delegates just two hours before. Also present was Hamilton's long time law partner Nina Burton, who had been appointed to be his Chief of Staff.

Hamilton leaned forward, and gestured to Nina. "We all understand now about the predicted unrest tomorrow in some of the U. S. cities because of the talk of welfare cutbacks in those three states. It's unfortunate, and of course, we'll be blamed. I don't trust Calista Meyers any farther than I can throw this building. Nina, you know how the states are coming along on their benefit transition plans?"

Nina nodded. "Nearly everybody is following the same template. They are taking the amount they had been putting in to match federal funds, and rolling everything into one monthly cash assistance program. Even the state match for the Food Stamp Program... all those other programs as well. Although state funds are being put in one pot, and all of the states have started the process of laying off staff, because with all the programs so simplified and consolidated, many are expecting that nearly seventy-five percent of the program staff at the state and county levels will be laid off.

"The money that was being spent for all the salaries and benefits will help to make up for the loss of federal funds. Most of the states are expecting that there will be some reduction in monthly benefits, but most are also planning workfare activities for the able-bodied recipients, like there used to be.

"So for the states adopting this model, there will be one simplified state program for assistance to the poor. Medical providers are being told to bill the state like they did for Medicaid for the first month, but states are putting out directives within a few days outlining what will be covered. Without all the federal mandates and interference, we think we can do pretty well in most states when it comes to covering the medical needs of the poor.

"At the same time, the states are planning to offer very basic benefit programs for the unemployed who have been laid off, and are able-bodied and expected to return to employment. However, it is likely that states will impose some public service work requirements as a condition of receiving unemployment benefits."

Hamilton leaned forward and began to rub his forehead. "And Nina... what about all those stories the media have been playing up about families fleeing the CSA because of these cutbacks?"

Nina shook her head. "It's no surprise that there have been some very shameless exploitation going on. It's hard for us to get numbers. Of course, the media has not really been covering the situation of St. Louis that much. I shouldn't be surprised... the story does not reflect well on Illinois. Most of the stories have covered the families who have left Texas for New Mexico, Arizona and California. Good luck to those state economies.

"We have to be concerned about unrest, but just not because of unhappiness over transforming poverty programs. There are a lot of people in St. Louis and some of the Texas cities especially, who are still hoping that some kind of public pressure or embarrassment will reverse the withdrawal of Missouri and Texas."

Hamilton leaned back in his chair and exhaled a deep breath. "There is a horrifying lack of understanding of economic reality among many millions of people, in both the CSA and the United States."

Tom Edelstein finally spoke up. "The dangerous thing... I think the most dangerous thing we will be facing for a while... is that opinion that some people should simply be exempted from supporting themselves. I'm talking about the able-bodied.

"It was before my time in government in the late 90's when Congress passed a welfare reform bill with all the work requirements. But I understand that worked."

Patrick Bridger nodded. "I was a young state representative at the time. I remember the angst I felt, because... let's face it... most of that came down hard on the mothers on welfare. After all, most of the welfare families did not have a man in the family.

"I voted to enact our state plan that included all those work requirements. At the same time... I really felt queasy about it all. I always felt that it was a cultural thing, that the mother was left with the children while the father was out doing who knows what.

"One of the old wise owls in the legislature knew I was getting wobbly about it. He took me to alocal bar that evening and bought me a beer, then confided to me that he felt the same way. But then, he told me that he was voting for the plan out of a tough love approach. He said it was unfair to the welfare mothers on the rolls at the time, but he believed deep in his heart that it would break the cycle, and the children that were on welfare at the time, would grow up seeing a parent go to work because that's what a parent was supposed to do. Then, they would not follow the pattern and go on welfare.

"It's too bad that so many of those requirements were done away with. Because, we are now back to the same fix we were in before 1997. And now we have to do it again, but I think we will only have to do it once in the CSA. But I will have that same queasy feeling in my gut that I had then.

"I still remember when we were working on that legislation. I lost my appetite, and I had a lot of trouble sleeping. I can't remember how many pounds I lost. I think my wife thought at first that I was having an affair. It's one thing in theory to reduce payments to the poor, then tell them it's either work for your benefits or go without.

"But it's what we have to do. Philosophy aside... we all know that neither the CSA or the United States has the money to maintain the status quo. And while I think that as years go by, the CSA would be able to provide generous benefits, we could not do so for the sake of the children who need to grow up with self-sufficiency as a goal. And we would dare not do it, lest we become a magnet for those in the United States who would simply rather not work."

Hamilton responded to Bridger's remarks with a brisk salute. "Very well said. I should have arranged for this meeting to be taped. I think even Calista Meyers would feel consoled this evening by hearing those words."

Nina spoke up again. "But what about those who simply are not willing to go quietly into the night? I am very concerned about demonstrations... even violence in St. Louis and Texas.

"There are all kinds of rumors, and we all know how much value rumors may or may not have. But police in several cities are watching some militant groups, many just newly formed, who may be very anxious to wreak some havoc. But I'm also hearing that the Texas law and order crews are not likely to give an inch. And I suppose, they need to set a hard tone right from the start."

Calista Meyers woke with a headache the following morning. The new mattress that had been delivered to the main White House bedroom seemed a little too soft for her liking, and a lack of sleep seem to always bring on a migraine. Throughout the night, she had relived the funeral over and over. When she was not awake and remembering the service, she dreamed of it.

Just as she was about to get into the shower at 6:30 AM, she heard her bedside phone ringing. "Madam President... Helen Gibraltar. Just wanted you to know... it's beginning."

The President sat down on the edge of her bed. "How bad is it already... this early in the morning?"

"There are several thousand demonstrators gathering in a park. It's below freezing here this morning, but they have so many children with them, they must have borrowed more. Great dramatic effect."

The President spoke slowly, choosing her words carefully. "I will not insult your intelligence, Governor, by asking if there's anything I could do to help. But I will wish you good luck. I understand it is going to be a difficult day, and I wish you weren't having to go through it."

"Thank you, and I will make sure my staff keeps you aware of anything major."

"Welcome back to NewsNet. My name is Cynthia Warren and we are monitoring events in Boston. Last evening, Massachusetts Governor Helen Gibraltar commented on the hearings being held in the Massachusetts House of Representatives on the possibility of reducing welfare benefits. The Governor's comments left open the distinct possibility, if not the probability, of benefit reductions taking place very soon.

"The reason for the benefit reductions is the sudden deterioration of the bond market and the nation's debt capacity. While Massachusetts and federal officials are hinting that the crisis has been brought on by the secession of states and establishment of the CSA, it is known that two other states, Illinois and New Jersey, are considering similar measures on an emergency basis. And now we are switching to Samantha Holloway of our Boston NewsNet affiliate."

A tall brunette woman suddenly appeared on the screen as police officers stood in the background. "Boston police, in conjunction with Massachusetts state police, are conducting surveillance from the air of the crowd gathering several blocks away from the Boston City Hall, which has for some reason become the announced focal point of the building demonstration, perhaps for maximizing media coverage.

"A spokesperson for a hastily – organized coalition of community organizations told me a few minutes ago that the gathering protesters consist of people from many neighborhoods in the city of Boston, and are being joined minute by minute by others coming in from various corners of the state.

"She told me that the purpose of the protest is to bring a national focus to the plight of the poor in Massachusetts, who she says cannot suffer the loss of any of the monthly income provided by the state and federal government. To complicate matters, it appears that Massachusetts officials were told by Vice President Eli Skinner by telephone that the funding situation is grave. According to an aide to Governor Gibraltar, the Vice President related nothing but bad news.

"Supposedly, Vice President Skinner went so far as to say that the Food Stamp Program benefit levels could also see reductions, as could federal funding to the states in general. Even worse, it appears that reductions could go in effect as early as December 1, just in time for Christmas. To say the least, anger over the secession is mounting, although a member of the Massachusetts State Treasurer's office who spoke off the record, acknowledged that the secession only accelerated the deterioration of the nation's solvency.

"Not everyone in Boston is sympathetic toward those protesting a reduction in assistance benefits. As we had been standing here for about an hour in front of City Hall, numerous motorists passing by aware of the impending protest, have shouted a variety of comments, many of which referred to the need for benefit recipients to simply get a job, while others offered some rather colorful advice on the matter of having children that cannot be supported without taxpayer assistance.

"As we speak, Governor Gibraltar is meeting with top officials in an attempt to figure out a way to avoid a cut in benefits to the poor of Massachusetts. In any case, it is known that Massachusetts shares a dilemma with Illinois and New Jersey, and word is that Vice President Skinner delivered the same stark message to the governors of those two states. This is Samantha Holloway for NewsNet, Boston. And now back to our New York studio and continuing coverage with Cynthia Warren."

"This is Cynthia Warren back in our New York studio for NewsNet, and we are keeping our eye on several developments. You just heard our report from Samantha Holloway in Boston about the demonstration that is being organized and is supposed to result in a massive march on Boston City Hall this morning to protest what are being called unavoidable reductions in public welfare benefits in the state of Massachusetts, likely to go into effect on December 1.

"We are also monitoring reactions from the governors of Illinois and New Jersey, whose states are now facing an almost identical dilemma as Massachusetts. A call to the United States Department of Health and Human Services to inquire as to whether any other states are grappling with similar circumstances has not yet been returned.

"At any moment, we are expecting some footage of the Boston march on City Hall, for we are told that the crowd is now about one block away as we are at just about 10:00 A.M., and we understand the marchers began leaving the park at around 8:30, and we know... I am getting... I'm being told that we have some urgent news to report... Okay, I am now reading on my monitor some breaking news from Houston, Texas... a report of a large blast. Let's see... the report says that an explosion took place in front of the headquarters of Magnum Oil... in Houston.

"I am being told that… Magnum Oil is the largest oil drilling and exploration company in Texas… a quick view of their website tells us that Magnum has nearly 12,000 employees. Our producer… I understand our producer is now on the phone with someone in Houston, so as we gather more information, we're going to take a very brief break, and when we return, we hope to have more information for you."

"Thank you for staying with us, I am Cynthia Warren in our NewsNet studio in New York, and we are receiving some very unsettling and sad news from Houston. We have verified that a large explosion, assumed to be a truck bomb, exploded in front of the Magnum Oil headquarters. We understand that this was a multiple story building, and that nearly 3,500 people work in that facility.

"Reports indicate that the bomb exploded at around 9:40 AM Eastern time, just after many of the employees there would have reported to work. And any time now, we should have… my God, there it is. Can the viewers see it now? Okay… as you can see… oh my… it appears that the entire front half of this large building is gone. I don't know if you can see this at home, but there is a large twisted and shredded vehicle on its back in front of the building, I am not an authority on explosions or bombs, but at first glance, it appears that this may have involved a semi tractor-trailer.

"I am now being joined by NewsNet correspondent and analyst Mike Silver… Mike… this is eerily similar to the scene of the Oklahoma City bombing so many years ago."

The obviously rattled man nodded his head. "And Cynthia… we have more information that has come in from a witness in a nearby building who was standing at a window making copies when the blast went off. According to this witness, the entire front half of the Magnum building is gone as you said, and he seems to verify that it was indeed a semi tractor-trailer rig that exploded. This witness supposedly called 911, then the local NewsNet studio. He had the number in his cell phone, because his wife is supposedly employed there.

"As we can see as we watch this unbelievable scene... I understand that what we are watching is a shared feed from a traffic helicopter... we can only imagine, as we watch all of the flashing lights as first responders pour onto the scene... the loss of life is going to be immense. Let's watch for a moment...

"It should take just a few seconds for the helicopter to circle round to the back of the building and... oh my gosh... there are huge chunks blown even out of the back of the building... this is going to be a very tragic outcome, I am afraid."

Viewers were suddenly seeing the image of Cynthia Warren once again. "And we are now getting reports of more major developments out of Texas, as there are now police swarming downtown Austin at the state capitol building, a reporter from our local affiliate is heading for the scene... I am being told that several thousand demonstrators are disrupting traffic in the area of the capital building in Austin, and that... I am being told in my ear piece that shots are being exchanged between some of the demonstrators and Austin police officers.

"This apparently took place with absolutely no warning, but initial reports are that there are several of these protesters who are armed. We need to take into account that initial reports are often rushed, and frequently inaccurate, however, an eyewitness... just a minute. Austin police have been forced to retreat into the capital building in Austin. This is confirmed by our NewsNet correspondent on the scene.

"Now she is verifying for us that the police did indeed retreat into the capital building. Okay... she is reporting from the third floor of an insurance agency building near the capital, but she is willing to verify... I repeat... she is able to verify that it appears to be that there are indeed many protesters with guns. Good... we have her on her cell phone, so we now have Connie Sinclair on the line... Connie, go ahead... you are on the air on our broadcast and simultaneously on NewsNet Radio."

For several seconds, the words were not understandable: "... and now there is a group of... I don't know, maybe forty or so demonstrators who have advanced to within 30 to 40 yards of the

Capitol, and they are firing wildly at windows and doors. Of course, there is return fire coming from inside the large building.

"I see what appears to be the bodies of let's see… I think I see the bodies of two police officers on the ground, and there must be around four bodies of the demonstrators on the ground. This is hard to believe, but this is nothing other than a pitched gun battle going on here in Austin.

"Now there are more police arriving on the scene, but these officers are dressed in protective riot gear. I'm also now seeing Texas Rangers arriving on the scene. This is going to be problematic for the police, as there are probably a couple of thousand demonstrators, and many have taken cover behind or under vehicles, and some of them are also firing at the building, although from farther away. There are many hundreds of apparently unarmed demonstrators who are caught in the middle of this. One has to wonder just how many of these demonstrators went into this situation expecting for there to be gunfire.

"I want to mention that the demonstrators who are armed are using handguns. I have not seen a single rifle, and to my knowledge, there have been no explosives used. In any case, most of the action is taking place in front of me, and I see the newly arrived riot police and the Texas Rangers… I probably should not say any more, because I'm afraid I could inadvertently give help to these violent demonstrators.

"I do think that I can report that police are taking dramatic steps to deal with the situation. And it is obvious to anyone in this area, that a very large number of police and Rangers have joined the gun battle. If anyone in the vicinity of the Capitol is listening to me on the radio… please do not go near downtown Austin, especially near the Capitol. The scene before me is simply surreal. This is a significant gun battle going on here."

Viewers were once again seeing Cynthia Warren. "It's hard to believe that we have to break away from that report for an update on another situation, but we have just been told by our Houston NewsNet Bureau that our worst fears have been realized. Initial reports from police and rescue personnel on the scene at the

Magnum Oil headquarters explosion include estimates that well over two thousand people were likely killed in that explosion. While it is too early for police to have any official theories on a motive for this horrendous crime, it is no secret that Magnum Oil had to be counted among the major beneficiaries of the new opportunities provided to the energy industry in the wake of the establishment of the CSA.

"The company is known for... I think we're going to break away now for a special report from Megan Howard, who right now is standing outside the Army National Guard Armory in Omaha, Nebraska. Megan...".

"Thank you Cynthia, and I am indeed standing outside in this cold wind, because security has been suddenly tightened up in this building where the delegates of the CSA states are still meeting and conducting the business needed to get the new nation underway. Last evening, President Hamilton and several other top CSA officials were on hand for Hamilton's press conference at the Great Plains Conference Center on the outskirts of Omaha, and although we know that the President was here earlier this morning, his location is now a matter of great secrecy.

"Ever since the CSA delegation arrived here at the Armory for the sake of security, there were many armed soldiers on duty. To say the least, there are now even more. We are assuming that once officials feel that security arrangements are sufficient, there will be some kind of a statement from President Hamilton regarding the staggering array of events this morning.

"Police here in Omaha have been quick to flood the streets with officers, and have provided an extra dose of security here at the Armory. Omaha has already been the scene of one deadly and large demonstration, and that experience is certainly fresh in the memories of the Omaha police force, for those memories include the loss of some of their comrades. This is Megan Howard for NewsNet, in Omaha."

The Governor had not even had the opportunity to leave his official residence in Austin before the report of this explosion made its way to him, let alone the subsequent news of the shooting going on within his own city, around the same building he would normally have been working in by that time of the day. The First Lady was suffering with a stomach virus, and he had texted his secretary to tell her that he was going to be arriving a couple of hours late that morning so that he could tend to her himself.

He listened on the telephone for a while, and remained silent for a few seconds after the voice on the other end had ceased speaking. He closed his eyes, then looked down at the floor, and then in a tight voice, responded, "Yes."

"This is Connie Sinclair for NewsNet... I'm still on one of the higher floors of a building near the Capitol here in Austin... I can only tell you that this is a shocking and bloody battle. As I reported earlier, the demonstrators, perhaps still a dozen... armed with handguns are still firing at the building, and are exchanging fire with a growing contingent of Austin police and Texas Rangers.

"I tried once again to count the number of demonstrators on the ground and lying in the streets. I think the number is around ten. However, most of the demonstrators are now in a large parking lot, taking refuge behind and under a lot of very bullet – riddled cars. In addition, across the intersection, there were a couple of scuffles when demonstrators tried to retreat into businesses. At least one demonstrator died while I watched as someone from inside that business fired through the window and killed him.

"From time to time, I have seen demonstrators surrender to police, or have found themselves being apprehended, but in either case they are going to be nursing some bruises tomorrow. The gunfire is still heavy and constant, and there is a continuous build up of Texas Rangers and riot police... I now see the first National Guard unit pulling up, and these guys are in an armored personnel carrier. Now, I see another one rolling up... now another one. Now those three vehicles are moving, and they are pulling up in front of the Capitol...

"Now there are... I couldn't see them before because of the angle, but now there are more troops in what appears to be full combat gear pouring into the street carrying their rifles. Now, the police, the Rangers and the troops are all backing away from that parking lot where many hundred demonstrators are clustered.

"They are backing away further and further, but appear to be ringing the area where the demonstrators are holed up. I want to emphasize, the gunfire has not abated one bit. Every once in a while, I have seen a trunk lid pop open in that parking lot, and that probably explains how the demonstrators could have so much ammunition.

"I wish I could give you a video feed of this incredible scene, but there are simply too many bullets flying for a crew to be able to operate safely. Now I see a National Guard soldier with a loudspeaker. He is shielding himself behind a police squad car, and I cannot make out what he is saying through this closed window. However, he is still speaking.

"He has now stopped talking and has walked away to rejoin his fellow soldiers, now the police, Rangers and troops seem to be moving a little further away, and now it appears that they have stopped firing, but are simply taking cover. I still hear some firing however and I see from watching the movements of the police that they are still being fired upon.

"Now I hear… I think I hear helicopters… I can't see any, but… Now I hear more rapid gunfire, but this seems louder… Oh, wow… Now I see them as they're circling around, there are two helicopters and they're firing down on that parking lot. I see demonstrators firing their pistols upward, but there are…

"That parking lot is now a scene of carnage. Several cars are now on fire, and the vehicles are just being chewed up by the machine gun fire coming out of those helicopters. Now there are several people trying to crawl out of the parking lot, but some of the demonstrators behind them keep firing at the police, and the troopers in that ring of police and Rangers are firing back out of self-defense.

"This is a nightmare for anyone trying to get out of that situation. It's probably not possible for the officers and troopers to differentiate between those trying to escape or surrender and those still shooting at them. Wait... I now see a group of about eight demonstrators... They are running with their hands up toward a group of Rangers. Now the Rangers are waving them to get down on the ground. As I watch, the surrendering demonstrators are being searched, and now they're being taken away behind police lines.

"I'm really not optimistic about how many of the demonstrators will be that lucky. The remaining ones either seem to be unable to decide how to surrender under the circumstances, or are themselves engaged in this battle with the police. But watching those helicopters continuing to riddle and tear up that parking lot, this is not going to end well for a lot of people."

Viewers were once again seeing Cynthia Warren and Mike Silver at their news desk. An obviously emotional Cynthia Warren spoke first. "We wanted to bring you back for a moment to give you an update on the Magnum Oil explosion in Houston. We reported earlier that it was estimated that over two thousand people were killed in the Magnum building. We are now being told that at least one hundred twenty-five people died in neighboring buildings, but that number is expected to rise dramatically as the rescue effort progresses. The total number of known wounded in the Magnum building and others surrounding it, currently totals over one thousand two hundred, with over five hundred of those listed as being in critical or serious condition.

"All Houston hospitals are overflowing, and any other individuals needing emergency care are being taken to hospitals in the Houston suburbs and surrounding cities. Trauma teams are being flown in from many other Texas cities, as well as from Oklahoma, Arkansas, Utah, Colorado, Arizona and New Mexico. Trauma surgeons from two of the largest hospitals in Mexico City are also being flown in. In addition, medical units from military bases in Texas and Oklahoma have been scrambled.

"A spokesperson for the Houston Police Department says that their bomb squad has verified that the explosion was caused by a semi trailer filled with dynamite. The manner of detonation has not yet been determined. Police have verified that they have a recording of a call from a security guard at the Magnum building who was going to investigate why such a truck would have pulled up in front of the building. Five seconds after that call, the trailer exploded.

"The next order of business for authorities will be to identify the truck and its owner. However, initial indications are that the truck resembles the type that is available for rental in the Houston area. Although they do not make any statements to this effect, police have to be concerned that false documentation was used to obtain this truck.

"Naturally, efforts are being made by some to link this act of terror to the secession. Police caution everyone to remember that the obvious answer can distract the public. They also caution against making assumptions about individuals who may have done nothing more than express opposition to the secession. They further asked that anyone who hears or sees anything that could be of even remote value, report it right away to the Houston police."

Cynthia Warren appeared on screen. "Welcome back to our NewsNet studio in New York, as we try to make sense of a tragic day. My name is Cynthia Warren, and I have been joined now by NewsNet contributors Joshua Simmons of the Potomac Review, and Mason Howell of the Washington Times. So Joshua, let me ask you, were you expecting violence of this nature?"

"As for the bombing in Houston, I am totally at a loss to understand what anyone would think they could gain by such an act. There is no way that a rational person would think that doing this would cause the state of Texas to reverse its secession. I think it more likely that a right wing extremist element did this to solidify hatred for those who opposed the movement.

"As for the riot and urban warfare going on in Austin as we speak, I can only speculate that these people see themselves as some kind of freedom fighters, the last bastion... almost the Alamo, if you will... of wishing to remain part of the United States. Perhaps they felt that it would take such a dramatic event to bring the focus back on the plight being faced by those forced to choose between leaving the only home they have ever known, or staying in a new nation formed to be plundered by wealthy special interests."

Cynthia looked over at Mason Howell. "I have a feeling you're not going to agree with what Joshua just said."

Howell simply shook his head at first. "I suppose that in a situation like this, it would be contrary to human nature to try to refrain from affixing blame for such a monstrous act of murder. What we do know is that Magnum Oil had been energetically lobbying federal lawmakers and policy makers to ease up on restrictions on oil drilling and exploration.

"It really did not receive much attention outside of Texas, but for several months the Magnum headquarters has been the subject of small protests and some picketing. That was because Magnum, being a large and very visible mover and shaker in the oil industry, was a perfect foil for environmentalists. However, I am in no way implying that the bombing was an act of some type of eco-terrorism. It is far too early to try to attach blame to any group or ideology.

"As for this incredible shootout going on in Austin as we speak, we are probably not going to know the motive for this attack on the state Capitol complex until some of the protesters are questioned and their recent activities examined. Such an attack just defies all logic. It looks to me to be some type of act of martyrdom."

Cynthia Warren was once again peering at a monitor. "We are going to return right now to Connie Sinclair, who I understand is still observing this bizarre gun battle going on in Austin... I am now being told that we're going to Connie, but watch a video feed from a traffic helicopter courtesy of the Austin Police Department."

Suddenly the image on the network was the sight of a large parking lot in which several vehicles were burning, and most of the rest a mess of torn metal and broken glass. The parking lot was being swarmed by police, soldiers and Texas Rangers along with medics.

"This is Connie Sinclair, still on the upper level of an insurance office overlooking the carnage. The shooting seems to have ended, but the outcome is going to be very grim. I have seen perhaps a couple of hundred protesters either surrendering or being apprehended, seized and taken away by the authorities.

"However, it has been alarming and quite disturbing to see a constant stream of stretchers and gurneys leaving the parking lot, transporting bodies covered by sheets. Just before going back on the air, a contact with a local news organization told me that an officer with the Austin Police Department had told her that around forty of the demonstrators were killed in the gun battle. We also got word that around a dozen police, Rangers and National Guard troops died as well.

"Although this cannot be verified at this moment, supposedly more than two hundred wounded individuals from both sides of this gunfight have been taken to local hospitals. Of course, once the helicopters arrived on the scene and entered the fray, the previously outnumbered police immediately had the advantage.

"We understand that police used a loudspeaker in an attempt to get the protesters to lay down their arms, and even warned them that more lethal force would be used. Unfortunately, the firing from the protesters continued, to such an extent that very few could probably even hear the message being broadcast. It is going to take some time for us to begin to understand just how this happened, and truly why."

Cynthia Warren reappeared on the screen, along with Mason Howell and Joshua Simmons. "Joshua... I don't know that anyone would have expected such a level of violence and loss of life as we have already seen today. In addition to what has happened in Houston and Austin, the city of St. Louis is in great turmoil, and while there have been some altercations there, most of the trouble has been in the form of civil unrest. However, are there not problems in Dallas and Tulsa as well?"

"Actually Cynthia, since the effective date of the secession, St. Louis had seemed to be the main flashpoint, but nothing there compares to the horrendous bombing in Houston and the bloody battle we have just witnessed in Austin. A truck bomb can be set off anywhere. The problems in the other cities are of another nature.

Apparently the protesters in Austin really felt that they could make secession appear to be costing too high a price.

"As it turned out, the authorities responded with a level of force, and this is my word... brutality... that will come to shock the citizens of both Americas in the coming days as the images and death toll settle in. But if Texas authorities made the decision to put the attack down with a show of force that will deter any further such situations, they probably succeeded."

Cynthia turned to Mason Howell. "Mason, the situation in Tulsa seems to be contained to protest marches, and a couple of buildings being set on fire. In contrast, St. Louis is, of course, a much larger city. It has a mayor who tends to be liberal, and the governor of Missouri is a Democrat, so while the legislature voted to secede, that action was opposed by both the governor and mayor of St. Louis. In addition, there is the Democrat – controlled state of Illinois right across the river. How do you expect that to play out?"

"Cynthia, I have heard suggestions that St. Louis should secede from Missouri and asked to be annexed by Illinois. Of course, that is not going to happen. St. Louis is a large city with many crime issues, and a significant population of people on public assistance. Illinois can afford neither. The city and its residents are going to have to come to terms with reality.

"Missouri, and St. Louis in particular, is simply going to continue to present complications for the Hamilton administration. Tulsa will settle down. As for the situation in Texas, I tend to agree with Joshua, and that the outcome of this morning's bloody confrontation likely was the last large and violent protest to be seen in that state. But Missouri is too divided, and things may not settle down there in the near future."

Cynthia turned once again to Joshua Simmons. "Mason just made a reference to the likely cessation of large and violent protests in Texas. But what about the possibility of smaller, more contained acts of protest in Texas, Missouri or other states for that matter?"

"Actually, I have a great deal of concern about that possibility. With each passing day, and people have a chance to look around and see where fate has planted them, people would begin to reevaluate their condition. Now if you are living in a state that became part of the CSA, but you don't want to be living in a secession state, it would seem there would be two logical choices: you move to the United States, or you simply adjust and make the best of your new government.

"The same would go for residents of the United States, who wish their state would've seceded. They could move to Nebraska or Montana, or stay in Ohio or New Jersey and make the best of things. The concern lies with those individuals who may see their role to be one of disruption. There are likely to be people who want to try on a small scale what the Austin protesters were most likely trying to do. For the governments of the United States and the CSA, such situations will not be neat and tidy."

Cynthia Warren turned back to the camera. "We're going to go to a break, but please stay with us as we continue our coverage of the dramatic and violent events rocking the state of Texas this morning. This is NewsNet."

President Bryce Hamilton, Vice President Franklin Chiles, Treasury Secretary Tom Edelstein and Commerce Secretary Patrick Bridger had been taken by the Commanding Officer of the Omaha Army National Guard Armory to a small meeting room in the facility upon hearing of the Houston bombing. The Major felt that the small, more secluded room provided the highest level of safety within the Armory.

In the hallways in that section of the Armory, soldiers with loaded weapons stood nearby, while others surrounded the building. Even more patrolled the perimeter of the grounds both inside and outside the high, barbed wire fence. Helicopters flew low overhead carrying infantrymen with sniper rifles, while Air National Guard jets high overhead made sure that no unwelcome aircraft made their way into what was now a restricted zone.

The four men who were the core of the the leadership of the Constitutional States of America sat down to relax at a table holding coffee and a selection of soft drinks. Hamilton and Edelstein had just taken off their suit coats in response to the warmth of the room, and were beginning to loosen their ties when they were joined by Nina Burton.

Nina sat down with an exaggerated sigh. "Nothing new on the casualty reports. The Governor just issued a statement offering sympathy to the survivors of those killed at the Magnum building. In the same statement, he condemned the armed demonstrators who tried to take over and capture the Capitol building. He emphasized that the demonstrators were given a chance to surrender, but that they chose to keep firing at police and the Capitol. I would suggest that we issue a statement of support for his actions.

The President stood and stretched. "I agree, but this is all so horrible and senseless. That bombing was just… so craven. As for Austin… I have a hard time grasping that level of zealotry and extremism."

Edelstein spoke next. "Of course, the media will label the counter attack against the demonstrators as the extreme act."

Vice President Chiles softly rapped his knuckles on the table. "I know that the killed and injured is the most important thing right now. Still… I'm just starting to realize how much we have always taken into account media reaction. But what about now? There will still be a media covering news across both American republics. But are the liberal media outlets going to expend a lot of energy and air time covering events in the CSA? Will their viewers in Pennsylvania, Massachusetts and New York want to hear about what's going on here? I mean, a mass murder and a pitched gun battle are always going to be headlines. But now, do even events like these take on the same meaning to the media?"

Nina responded. "I have a niece watching the news for me today. According to her text messages, all of the major networks are covering Houston and Austin, but it's interesting that the 24/7 networks are giving a lot of time also to the welfare cutbacks. Not equal time by any means, but the broadcast stations have abandoned their regular programming for Houston and Austin, while the news networks are alternating their topics to a higher degree as it is to be expected."

Bridger leaned forward and stared down at the table. "There is so much going on... the media is going to try to show that our new Republic has already descended into chaos. Even if all of these problems turn out to have been created by people who were opposed to the establishment of the CSA, it will make no difference to the media. Perhaps, if we are lucky, they will declare us a failure and walk away and leave us alone."

President Hamilton resumed standing, and then leaned on the conference table. "For all practical purposes, we have been attacked by domestic terrorists. That is the tone and the theme of all further public responses, and to all press inquiries. We will emphasize that our newly established and sovereign nation has suffered a terrorist attack in Houston, and an attempted overthrow of our government in Austin. We will keep using those words, repeating them over and over to everyone we talk to."

The Vice President began to drum his fingers on the table. "I understand that a few minutes ago, NewsNet played a tape of the audio from that National Guard officer trying to talk the demonstrators into surrendering. It's pretty dramatic... he tried several times to tell them to give up... he told them at least three times that they didn't want anyone else to be hurt. But all the time, they continued shooting... the demonstrators I mean. That poor guy with the loudspeaker had to keep ducking."

The President began to pace the floor. "One thing I am not going to do... I'm not going to throw the Texas authorities under the bus. That part of town was turned into a war zone... literally. There were lots of demonstrators with handguns attacking the state government. Those demonstrators created a free fire zone where thousands of innocent people were working and doing business, and all of their lives were put in jeopardy."

The President halted his pacing, and then turned to face the others. "Not only will I not fail to support the Texas authorities... I am going to complement them on their decisive and proper actions.

If we want to set a tone, that should do it. Nina... I think it's time to call a press conference. Please arrange that with the Major."

Bryce Hamilton stood in a hallway just off from the Armory assembly room where the delegates had concluded their business for the day. The delegates were ready to move to the Conference Center so that they could sleep in beds rather than cots, and eat food ordered from a menu rather than from a small cardboard box. As the last of the delegates filed out, reporters and video operators began to filter into the room after being searched.

Nina had worked her typical magic. Within two hours, she had made the security arrangements, contacted the media and received assurance that the President's news conference would be broadcast on television, at least throughout the CSA states. Now she stood by her boss as he peered around the corner of the door, awaiting the signal that the broadcast time was at hand.

The assembled media had settled into chairs and chatted enthusiastically with each other regarding the events of the day. Finally, Hamilton and Nina received the signal that it was time to begin. More nervous than Hamilton himself, Nina entered the room first and faced the assembled media: "Ladies and gentlemen... the President of the Constitutional States of America."

Nearly all of them immediately rose, and when Nina spotted two who remained seated, they received a glare that made them almost stumble over themselves as they stood. When Hamilton had arrived at the podium and microphone, Nina nodded to the crowd: "Please be seated."

The President slightly lowered his glasses on his nose as he looked down at his notes, knowing that he would in all likelihood ignore them anyway. "First of all, I wish to extend my sympathies and prayers to the families of those murdered in the cowardly and senseless act of terrorism in Houston this morning. The loss of life is tremendous, and I extend my hopes for full recoveries to all of those injured in and near the Magnum building.

"My administration will provide all possible assistance to the authorities investigating this heartless and brutal act, and we trust that whether this was an individual terrorist acting alone, or part of a terrorist organization, all guilty parties will be brought to justice.

"I also wish to extend my sympathies to the families of the law enforcement officers and members of the National Guard who died this morning in Austin, defending the government of the state of Texas against what appears to be an attempt to negate recent decisions by the state government. There were also very many police and National Guardsman injured, and I pray for their speedy recoveries.

"We also understand that a number of innocent civilians in nearby buildings and on the sidewalks were injured as a result of this violent siege attempted by armed attackers. We hope for their recovery and rapid healing as well.

"I want to take this opportunity to express my appreciation to Texas state officials, and the municipal leadership of Austin, for their firm and swift actions in neutralizing an armed assault by extreme and zealous elements hoping to destabilize the government of the largest state within the Constitutional States of America. Unfortunately, the attackers refused a number of pleas for them to surrender and halt the violence and bloodshed. Their response was to continue firing their weapons at the Capitol building, and police and soldiers who had backed away to await their response to that opportunity to surrender peacefully.

"However, it was the duty of the authorities to ensure that the violence was contained and not allowed to spread. Absent a willingness of the attackers to cease their violent activities, authorities were forced to bring the attack to an end to prevent further injuries to police, Guardsmen and the general public.

"The Constitutional States of America is in its early days, and we know that there will be challenges. However, challenges of a violent nature will be met with resolve and a dedication to the preservation of the safety of our citizens. We know that there are differences of opinion, and we respect those differences when they are expressed in a peaceful manner. However, we will not be deterred from establishing this new Republic in accordance with the principles of its founding, by acts of violence and intimidation. I will now take some questions."

To the surprise of no one, in light of the day's events, nearly all the reporters present began to shout to be recognized. Hamilton sighed and pointed to the correspondent from CBS.

"Mister President... you just seemed to endorse the amount of force used in Austin this morning. Some are saying that the actions by the police, the Texas Rangers and National Guard were excessive and brutal."

Hamilton looked directly back at the reporter. "Some are saying...? Who is saying that?" Off-camera, Nina was standing in the doorway chuckling.

"Well... some are saying that the actions were excessive and uncalled for....".

"Young man... you said some are saying that. It may be helpful for me to know who is saying that, so I would have a better understanding of the context and qualifications of those evaluating the actions of the authorities this morning. Perhaps you would like to elaborate?"

"Well... Mister President... do you want to restate that you approve of their actions?"

"Thank you. Yes, I do support the actions that were taken. Heavier force was brought in to counter a determined group of armed attackers. The authorities had no way to know if this was part of a larger action, and several thousand innocent people were in danger. The attackers disregarded opportunities to walk away unharmed, and decided to continue firing their weapons. The local and state authorities did the right thing."

Hamilton pointed to a correspondent from ABC. "Mister Hamilton... do you and the rest of the leadership of the CSA feel any responsibility for the deaths that occurred in Houston this morning?"

Hamilton slowly shook his head. "I'm sorry... I'm afraid I don't understand your question."

The reporter followed up. "Do you feel that this bombing would never have taken place if there had not been a secession movement?"

"It will be up to the police to determine what the motive was behind this senseless carnage. If the motive was to protest the withdrawal of Texas and the establishment of the CSA, then logic would dictate that the bombing would not have occurred, had those other actions not taken place. This places no responsibility on those of us who took the initiative in establishing our new nation. This was a terrorist attack, and it may very well have been an act of domestic terrorists. Whoever committed this almost inconceivable act, the blame lies with that individual or group alone."

Hamilton pointed to a reporter from the Associated Press. "In the wake of the bombing in Houston, and the bloodshed in Austin, do you feel any regret over your actions during the past couple of years that led to the establishment of the CSA?"

"No. But I am overwhelmed by sadness that extreme zealots felt a need to express their disagreement through terrorism and violence. I also feel anger that our nation was attacked."

Hamilton pointed to a Fox News correspondent. "President Hamilton… we have heard anecdotal stories about people wanting to move from St. Louis, across the river into Illinois, where they have been greeted by what appears to be a handfull of bigots discouraging them. What can you offer to St. Louis residents in that predicament?"

"I must say, I have been very bothered by that situation. Although there are now two Americas, I hope that people can always feel free to choose where they wish to live. I have no authority over what happens in Illinois, and I know that the discriminatory and threatening actions of a few in no way reflect the viewpoints of others in that state.

"As for what I offer to the residents of Missouri, I offer them the opportunity to pursue their dreams, to seek the manner in which they wish to earn a living and raise their families with a minimum of government interference in their lives, and a pledge that we will only take the smallest possible portion of their earnings in the form of taxes, and take great care in the use of that money. I also offer them their government's respect for their religious beliefs, and their government's respect for the right to defend themselves."

The President pointed toward a correspondent from CNN. "President Hamilton, what do you say to the families of the protesters who were killed in Austin today?"

Hamilton hesitated for a moment to look down. "It has always been my tendency to feel a special type of sympathy for families who lose loved ones when the loss was especially unnecessary. That is the case in those deaths. I am yet to receive any details about who they were. I know that it must be distressing to their families to not only have lost them, but to have them die in the conduct of such an act of violence. I know that unarmed demonstrators died in that conflict. I wish that their armed compatriots had not put them in harm's way."

The President called on a reporter from an Omaha television station. "President Hamilton, have the events of today caused you to consider accelerating the formation of a comprehensive military force?"

"Thank you for your question. As you know, a defense secretary was appointed just yesterday, but he is in the process of coordinating National Guard organizations. In fact, those commanders are also working in conjunction with and guidance from some Pentagon officials. We expect that when all is said and done, our military structure will be ready to work in close cooperation with the United States military on a moment's notice.

"In the aftermath of today's violence, there has been communication with some of the United States military bases located within the CSA. So far, we have made no requests for any type of assistance from the commanders of those bases, but it should be noted that those commanders have been quick to provide medical personnel to deal with the casualties from both of these tragic situations."

More shouted questions echoed through the room, but Hamilton held up his hands and leaned into the microphone:

"Thank you for your questions. I hope you understand... I have many urgent matters to deal with, and I will try to have another press conference just as soon as possible." As fast as he had entered the room, Hamilton strode out into the adjoining hallway.

"Welcome back to a special edition of America in Real Time. I am your host Ben Stirling, and it has been a very troubling and sad day of news coverage, and we have some updated information. The death toll in the bombing of the Magnum Oil headquarters in Houston has risen to two thousand nine hundred and forty-nine, with another one thousand one hundred and twenty-seven listed as injured. The reason for the growth of those numbers is due to additional information coming in throughout the day concerning casualties in neighboring office buildings.

"The numbers have been inflated to some degree by a large number of individuals in those neighboring structures who were injured by broken glass, but who had not reported to have their own wounds treated until later in the day, after having spent hours trying to assist those more badly injured. A nearby building that was constructed to be a new sporting goods store but was largely spared of any damage, has been turned into a triage center, and medics from area towns and military bases have staffed that facility.

"Police in Houston have not yet issued any statements regarding suspects in the bombing, but they have been closely examining the remains of the tractor trailer that exploded. Police maintain that they are not ready to speculate on a motive, in spite of the role Magnum Oil has played in promoting oil exploration projects that have been identified by some environmental groups as being particularly problematic.

"Moving on to the unbelievable happenings in Austin this morning, we now know this much from police reports and eyewitness accounts: demonstrators had apparently arrived in the area of the capital building individually throughout the morning. There were no groups or clusters that would have drawn attention, and it has been verified that most of them were dressed in business attire.

"Members of a crew repairing the roof on a five-story building near the Capitol were taking a break at approximately 10:00 A.M. Central Time, when they noticed that hundreds of people suddenly started to walk to and fill a large parking lot. A minute later, a group of them began running toward the Capitol, firing handguns. Police officers and Texas Rangers who were guarding the building and patrolling the grounds, had to immediately retreat inside.

"The officers returned fire and immediately called in reinforcements. More demonstrators produced handguns and joined in the battle as more police and Rangers arrived. Intense firing continued for some time, and it has been discovered that some of the cars in the parking lot belonged to the demonstrators, and were used to bring in large amounts of ammunition.

"Witnesses stated that they were amazed at how long the battle lasted. People in nearby buildings who were trapped inside had to take cover, said that it seemed to go on forever. However, with the protesters shielded behind and under a large parking lot full of cars, and the police and rangers inside the Capitol, there was a virtual stalemate until a hastily – assembled unit of National Guard infantry from an Austin suburb arrived, and that was when the demonstrators, while still not outnumbered, found themselves trapped and encircled.

"The next few minutes were described by both authorities and witnesses as surreal and perplexing. That was when a National Guard officer used a loudspeaker to encourage the demonstrators to surrender and be taken safely into custody. Instead, the demonstrators maintained their same level of gunfire, before the police and Rangers and Guardsmen pulled back and ceased their own firing to give the demonstrators one last chance. Some demonstrators, individually or in groups of two or three, did manage to make a run for safety to surrender to the police.

"Then, a tragic and unbelievable scene unfolded. The demonstrators continued firing at the Capitol and the ring of officers and troops surrounding them. That was when two helicopters from the Texas National Guard moved in with soldiers armed with automatic weapons and sniper rifles, and brought the battle to a conclusion.

"Our latest reports indicate that four Austin police died, along with two Texas Rangers and two National Guardsmen. We also have unofficial reports that there are twelve Austin police officers who have been treated for wounds, along with seven Texas Rangers and seven members of the Texas National Guard.

"The Austin Police Department is now officially reporting that thirty-five demonstrators died, with one hundred seventy-nine wounded. There were also seven hundred sixty-seven demonstrators taken into custody, and they are being held under tight guard in a gymnasium at a large high school that has been commandeered by the National Guard.

"Once again, downtown Austin is under martial law, and several additional National Guard units are now in the city to help maintain order and guard those demonstrators taken into custody. We also just received a report that several thousand demonstrators who had originally assembled on the campus of the University of Texas are now converging on that high school. There are large numbers of police and National Guard troops on the premises, and we are being told that teargas is being used to disperse the demonstrators.

"This information is coming to us in bits and pieces... there have been several firebombs or Molotov cocktails thrown at the Guardsmen by the demonstrators... We are going to take a quick break, and we will be back with you in just a minute."

"This is Ben Stirling on a special edition of America in Real Time, and we want to give you the most recent information that is coming in right now from Austin, Texas. We can now confirm that several gasoline bombs were thrown at National Guard troops by demonstrators who were attempting to converge on a high school where several hundred arrested demonstrators from today's gun battle are being held.

"Several National Guard soldiers were badly burned by the gasoline bombs, and the Guardsmen fired into the crowd. We now have verified reports that the Guardsmen are pursuing the demonstrators as they are attempting to retreat. For matters of security, we can only say that we have a correspondent in the vicinity in a position to see what is happening. Although night has fallen in Austin, normal lighting coupled with security floodlights set up by the National Guard units is assisting in her reporting, and our correspondent confirms that there are significant casualties among the demonstrators, in addition to the burned troops.

"Forgive me while I listen for a moment to the report coming in through my earpiece... I am being told that the troops are still pursuing the demonstrators through the adjacent streets, and some are still firing upon the fleeing demonstrators. I am being told that after approximately nine Guardsmen suffered burns from the makeshift bombs, many of the other troops went into virtual combat mode.

"Now I... I'm sorry... I'm trying to get this straight... I am being told now that the retreating protesters are breaking windows in office buildings and throwing firebombs inside. There are now approximately five... I am now being told that six buildings are on fire, and gunfire is still being heard... I am being told, automatic weapons fire is being heard, and that would indicate the gunfire is being conducted by the troops. What we do not know yet is whether these demonstrators are armed aside from the gasoline bombs.

"Now we are getting... please stand by... Mike Silver is going to join me now, and I understand that he has the text of a statement from the Austin Chief of Police... Mike, what do you have?"

The older correspondent sat down at the desk and began to read from a printed text: "The Austin Police Department wants to remind all citizens that the city is under martial law, and until further notice, there is a curfew from 8:00 P.M. until 5:00 A.M. within the city limits, except for individuals traveling to and from employment.

64

"We are also notifying all residents of the city of Austin that until further notice, the city is under a state of emergency. The entire downtown area should be considered too hazardous for anything but emergency travel. There are now several fires burning in the downtown area, and riots have broken out in several parts of the city.

"Citizens and businesses or homes within a ten block radius of the Texas Capitol building, are urged to take cover and avoid being near windows. Citizens in that area who have a means to block doors that open in are urged to do so. There have been numerous reports of rioters with gasoline bombs in that section of the city and several reports of armed demonstrators firing not only at police and National Guard troops, but also at civilians who have confronted them.

"There have been many injuries reported during the past hour. Residents are encouraged to turn off lights and televisions to discourage looting. Emergency information will be provided by local radio stations."

Mike Silver leaned back in his chair and shook his head. "And Ben, before I walked in we got a report that as many as twenty-five demonstrators were wounded or killed outside that high school after those gasoline bombs were launched at the troops. And I understand that our person on the scene has heard three more explosions, and those could be more of those crude bombs."

Ben Stirling began to speak, but a producer stepped into the camera's view momentarily and handed him several sheets of paper. "Okay... now there are reports of armed civilians engaging groups of armed demonstrators in different areas of the city... Oh, boy... here we go. A newspaper reporter who will remain nameless for the sake of his own safety, has called into our Austin affiliate, and is confirming that armed citizens are in some cases capturing individuals believed to be retreating protesters, tying them up and leaving them on sidewalks, then calling 911 to inform police of their location. Oh... yeah. I'm sure that's going to work out really well. I guess it could be worse.

"Mike... what did you just get handed to you?"

"Ben... we now have the first release of information from the Austin Police Department regarding the demonstrators. Authorities have had the opportunity to identify and question many of the demonstrators. I have never heard of this group... the name of a group that was heard several times during interrogations is The Pact.

"According to a police spokesperson, this organization called The Pact was formed the day of the secession, and this group is described as an underground organization, formed by individuals willing to give their lives in a last – ditch effort to overturn the decision by Texas to leave the United States. Wow! Sounds like this is almost a suicide pact.

"Anyway, this report goes on to say... let's see here... a leader has been identified by several of the interrogated demonstrators, and is said to have died today. His name is Charles Cushman, said to be a writer, activist and lecturer with a rather substantial cult following among those in academia and in the field of revolutionary studies in particular. Cushman has supposedly taught some seminars on civil disobedience at various universities, and did substantial amounts of ghostwriting in addition to having published several books under his own name, most of them devoted to matters of promoting an anarchist society and disrupting law enforcement processes.

"While I have been speaking for the past couple of minutes, our producer has been busy with the Internet... here is some more information about Charles Cushman. He was sixty-five years old, and was a founding member in 1972 of the Indiana Students Coalition Against Imperialism, a group opposed to the war in Vietnam. Cushman went on to make contacts with other antiwar groups and activists, but as the war was winding down Cushman became involved with some radical environmentalist organizations.

"In 1978, Cushman began a three-year federal prison sentence for his role in blowing up a fueling facility at a large logging company in the state of Washington. Seven years after his release, Cushman was investigated for, but never charged with, setting explosives that destroyed an Oklahoma oil refinery.

"Although he was never charged with any other crimes, Cushman was questioned by the F.B.I. three times over a thirty year span for his connections to radical groups being investigated for attempting to rob banks and armored delivery trucks to support the activities of various anarchist groups and Marxist organizations dedicated to overthrowing the government of the United States.

"Cushman was married for fifteen years to Belinda Cartwright, a member of a Chicago-based Marxist group. She was killed during a foiled bank robbery in Dallas in 1987 when she fired a gun at a bank security guard and wounded him, but then died when he fired back and killed her.

"Cushman had been holding a series of free lectures around the campus area, but it is said that most of his following consisted of activist wannabes and hangers on who were mesmerized by his philosophies, or people who just wanted to be on the inside with one of the classic anti-Vietnam radicals. However, he is said to have also had a significant number of students hanging onto his every word. We are also finding out that local authorities have had Cushman under surveillance for several years based upon his past activities.

"When it became evident to local authorities that Cushman was developing a loyal following through his lectures and impromptu brainstorming sessions in places ranging from libraries to coffeehouses, they made unsuccessful attempts to infiltrate his following.

"So the initial indications are that this Cushman was able to somehow assemble a small but fierce group of followers, and the secession allowed him to whip them into a frenzy to the extent that they were willing to take up arms and go into a firefight they could not possibly win."

Ben Stirling shook his head as he looked down at some papers on the desk. "At the risk of making a perilous link out of what may be nothing but coincidence, I would imagine that authorities will now be exploring the possibility that Cushman was linked to the Houston bombing, considering his past forays into environmental extremism. And now we must take a brief break... this is NewsNet."

It was near midnight when an exhausted Bryce Hamilton sat down at a small green desk in the armory supply room. He was waiting to be joined by Franklin Chiles and Nina Burton, and in a quiet moment he looked around at his surroundings and experienced a wisp of nostalgia for his days as a young soldier. The President of a new nation was sitting behind the borrowed desk of a Staff Sergeant, gazing at racks full of helmets, canteens and mess kits. The Major had offered use of his office, but Hamilton felt that the National Guard unit that was suddenly thrust into the role of protecting the government, would function better without his adding to the already considerable disruption.

His Chief of Staff and Vice President walked in and took seats on two folding metal chairs. Allowing himself to chuckle for the first time in a couple of days, Hamilton smiled as he gestured at the surroundings. "Finally... tomorrow afternoon. We go to the Conference Center. In the morning, there will be frequent movement of those troop carriers leaving and entering the armory grounds. In the middle of the afternoon, we will all be loaded onto them and taken to our new, temporary headquarters."

Nina Burton let out a shout. "Beds... private showers... a bar. At long last. And did I mention a bar? I know it's only been a few days...".

Hamilton continued. "And tomorrow evening, the Congressional and Senatorial delegations will arrive. The Governor and the National Guard commander have coordinated some remarkable security arrangements. Of course, there will be no announcements until everyone has arrived and we are declared to be secure. We need to hold a special session to recognize and thank the delegates, but I think that most of them are more than anxious to get back home."

The Vice President leaned forward. "I do want to make you both aware of a situation within the delegation from my own state. I just got finished with a lengthy phone call from the Speaker of our state House of Representatives. Two days ago, one of the House members from Oklahoma resigned. This evening, they appointed his replacement, and she has a rather dramatic story to tell about her life.

"Her name is Colleen McBride. She is an extremely conservative Tea Party leader, and she made a lot of waves throughout the state after she gave some rather impassioned and well-publicized testimony in front of the House and Senate in the days leading up to Oklahoma's withdrawal.

"Well, when the Congressman resigned, the media in our state went into a frenzy focusing on Colleen. They were right on the mark: there were only two people nominated yesterday morning to fill the slot, and she got nearly unanimous support in both houses.

The President shook his head slowly. "I'm sorry to say I don't know of her, but now I'm looking forward to meeting her."

Chiles began to laugh. "She is a true believer... a real firebrand. And I mean that as a compliment to her. Her convictions are unshakable, and we should all be blessed with her depth of common sense.

"Nina... forgive me if these next comments are sexist. But there are certain realities about Colleen McBride that are going to bring her even more attention beyond her solid conservative words and deeds. Colleen is forty-five years old, and she is an extremely attractive woman. In fact, she is a former model, and that is how she helped pay her way through college, because her family was one of modest means.

"Today she resigned from her position as a county commissioner. She has been in that position for twelve years, and she has received a couple of awards recognizing her talent for cutting budgets. Right after she graduated from college, she served four years in the Navy, and that was where she started her medical training.

"Her hobby is rodeo competitions on horseback, and she has even won some trophies in that field. She is a physician's assistant, and her husband operates a horse breeding operation. They live on a small ranch about sixty miles from Oklahoma City, and they have two teenage daughters.

"It's inevitable that she's going to receive a lot of media attention. I am not aware of any blemishes in her background, except that when she was in college she was known for being a rather avid partygoer.

"Most of all, she is solid in her convictions and she is extremely bright. She also has a spine made of steel. She was a lock to be one of the initial delegates, but the day before the selection was to be made final in the legislature, her father-in-law suffered a stroke, so she felt an obligation to withdraw her name and stay with the family until they knew how serious it was."

The President nodded and smiled. "I'll make a point to seek her out tomorrow evening. Thank you, Franklin." He then turned toward Nina. "It's hard for me to talk about these things, but how are things in Austin right now?"

"That big parking lot is a nightmare. Bodies are still being cleared out after photos are taken and their locations marked. It is expected that all the bodies will be removed by late tomorrow morning, and once all the photography is finished, there's going to be a slow and massive process of taking the cars away to an area fairgrounds where they can be processed for evidence.

" The local authorities have a concern that once everything is removed, there is going to be this big, bloodstained asphalt lot riddled with bullet holes that could serve as a rallying memorial for protesters. They are trying to get the okay of their prosecutors and judges to tear up and reconstruct that parking lot. For the moment, it is a crime scene.

"By the way, the police did not seem to be disavowing a story that they're looking at that Cushman guy and his movement for being behind this attack today, and the media is starting to link Austin with the bombing in Houston."

Hamilton shook his head. "I'm afraid to ask this... is there anything else?"

The Vice President responded: "When Elaine Ford popped off about doing away with the Constitution, she seemed to stir up a hornet's nest. And all this could affect us significantly.

"I'm not surprised that she would get some support from members of the House and Senate from her party to bite, but they seem to be heading toward serious consideration. I've been making a lot of calls, and believe it or not, this thing is gaining traction… quickly. In fact, I am picking up that it gained a lot of momentum today. Apparently, some of the members of the U.S. Congress who are entertaining this idea, used the media distraction for the day to operate a little more freely in lobbying their fellow members to see it their way.

"The direct impact for us would be that, it could very quickly bring two or three more states to our doorstep asking for admission. It can also accelerate migration to the CSA. And even though it would not be our problem, some states would be subject to some very serious internal struggles should the United States abandon the Constitution."

Nina Burton seemed to stare off into space for a moment. "The United States, at least in the electoral terms, is now a dominantly liberal nation, with just a handful of solidly conservative states remaining. I am concerned about places like Ohio and North Carolina. I think that states that have liberal metropolitan areas surrounded by very conservative rural areas are going to be quite problematic. Take Ohio for example. President Obama won the state twice, and John Malcolm squeezed out a narrow victory as well. But Ohio has wide swaths where the rural populations are very conservative, and would be horrified at the prospect of seeing the Constitution abandoned.

"Northeast Ohio, and other places like Toledo may be liberal bastions. But geographically, the state countryside is filled with people who are outspoken, faithful and fiercely protective of tradition and their rights to gun ownership. There are also portions of the state that are among the most pro-life regions in either of the Americas. They still hope to see abortion declared unconstitutional someday, and if there is a collective decision made to scrap the

71

Constitution that is one state among several that is in for some serious backlash."

"Thank you for being with us today on the special edition of American Morning here on NewsNet. This is Robert Carter reporting.

"We are continuing our coverage of the bombing in Houston and the startling attack by armed demonstrators on the state Capitol building in Austin. Law enforcement authorities of those two cities are now hinting that they are viewing these two attacks as being coordinated. In light of this development, the Texas Rangers have assumed coordination of the investigations.

"One major lead being followed points to a movement led by long time revolutionary activist Charles Cushman, who died at the Austin shootout, and who was involved in the movement to end the war in Vietnam, then went on to become involved in extreme environmentalist activities, and had been questioned about, but never charged with some acts of eco-terrorism. Cushman was also a prominent lecturer in his advocacy of anarchy and resistance to government. He also published several books outlining his political theories.

"We are also following several other stories of interest. Yesterday in Boston, thousands of marchers stood outside the City Hall, protesting plans by the state of Massachusetts to reduce welfare benefits effective December 1. Governor Gibraltar has made an urgent plea for additional funding from the federal government, but Massachusetts, along with Illinois and New Jersey, are being told that there are insufficient federal resources available to help them avoid benefit reductions. The situation is being blamed on a complex debt crisis related to a sudden downfall in global confidence in the United States bond market.With a live report from Boston is Clarissa Higgins from NewsNet Boston."

A petite brunette came on the screen, standing in front of a large building. "Various community organizations in Boston came together yesterday to sponsor and coordinate a march of several thousand people to express their displeasure with impending reductions in assistance payments to low income families. Unless Governor Gibraltar and the legislature can come up with some form of additional funding, Massachusetts residents receiving public aid will see their monthly benefit payments fall by at least 15 percent, and as much as 20 percent effective December 1.

"To add to the sense of crisis spreading through poor neighborhoods in Massachusetts, is news that funding for the Food Stamp Program may also be negatively affected. Right now, Massachusetts is facing the most immediate threat of reduction in such benefits, but it is also known that Illinois and New Jersey are facing similar crises within the next couple of months.

"Governor Gibraltar met last evening at a local drop-in center for youth with several representatives speaking on behalf of low income families in Massachusetts. She explained that the federal crisis of debt and bond valuations by the secession has precipitated this state of events.

"During that meeting, Marie Simpson, a volunteer for an inner-city food bank, told the Governor that finding the funding to avoid benefit cuts had to be the first priority of the state government. Margaret O'Malley, an employee of a utility assistance program, says that poor families in her South Boston neighborhood simply cannot get by on reduced income.

"While observing the march yesterday, there were several critical comments shouted by passing motorists. Also, a group of five individuals were walking through the crowd handing out copies of lists of available jobs in downtown Boston, so I stopped one of them and asked where they had obtained those lists. I was told that they had received the information from the local office of the Massachusetts Labor and Workforce Development office, and were available to anyone wishing to find employment.

"I later walked up to a man who appeared to be in his late 40's, and was leaning on a cane. I asked him if he were here to protest the cuts as well. However, he went on to tell me that he came out of curiosity, trying to simply understand why people felt they were entitled to other people's money. He told me that he is self-employed, and has a shop in the downtown area where he rebuilds engines for people restoring what he called muscle cars from the 60's and 70's.

"He went on to say that he does not object to helping the disabled or people facing an emergency. But he says that he fell on the ice two years ago and injured his leg and knee, and works six days a week to support his family in spite of his constant pain. He says that he fears our society has lost its sense of self-reliance and responsibility for personal actions and decisions. This is Clarissa Higgins for NewsNet Boston."

The face of Robert Carter reappeared on the screen. "I have now been joined by Simone Dickerson from the NewsNet Business Channel. Simone... can you provide any further explanation of what is happening?"

"Thanks for having me on Robert. When it became inevitable that the nation was going to fracture, bond investors around the world, including in the United States, saw the safety of a government issued bond in a much less favorable light. When investors saw many of the more fiscally conservative states leave the nation, it rattled confidence in the remaining United States. As a result, fewer investors were willing to purchase not only United States government bonds, but even corporate bonds issued by companies located in the United States. At the same time, some investors who already owned such bonds wanted to sell them, so they, in effect, went on sale.

"So as of yesterday, our bonds are seen as a riskier investment. Subsequently, for the government to now sell bonds, those bonds must offer a higher interest rate to offset the risk of possible future devaluation or even default. So you have a vicious circle coming about.

"Paying higher interest rates reduces the money the government has available, because it's being paid out to bondholders. Because our income is reduced, fears surface that the government will simply print more money, but that only further reduces the value of those bonds and our currency in general.

"As a result of all of these factors, the government of the United States ran into a wall. Our spending far outpaces our available revenue, and our credit card has just melted."

Carter raised his hands as if he were surrendering. "Are we now in a state of default?"

"This is where we arrive at the most incredible state of affairs one can imagine. The secession became inevitable when Congress rejected that Last Chance proposal from that coalition of Blue Dog Democrats and Republicans. I could yet be proven wrong... but I think that we are heading toward seeing President Meyers and her party having to wrap their arms around the very proposals that were contained in that suggested legislation."

"The Last Chance package included what are too many... unthinkable reductions. Twenty... thirty percent reductions to all federal agencies? Elimination of the healthcare legislation President Obama put through... elimination of some federal agencies. Can that really happen?"

"Of course, it can happen. In fact, this situation we are in is much more critical and dangerous than the public realizes. We could be facing a catastrophic collapse of our government's finances within the next two weeks."

Carter sat silent for a moment. "So if... okay... why has the government not made this known, and why have we not heard more about this?"

"Alright, Robert... I'm really going to step in it now, so remember this moment. First of all, we continue to have an administration in Washington that has a dismal understanding of economics. They simply do not have a grasp of the concept of unintended consequences. Second, most media outlets are currently in such a philosophical trap that they would be loath to even raise the possibility in a Presidential press conference that spending by the government could be an irresponsible thing, unless of course, we were talking about defense spending. There."

Carter found himself laughing. "Is there any chance of avoiding such a train wreck as you describe?"

Now Simone found herself laughing at her own comments. "There is no way that the administration or Congress are going to pick up the Last Chance proposal out of the trash can, dust it off and say they should try it. But I do hear rumors that Congressman John Perkins of Virginia is working on some type of proposal for a major scaling back of federal spending. We expect to possibly hear something about it today, but all of the tragic news coming out of Texas, and the odd circumstances centering around St. Louis are rather monopolizing available media coverage. If I were the Congressman I would give things a little time to slow down so that his ideas do not get lost in the midst of all the breaking news."

"Thank you, Simone Dickenson from NewsNet Business. And we will be back in just a minute, but we will continue to provide you with information up-to-the-minute, on all the breaking events."

John Perkins paced the floor of his office, sipping on a cup of coffee as he looked out a window of the Longworth House Office Building. He had served his rural Virginia district as a Member of Congress for nearly twenty years, but had never felt such an exhilarating combination of excitement and anxiety.

He nearly jumped when there was a rap on his door, and his budget aide entered the room with a file folder. Sherry Mandell had worked for him for ten years, and had a clear understanding of his attitude toward expenditures of tax money. He quickly headed for his chair behind his modest oak desk, and animatedly motioned for her to sit down.

"Were you able to add much to the list?"

The fortyish black woman nodded and handed him the folder. "Just a few things. You seem to have a good memory for when things happened. You didn't miss any of the major ones."

"Thank you for all your work. I suppose you can imagine the venom that is going to be flying this way... even from members of my own party."

Sherry stood. "I have one question before I go... do you have a title for this proposal? Just curious."

The Congressman laughed. "Not yet. However, I'm certain that there will be no shortage of quite complementary suggestions coming my way in the next few days."

Sherry began to walk toward the door, then halted. "To wish you good luck would sound too anemic." Perkins laughed as he watched her leave. He opened the file folder to find three sets of a list of major programs and regulations enacted year by year since 1975.

He pulled highlighters in three different colors from his desk drawer and placed them on the desk next to the folder. They would be used to identify the priority he would assign to each line item. He spent two hours going through the list, reliving some of the battles that were fought in the House Chamber when some of those bills were passed. As he perused the list, he estimated as he went that he had probably voted against 85 percent of the ones he had marked in red, over 90 percent of the ones he had highlighted in yellow, and 100 percent of those now marked by blue.

He sent an email to Sherry, telling her that he was ready to have her begin gathering the budget figures for the current annual cost of each item of legislation he had designated for review. Then he picked up his phone and called his secretary on the intercom: "Patricia... please get Minority Leader Benson on the line for me."

President Bryce Hamilton finished gathering his sparse belongings to be loaded onto an army truck for transport to the Great Plains Convention Center. He was ready and eager to be transported to a place where he and his fledgling administration could operate more efficiently and in more comfort.

There was one more item of business he wanted to take care of first. He pulled out his cell phone and punched one number, then smiled when the soft and welcome voice answered. "Oh, Bryce... I have been so anxious to hear from you."

"My Sweet Cynthia... I can't tell you how much I miss you. I love you very much. I'm sorry I haven't called sooner. Things have been going on."

Bryce could hear his wife softly crying. "I've been so afraid that somebody would do something to you."

"I have a lot of soldiers around me. We're okay here. And in about five minutes, we leave for the Conference Center. And I have a room waiting for me... for us. That's if you are up to living for a while in a convention hotel that's also serving as a national capitol."

"Make the arrangements... I'll be there."

John Perkins and Myron Benson eyed each other warily as they shook hands and sat down in matching leather high back chairs in the office of the Minority Leader. Benson was already in a deep well of disappointment, for prior to the secession he had been the heir apparent to become Speaker of the House within a few years. While the Democrats seemed to have a tight grip on the White House and the Senate for the foreseeable future, at just fifty years old, the Republican from California felt convinced he would eventually ascend to the post of Speaker.

The secession had taken that dream from him. Republicans in the House were now relegated to a permanent minority status, serving as punch lines for late night comedians and providing unwilling foils for liberal pundits and talking heads. The last thing he wanted at the time was a member of his own party proposing an extreme and unpassable budget scheme that would only reinforce the media theme of his party being a collection of relics yearning for another time and place.

On this day, the Minority Leader exhibited less class and patience than usual. "Okay... let's hear it."

Perkins opened the folder. "First of all, can we stipulate that we are in agreement that we have to take drastic measures immediately?"

Benson rubbed his eyes impatiently and let out a theatrical and exaggerated sigh. "Just give me your damned idea."

"I want to establish a point in time... a base year. Just for arguments sake, let's take 1975. I think we could all agree that prior to nineteen seventy-five, our nation was meeting all the basic needs of its citizens."

Benson threw his hands up in exasperation. "Now aren't you just taking up an argument Bryce Hamilton or one of his friends tossed out there before the secession? We do away with everything new after that point in time?"

"How about we discuss the merits of the idea rather than who originally brought it up? Come on, Benson... have we really enacted anything since that year that we could not survive without? But is it not true that if we don't do something big right now, we will not survive economically?"

"What you are proposing would result in the layoffs of thousands and thousands of federal and state employees. Do you know how many programs would be done away with?"

"That's the whole point, you dumb ass. The numbers are still being worked up, but it looks like if we wipe out everything new since that year, we would have a budget reduction of nearly sixty percent, and we could have our deficit taken care of in five years. Of course, if you just move the baseline forward in time, you still get great results. For that matter if we would go clear up to 2005 and do away with everything enacted after that, we could probably be in balance in a few years if we froze spending. Would that not be preferable to seeing the nation go under?"

"That will never pass in Congress. If you introduce a laughable piece of shit like this, all that you're going to accomplish is to play into the hands of the media that will portray this as just another example of our extremism."

"Then why do we even bother coming here and drawing a paycheck?"

"We do it because it's our obligation. We come here to give the people in our districts a voice."

"If that's the case, we're speaking in a whisper. Because what you're telling me is, Bryce Hamilton and his crew were right."

Benson slammed his open hand loudly upon his desk. "You are nothing but blind to everything going on in front of you."

Perkins gazed at the Minority Leader in silence for several seconds. "No, my old friend... I'm quite aware of everything that's going on in front of me. Particularly... at this moment."

"This is Mike Silver here in our NewsNet New York studio, with a wrap up of today's developments. It is now noon in Texas and much of the CSA, and we now have some more information on the startling and violent events over the past forty-eight hours.

"The Texas Rangers are still questioning individuals with ties to Charles Cushman, former antiwar activist and longtime activist in various radical movements who was killed in the shootout at the Texas Capitol in Austin. It is now coming out that in his most recent lectures regarding the possibility of Texas secession from the United States, Cushman began to present the concept of Austin refusing to join the rest of Texas in such a move.

"According to a young woman whose name has not yet been released, Cushman had become quite excitable when the secession actually happened, and was telling his followers that a show of armed strength on their part, would allow Austin to be to Texas and the CSA, '... what the Vatican is to Italy and Europe'. Two evenings prior to the gunfight, he had spoken to a large crowd assembled at a union hall, and painted a picture of Austin as an island of culture and enlightenment within Texas.

"Under further police questioning, the young protester related how Cushman had convinced a core of individuals that, while they needed to be ready to become martyrs, the reality was that they would be able to easily buy time in a standoff, and be able to bargain with Texas authorities.

"Rangers are now looking into the possibility that the timing of the Houston bombing was coincidental after all. Experts in examining documents have already verified that the tractor-trailer that was leased and used in the bombing, was leased under a false identity. The identity of the individual who arranged for use of the truck, and all of the financial elements of the lease, appear to have been accomplished through an elaborate web of falsification.

"In spite of the secession, the F.B.I. has continued to maintain a field office in Dallas, and that agency is working in cooperation with the Texas Rangers. Although neither the Rangers nor federal agents will comment, an expert on domestic terrorism has told our Omaha NewsNet Bureau that circumstances surrounding this bombing are very similar to a much smaller truck bomb attack on another Texas office building several years ago, and that also involved a company in the oil business.

"No one was ever charged in that bombing, and while it did result in some significant property damage, there were no serious injuries. Two members of a group suspected of environmental terrorism were questioned, but no forensic evidence could tie them to the crime.

"Also, on this busy news day, we are picking up reports that Pennsylvania Senator Elaine Ford's suggestion that the United States consider abandoning the Constitution is gaining some traction. No Democratic members of Congress in either house have so far been willing to go on the record regarding the proposal. Right now, I am being joined by Bradley Walsh, our Washington correspondent, reporting today from the lobby of the Capitol. Bradley... what are you hearing?"

"Good day to you, Mike. To say the least, the Senator has Washington buzzing, and that is remarkable in and of itself in light of all the breathtaking news from the past two days. Of course, that is now part of the reality of the secession: Austin... Houston... St. Louis... Tulsa... these things are happening in places that are no longer part of the United States.

"As a result, an idea has been floated that would have been unthinkable a year ago. As you mentioned Mike, no Democratic members of Congress aside from Senator Ford are willing to comment on the matter, although most Republicans are condemning the idea. However, what I find most stunning is how few Democrats are commenting either way. There are also a handful of Republican Senators and Representatives refusing to comment.

"In the handful of what we would call Red States remaining in the United States, the Governors and members of state legislatures in those more conservative states are making up for them. Members of state legislatures in Kentucky, Indiana, Florida, North Carolina and Georgia are already vowing to introduce resolutions for secession the moment the United States of America dispenses with the Constitution.

"At the state level, there is some bitterness over what one Georgia State Senator referred to as Washington's cavalier attitude toward the states. Senator Lawrence Bigelow says that some of the leadership of the CSA warned in the days leading up to the secession, that people in Washington had lost their understanding of history: the states created the federal government, and by the Constitution, the states assigned duties and powers to it. Bigelow fumed in an interview with an Atlanta television station over what he views as a total disregard for the 10th Amendment to the Constitution, that limits the powers of the federal government.

"Bigelow noted that Senator Ford is in favor of scrapping the Constitution and simply operating the federal government through its code of regulations. Bigelow added that, when one steps back and views the actions of the federal government over the past several years, one would think that such an arrangement is already in effect. This is Bradley Walsh at the U.S. Capitol... Mike, back to you."

"Thank you Bradley... and now we want to mention a bit of a stir being created by another member of Congress, that being Representative John Perkins of rural Virginia. A rather brief press release issued by Perkins' office earlier this afternoon indicated that he would be introducing a proposal to curtail federal expenditures and alleviate the immediate debt and bond market crisis, which appears by the hour to be more critical.

"That crisis has effectively frozen the ability of the government of the United States to issue and sell any bonds or to extend our debt in any way. And investors are beginning to panic at the prospect that the government will simply increase the currency supply. And mixed up in all this mess is the inability of the federal government to provide any cash relief to states facing the prospect of reducing welfare benefits, and furloughing large numbers of employees in many state agencies.

"To explain the situation better, I am being joined by NewsNet Business Channel anchor Simone Dickerson, who is right now at the New York Stock Exchange. Simone…".

"Thank you Mike. Here at the Stock Exchange, the Dow Jones Industrial Average has fallen another 1097 points on the speculation that Congress will be unable or unwilling to meaningfully address the debt and bond crisis. Right now, the only people who appear to be geniuses are the ones who had invested in precious metals. Everything else appears to be going into the tank, except that small company stocks in what are called the emerging markets are holding their own, but not gaining. Some analysts are telling me that the emerging markets are steady because they are considered to be the least directly tied to the U.S. economy.

"And in a development that to some will be seen as icing on the cake, several European finance ministers sent a joint communication to President Meyers asking the United States to exercise fiscal restraint to prevent European economies from suffering in the process. And some of those finance ministers are from countries that just several years ago experienced critical situations because of their own runaway spending.

"Another thing generating some modest optimism is a report that Congressman Perkins of Virginia will introduce a proposal to cut back on spending. However, it is known that he is doing so without the support of the Republican leadership in the House of Representatives. While we do not have anything official from Perkins' office, we understand that the proposal is based upon setting some year in the past as a baseline, then eliminating any federal programs or costly mandates enacted after that date.

"House Republican leader Myron Benson told me in a telephone call that he was unable to speak to any of the details of his colleague's proposal, but that he would keep an open mind for any ideas to help bring fiscal discipline to Washington.

"On an afternoon news program on another network, Democratic Party Chairman Lowell Masterson was asked about the proposal that would likely call for spending reductions of tens of billions of dollars per year. Masterson said that he was not yet briefed on any details, then went on to say that while he was skeptical, he would like to look at any measures that would, for example, contain taxation adjustments for the wealthy, or reduce defense spending so that the federal government could not only provide relief to states struggling to maintain benefit levels to the poor, but perhaps even be able to increase those payments. So Mike, I think that you see just how difficult it may be for any immediate and dramatic reductions in federal spending to actually take place."

"But Simone... I was just wondering... do any of the Congressional leaders of either party indicate that anyone is going to be willing to stand out from the crowd and support a measure that could prevent what could turn out to be a total collapse of our economy?"

"Not so far, Mike. The only person out there with a desire to go so far out on a limb is John Perkins. I have talked to as many as seven members of both sides of the Congressional leadership or their aides over the past several hours. When asked if they were willing to take dramatic actions to avert a total meltdown, all responded to the effect that they were still studying the situation, but had confidence in the American economy. As for any specifics, all that we have is the so – far unseen Perkins proposal. And by the way, just in case you're wondering... although the proposal has not been released, here at this Stock Exchange it has already gained a nickname: The Point in Time Proposal."

"Thank you, Simone... when we return, we will have a review of the day's developments from Texas. This is NewsNet."

It was nearly 5:00 P.M. when Congressman John Perkins was dropped off by his driver at the Washington studio of the American News Channel. While sitting in the backseat as his driver fought the heavy traffic, he reviewed his notes and tried to anticipate the questions that would come from a program host not known for her favor for reducing federal expenditures.

A producer for the program was at a door at the side of the building watching for him, then opened the door and warmly greeted the Congressman and escorted him to the studio. They reached the studio, just out of camera range as the host, Lucinda Fowler was impatiently watching for her guest to arrive to open the segment that was scheduled to go live just 15 seconds later.

The producer quickly ushered the Congressman to a seat next to the attractive fortyish woman who displayed a preliminary obligatory smile before turning rapidly back to face the camera. "Good afternoon, and welcome to Washington Today here on ANC. I am pleased to have this my guest today Congressman John Perkins of Virginia, who is planning to introduce a proposal within the next day or two as I understand, to dramatically address what is being recognized as an impending financial crisis for the United States government. Congressman... welcome to Washington Today.

"Of course we are having another busy news day, so let's get right to your proposal. As you probably know by now, your idea is being nicknamed The Point in Time Proposal. Would you explain to us what your proposal would involve?"

The Congressman smiled. "For expediency, let's use that unofficial name for the proposal. Point in Time means that we would identify a specific year to use as a baseline. We would then look to eliminate and repeal all major programs that went into effect after that date. I would hope that it would be quite easy for us to agree that, prior to... let's say for example... 1985... we had already enacted Social Security... Medicare... Medicaid... all kinds of programs to provide for the basic needs of the citizens of our nation.

"What I am contending is admittedly what some of the founders of the CSA had contended as well... probably most programs and government activities that were created after that year could disappear, and most Americans would not feel that their lives had been in any way disadvantaged. I am not saying that there aren't some, but we are facing a crisis, and if we crash, millions and millions of Americans are going to face hardship."

Lucinda Fowler put her hands up as if she were pleading. "But Congressman... what you are saying in effect... is that it's okay for us to do away with programs created over the past forty years, because most of the programs created in that span of our history are meant to help the poor and disadvantaged."

The Congressman nodded. "I'm not necessarily disagreeing with your statement. It does happen that much of the legislative and regulatory activity over that span has addressed matters of social programs. But they have also addressed burdensome regulatory matters that have put a tremendous drag on our ability to create jobs, and caused states and municipalities to increase taxes and divert resources from public safety issues to adhere to new environmental mandates and employment regulations, rather than enhancing services to its citizens."

"So Congressman, what you are saying is that we should go back to the way things were in 1985, when the air and water was not as clean, there was less emphasis on safety and fairness for workers, matters of civil rights were far less protected than now, and medical care was a privilege, and not a right that everyone could expect to be provided. Am I correct?"

The Congressman smiled. "I am saying that in 1985, America was a great place to live, as it is now, although its future is now in grave danger. Yes, I do think we could live quite well with environmental protections that were in place at that time, workers were already being quite well protected, and we already had Medicare and Medicaid, local charitable organizations helping with medical needs, and the fact that hospitals, even then could not turn away someone with an urgent need.

"But included in your proposal, am I correct that you would be also doing away with the major healthcare provisions enacted during the Obama administration?"

"Absolutely. Once again, we need to do away with all of these programs we cannot afford. We need to let the free market take its course."

"And in the area of civil rights, what about the more recently enacted statutes and guidelines on all the various types of discrimination we encounter in America?"

"As for civil rights, I believe that the answer is found in the hearts of Americans, and great progress has been made. You cannot legislate or regulate a sense of basic decency into people. However, I do believe that overall, we have achieved that. But in any case, having well-meaning and costly laws and regulations on the books will be of little consolation if our economy crashes and we go into a deep Depression. We simply cannot afford to do what we're doing today, and I don't understand why we have this collective refusal among our elected officials to acknowledge that."

"But Congressman, you are one of the Republicans who has fought bitterly against recent tax increases on the wealthy. How can you, on one hand, cry out that our expenditures far exceed our income, and at the same time vote against the measures that would increase income?"

"Let me say something that would surprise you. I would vote for tax increases today, for all Americans, if I could receive, on the other hand, a guarantee... Wait just a second... let me qualify that... a guarantee that I could believe, that spending would be cut at the same time, and the savings applied toward reducing our debt. It would also need to be a tax increase that would require everyone, even those of lower income brackets, to contribute more. This can't be just another scheme to take more money away from the successful so that politicians can't stand in front of the camera and thump their chests and brag about how they stood up for the little guy.

"True, I've never said this before, but I would be willing to vote for tax increases with those conditions. I would vote for tax increases to try to fix this mess, if Congress would also enact the Point in Time package. But for decades, all we have ever gotten is the tax increase part of it.

"Of course, I would prefer that we simply dramatically and immediately cut our spending. But yes, I would accept some tax increases in combination with those dramatic cuts."

"But Congressman, three months ago you stood on the floor of the House of Representatives and soundly blasted a Democratic budget proposal that would have reduced expenditures. Have you suddenly become more trusting of your friends across the aisle?"

"Those were reductions in the rate of growth, not reductions in spending. There were actually spending increases in that proposal. There was shuffling of funds, and some flaky accounting that would have made some current expenditures appear to be set aside for future years. But we are now in a much greater condition of crisis. If there would be any tricks this time, we all go down the drain. And besides, I have been in Congress for a long time, and I know all the tricks. I am a bit too long in the tooth to fall for any...uhm... that was close... nonsense."

"So when will you be formally releasing your proposal?"

"I hope to have it ready by noon tomorrow."

"We'll be looking forward to it. Congressman John Perkins... thank you for being with me today. And please stay tuned, because after the break we are going to be having an update from our correspondent on the ground in Austin, Texas. Stay with us on ANC, for the latest and most accurate coverage."

The grounds of the Great Plains Conference Center had somewhat the appearance of a military base. The large facility was set far back from the access road, and since it was the first completed new construction in the complex that would soon house other hotels, restaurants and specialty shops, there were few buildings close enough to present any security concerns.

Armored personnel carriers provided a dramatic atmosphere at the entrance of the Conference Center grounds. Concrete barriers had been interspersed along the lengthy driveway to ensure that no approaching vehicles would be able to accelerate toward the facility. National Guard troops and Oklahoma State police, now joined by counterparts from Nebraska and Kansas, provided an intimidating force patrolling the outside and interior of the complex.

Although traffic was backed up for some time, eventually all of the delegations from the sixteen states, and the observers from the Upper Peninsula of Michigan made their way to a conference room where they received their room assignments. News correspondents were guided toward another set of suites on the first floor where their credentials and identities were verified. For the sake of security, the correspondents were provided with rooms for the first week of operations, so that there would be fewer people to be screened by security personnel on a daily basis.

Overhead, police and troops in National Guard helicopters from several states constantly scanned the Conference Center and the surrounding area, complementing the ban on commercial and private aircraft in the area. After dark, National Guard troops with night vision goggles would be stationed outside the large facility.

There was no formal dinner, and plans for a large reception had been called off out of respect for the victims of the recent violence. They would, however, open up a large ballroom that evening so that members of the new administration, those who had served as delegates to get the new government under way and the delegations of the House of Representatives and Senate of the Constitutional States of America could mingle and get to know each other.

As for everyone who had been confined in the National Guard Armory for days, they were quite relieved to be able to sit in the large restaurant and order something other than a boxed lunch. A closely scrutinized catering service would be bringing in food on an ongoing basis to be made available buffet style so that members of the new government, and the media covering them, would be able to dine well enough without leaving the premises. All looked forward to their informal gathering that evening, but most looked forward most of all to sleeping on a bed rather than a cot, and having more privacy while showering and using the bathroom.

At 9:00 P.M. the gathering came to its only formal moment. The President of the Constitutional States of America who had been walking through the crowd and chatting casually, stepped to a small podium to a round of rousing applause.

"I want to welcome all of you here, and I appreciate very much your willingness to take part in the greatest experiment in liberty that has taken place on the continent of North America since the year 1776.

"I'm sure that all of you join me in offering up our prayers to the families of all those who have died as a result of senseless acts of violence by those who would do anything to prevent us from reinstating and honoring the promises set forth by the Founding Fathers of the United States of America so many generations ago.

"It is up to those of us in this room, along with our fellow citizens in the Constitutional States of America, to honor those who have died, or are suffering from wounds, by ensuring that the light of liberty held out by our forebears not be extinguished. If Americans are to ever again have the opportunity to live in the freedom, and with the opportunities envisioned by our Founding Fathers, it will be because those of you in this room provided the vision and courage to make that happen.

"I understand that the staff of this wonderful facility are still working hard to finalize what will serve as a chamber for each house of our Congress. I know that when you meet tomorrow morning and select the leadership of those chambers, you will do so in a spirit of cooperation and keeping in mind the best interests of the citizens you represent. I wish you well in your work, and I look forward to working with all of you on a daily basis. Once again, thank you for your spirit and courage to take on difficult tasks."

Hamilton stepped down to another loud round of applause, and resumed working his way through the room shaking hands and introducing himself, with an air of humility that endeared him to people who had been so used to being around powerful people who thought themselves of a special and privileged breed. He happened to notice his Vice President Franklin Chiles waving at him from across the room. He made his way through the crowd, shaking hands and exchanging greetings as he went before finally reaching the former Oklahoma Senator.

Chiles put his arm on the shoulder of a woman who was turned the other way, and when she pivoted to see who was standing in front of her, she smiled widely. The attractive woman was dressed in a denim Western style dress, and looked stunning. The Vice President gestured to her. "President Hamilton… I would like you to meet Colleen McBride, the new member of our Oklahoma delegation I was telling you about."

The President and the newest member of the Congress shook hands before she spoke. "It's such an honor to meet you. Ever since you emerged as a leader of the Council for a Free America, I have been impressed with your philosophy and leadership. I was very pleased and honored to be a member of our Oklahoma Council steering committee."

"The Vice President has spoken highly of you." Hamilton laughed before continuing: "He has also warned me that you are very outspoken… and usually correct. Those are both qualities that our new government needs in our leadership. I understand from our friend here that you have a multitude of talents."

The new delegate laughed. "But I am most talented at running my mouth. At least that's what my husband tells me. I can't wait for you to meet him. He still can't believe the mischief I get involved in. But I can't wait to jump in and get going."

The President nodded and smiled. "I am very happy that you are so enthused, but most of all, we are pleased that you are willing to sacrifice time with your family to help out our new nation."

The Congresswoman shrugged. "It is entirely my privilege."

Hamilton smiled, and then once again took her hand. "I had better move on now, but I am looking forward to working with you."

As he began to walk away, Franklin Chiles walked alongside him. "You can see why I am so impressed with her."

"She is very charismatic. Very calm and confident. I think we need to consider her for some special role. The most outstanding thing about her, is everybody tells me she stays very cool under pressure. When she testified in the legislature in favor of withdrawal, one of the main opponents to the concept miscalculated, and thought he was just dealing with a charming symbol of rural Oklahoma.

"This guy had spent twelve years in our House of Representatives, and ten years in our Senate. He made the mistake of trying to talk down to her. She just had him for lunch. This guy had bullied people for years... experienced attorneys and longtime politicos. She had him so flustered, and there were a couple of people in the audience, people from his own party, who will swear that he was on the verge of tears.

The Vice President halted. "The thing is she was as cool... as calm... as polite as someone could be. But her command of the facts was withering. She kept shooting down his arguments, smiling and taking him apart with her soft, measured tone. I saw a video of it... nothing but remarkable. He never stood a chance."

Hamilton nodded and displayed a sly grin as he began to walk once again. "You're giving me all kinds of ideas."

It was not unusual for Elaine Ford to still be in her office in the Russell Building late into the evening. The Senator from Pennsylvania had a reputation for focusing like a laser on something that caught her interest, and such was the case with her own proposal of abandoning the Constitution. She glanced at her watch with impatience, and then heard a tap on her door before her secretary stepped in and told her that Senator William Morrow from Florida had arrived.

They shook hands, and then Senator Ford asked her colleague to have a seat. "I appreciate your coming by this late. I always tell myself there is no rest for the wicked."

The elderly, trim man with silver hair laughed. "In that case, Elaine, you must be an insomniac. I take it you want to talk to me about the Constitution."

"Yes. What are your initial thoughts?"

"It's no big deal. We would only be abandoning a couple of centuries of rules and traditions that dictate that the states must approve of any changes in the Constitution, let alone its abolition. Still, your idea is one whose time has come. It would seem a bit contradictory for us to ask the states to vote to get rid of the Constitution, when the Constitution says states must make such changes. It seems a little impractical and nonsensical to go through all that, especially in light of recent events."

Senator Ford leaned forward to emphasize her words. "I contend that through the course of the secession, we got rid of most of the hard-core Constitutional adherents. I know there will be some Representatives from your own state, and Georgia and Ohio who will go ballistic. I consider this will put Indiana over the edge, but I can live with that."

The elder Senator chuckled and looked up at the ceiling. "I think it can happen more easily than most observers would realize. But Elaine... I want you to tell me... what do you really want out of this?"

The elegant and impeccably dressed woman stood and placed her hands on the back of her chair. "We can make so much progress as a nation so much more rapidly. The elected representatives that the people send to Washington should be able to decide if people have the right to own guns. The representatives of the citizens should be able to determine how many terms a President can serve... they should be able to determine where to draw the line between freedom of speech and statements unnecessarily harmful and insensitive to others.

"But to have this archaic... almost medieval... for that matter undemocratic process of having all these assorted state assemblies have to pass or deny what those of us in Washington think best...". The Senator shook her head. "Not just because I brought it up. But you are right, Bill. It is indeed an idea whose time has come. Are you with me on doing this?"

The Florida Senator folded his hands together, pressed them against his forehead and nodded. "Okay. We can go for it." He looked up and sighed. "I wanted to talk to you some more before I mentioned this, but I have several others in our chamber willing to sign on. Two are liberal Republicans... the rest are all Democrats. But at least we can make a legitimate claim of bipartisanship. And I know at least seven from our party in the House who are on board, but no Republicans.

"We also have to consider this, Elaine. We can claim that the debt crisis is a product of our ancient and inefficient form of government. We could make the case that we could respond to problems more quickly and efficiently if we operated only by statute, with a Supreme Court only deciding whether the statutes were being followed correctly and, more importantly, fairly."

She sat back down and leaned close to Morrow. "I would like to call a press conference... soon... right away. I will state my intention to bring the resolution to the Senate floor and get this underway. Would you be willing to stand next to me when I do this?"

Morrow looked at her with a look of steeled determination. "You've got it."

Bryce Hamilton watched with an almost wistful gaze as he watched the last members of the newly arrived Congressional delegation filter out of the ballroom. Only a few people remained as he walked slowly toward the corner where Nina Burton and Tom Edelstein sat at a small table.

The new President had no more than sat down when Tom Edelstein pulled out a notepad. "The people from the Upper Peninsula plan to start their petition drive late this week. They're going to ask the Michigan Secretary of State to certify a referendum election on withdrawing from the state."

Hamilton shook his head. "From the rumors I'm hearing, Elaine Ford is going to drive Indiana into our open arms. Perhaps, Georgia, North Carolina and Kentucky as well. I would think that would be the extent of it all."

Nina arched her eyebrows as she looked back and forth at her two companions. "There are some very disappointed people in Ohio who would love to be a part of all this. They understand that it simply won't happen, but you have people in the western portion of the state, some on the east side and some in the southern part... that just aren't liking what the future seems to hold for them. I hear a lot about it through my sister in Marietta... she says that a lot of people in that state just feel so torn. People don't want to move from where they've lived their entire lives... it's understandable.

"But the sense of disappointment... Catherine says that being viewed as the big swing state, with a bad debt situation, now this chatter about the Constitution... She says it's one thing to want to migrate, but the economy is in a shambles again. It's hard to sell a house. It's ironic, but it's people who are renting their homes who can most easily head for the promised land. Businesses have had a tough time, so it's difficult to have enough capital to relocate an enterprise, under the best of circumstances.

"Catherine feels scared. She knows that a lot of people feel trapped, like they don't belong there anymore. And there are a lot of rumors about angry people. Everyone knows they can relocate, even if conditions are not optimal. But there are some who aren't looking at it like that. A lot of people feel betrayed, and Catherine is worried about how they will express that."

"This is Gwen Munro, reporting from the lobby of the Great Plains Conference Center near Omaha, Nebraska, the capital of the Constitutional States of America. On this sunny but brisk morning, several hundred people are now at work in this sprawling complex that is serving as a temporary seat of government. Just one hour ago, at 9:00 A.M. local time, the first sessions of the two houses of the Congress of the CSA were gaveled to order.

"President Bryce Hamilton opened the session of the Senate, and Vice President Franklin Chiles opened the historic first meeting of the CSA House of Representatives. The first act of the Senate was to select a chamber President. As you can imagine, as of this time there are really not distinct political parties in the traditional sense, as most Senators and Representatives sent to Washington by these states were Republicans.

"In the Senate, Jeremy Whitley of Missouri was elected from three nominated candidates to serve as the President of the body. In the House, things got a bit more complicated. There were seven members nominated, and while the session remained quite civil, it took several votes to narrow the field. In what has to be considered as a major surprise, and some may call it a compromise, Congresswoman Colleen McBride of Oklahoma was selected to be Speaker, winning by one vote over Representative Leonard Youngblood of Texas.

"What is remarkable about the selection of McBride, is that she was just named two days ago to fill a vacant House seat, when veteran Representative Ed Mallory decided to retire rather than take up a position in the new government.

"McBride has served several terms as a county commissioner, and made quite an impression upon members of the Oklahoma state legislature when she testified recently in favor of secession. Considering however, her lack of administrative and legislative duties beyond the county level, McBride may have to struggle to be taken seriously.

"Apparently, there was an informal meet and greet session held here last evening soon after the delegations arrived. It is said that McBride was quick to offer her philosophies and opinions to her new colleagues, and apparently many were so impressed as to be willing to promote her leadership in the chamber.

"That vote took place just five minutes ago, but McBride is now at her post, at the podium conducting the business of the House of Representatives of the Constitutional States of America.

"McBride will have to lead the House in its quest to put the new nation on a firm footing. There are matters of health care, economics, including a decision on a currency. The status of the military lends itself to many unanswered questions, and decisions must be made on everything from issues of air travel between the Americas, joint banking regulations, and even matters of how college and professional sports will be coordinated.

"As for the Senate, they will also be discussing matters of banking, commerce between the Americas and the status of treaties and trade agreements which had been entered into by the United States.

"And with all that on their plate, this fledgling nation is still in shock over the violence and loss of life that took place in Texas. And while the demonstrations in Tulsa, Oklahoma appear to have ended, there are still new outbreaks of arson taking place in St. Louis accompanying the unrest of large numbers of citizens who do not relish what they perceive to be the philosophy of their new government.

"In the meantime, several of the larger cities in Texas are seeing a continuation of peaceful protest marches by those who want to convince the new nation to not abandon the policies of the United States in terms of services to the poor and minorities. However, advocates for the poor located in the CSA are finding their protests being tempered significantly by seeing what is going on with assistance to low income individuals in the United States.

"Earlier this morning, I spoke with Tom Edelstein, who has been appointed as Secretary of the Treasury for the CSA, and asked if he and other CSA officials feel vindicated by what is happening in

Massachusetts, Illinois and New Jersey. He replied that the budget crisis should be of no surprise to anyone, and he emphasized that the current situation is what many of those who were active in the Council for a Free America had warned of but to no avail. And now back to New York, and Carol Rogers."

"Thank you, Gwen Munro, for that report on the first morning of business being conducted by the Congress of the CSA. This is Carol Rogers and you are watching American Morning. We are able to report this morning that Texas Rangers officials state that they now officially have no reason to believe that the bombing of the Magnum Oil headquarters in Houston was directly linked to the armed attack upon the Texas Capitol in Austin.

"It appears now that the deceased radical leader Charles Cushman was the principle driving force behind the Austin revolt, although he was joined in his instigation by a cadre of long time colleagues and friends in anarchist and revolutionary circles. As police continued to identify those killed in the Austin gun battle, they are finding that some of the dead had been known to the F.B.I. and major police organizations for as long as forty years.

"In fact, authorities have disclosed that at least three of the dead were fugitives, not at the level to be placed on the most wanted lists, but wanted nonetheless. One of the younger protesters taken into custody has related to investigators that Cushman had hyped his vision of such a confrontation as some type of Alamo for resistors against the secession.

"Rumors are running rampant in and around Austin, and there are unconfirmed reports that autopsies are being performed on protesters killed in the gun battle to see if they may have been rendered susceptible to manipulation through the use of drugs. Cushman wrote in an essay published in an underground newspaper and various websites, of his use of PCP and numerous other drugs. He had a reputation for being quite generous with such substances.

"There have been questions raised about the weapons in the possession of the demonstrators. A young female demonstrator is said to have given a detailed account of agreeing to spend the night with Cushman in exchange for a supply of drugs. She told investigators that after she and Cushman had sex, they began to ingest crack cocaine, then Cushman took her to the basement of his rented home several blocks from the campus of the University of Texas, and opened a metal cabinet containing several shelves full of handguns.

"Investigators have discovered that, while Cushman held himself out as a revolutionary living a meager existence, he rarely revealed to anyone that his father was the owner of a Colorado copper mine, and Cushman inherited a large sum of money at the age of twenty when his widowed father died. Soon after his father's death, Cushman entered the world of the radical underground, keeping his wealth a closely guarded secret.

"Authorities continue to try and determine who really leased the semi tractor-trailer that was filled with dynamite and exploded outside the Magnum Oil building in Houston. It had been reported earlier that the operation seemed to mirror an unresolved bombing from several years ago that also happened to target a company involved in oil production.

"I can also report that... we have a report... The Texas Rangers issued a statement just several minutes ago that they have identified a person of interest in the Houston bombing. They are not disclosing the name and are not stating that they have a suspect. But they are now acknowledging that they have a person in custody who is being questioned about the bombing. We will be following that development very closely, and we have news to report on many other topics as well. So please stay with us, and we will be back right after this short break."

"Thank you for staying with us. I am Carol Rogers and this is a special edition of American Morning here on NewsNet. The stunned city of Houston, still reeling from the deaths of so many hundreds of victims from the Magnum Oil bombing, is now preparing to make plans for funerals for some of the dead. Due to the nature of the crime, and the status of the investigation, it is expected that funerals will become a daily matter in that city over the course of the next two weeks. The mayor of Houston has pledged to make hundreds of city staff available to the victims' families to assist in the coordination of individual services and burials, in addition to a memorial event to honor all the victims.

"The death toll in that bombing now stands at an official count of two thousand, nine hundred ninety-seven, and over two hundred are still hospitalized.

"In Austin, the last of the bodies of the protesters killed were removed last night. Funerals for Austin police, Texas Rangers and National Guardsmen who were killed begin tomorrow. Twenty-three police officers, Rangers and Guardsmen are still hospitalized.

"And in Boston, Massachusetts this morning, peaceful picketing continues outside City Hall. Although the city government has little to do with the issuance of state welfare benefits, it has become a focal point for protesters seeking to bring attention to the plight of poor families facing benefit reductions effective December 1.

"Governor Helen Gibraltar was not directly available this morning to comment on whether any progress had been made by the state government in seeking to find funds to forestall or prevent such reductions. A spokesperson for the Governor told our Boston NewsNet affiliate that it will be impossible to prevent what he referred to as a human tragedy unless additional federal funds are forthcoming.

"Massachusetts, Illinois and New Jersey are all facing the prospect of benefit reductions within the next couple of months. But while these states are trying to avert an immediate reduction, we are now hearing that Maryland, Michigan, Ohio and Rhode Island are not far behind. In the CSA another approach in helping the poor appears imminent. To tell you more about this topic, we go to Megan Howard in our Omaha Bureau."

"Thank you Carol. I am standing outside the local office of the Kansas Department for Children and Families here in Emporia. People who come to this office to obtain monthly public assistance benefits are in for some big changes.

"Up until now, recipients of welfare type benefits in the United States could qualify for other types of benefits, in addition to the standard monthly cash grant, Food Stamps and Medicaid. Although it varied by state, around the country there were different forms of assistance for utility payments, housing costs in some cases, and even special supplemental benefits for families with young children, and it was not unusual for low income benefit recipients to be eligible for government provided cell phones.

"Critics of the welfare system often pointed to this list of income supplement programs as proof that the welfare system had gotten out of control, but now many states in the United States are finding their programs in critical financial trouble. But in the CSA, simplification and consolidation are being pointed to as a way to do more with less.

"Prior to the secession and establishment of the CSA, the Council for a Free America had many taskforces devoted to critical topics, one of them being the matter of public assistance and welfare benefits. A result of the work of that particular task force was to develop a template, but not a mandate, for states to follow. However, it appears that Kansas will be one of many, if not all of the states, adopting that guideline.

"For your typical and traditional welfare benefits, states are required to allocate a percentage of the benefit costs to obtain federal money, and that same match requirement applied to administrative costs. States are also required to chip in a percentage for Medicaid and now for administration of Food Stamps. Some other programs were operated out of federal funds, but required state and county employees and other administrative resources to implement them. In all, there are more than one hundred twenty programs in the United States that provide some type of assistance to families qualifying by a wide variety of eligibility rules.

"CSA officials are now going to be restricted to providing benefits without any federal funds. However, they maintain that a state can simply set aside the funding that was already going to such benefits, and have one simplified assistance program. They emphasize that the administrative costs of the old federal system were staggering, but money that used to go to administrators and a large number of case workers needed to handle such a complex array of programs, can now be rolled into the pot of money to be issued to the people in need.

"Kansas officials are also planning to institute a massive work for welfare initiative, and those who refused to work would be denied income through the system. Officials also go on to point out that recipients required to work will soon realize that conventional employment will provide much better for their families.

"A spokesperson for Governor Brackett was asked what would happen to children in the family if a parent refused to work, leaving the family with no income. She responded that such a situation would be considered child neglect, and handled accordingly.

"Tom Edelstein is the Treasury Secretary for the new nation, and when we contacted him for comment on this matter, Edelstein pointed to the difficulties being experienced right now in the United States. He said that neither American nation is in a position financially or morally, to allow the welfare system to be an option to self-sufficiency.

"Edelstein points to what is happening in Massachusetts and other states as the inevitable result of a society's willingness to seize the earnings of some people to compensate for unfortunate choices of others. He says that he likes to remind people, that the welfare system originated during the presidency of Franklin Delano Roosevelt, and was intended to provide for the needs of widows and orphans.

"Edelstein feels that the United States was such a successful nation, that it was able to generously expand what he calls the welfare state to those who were without regular income for an almost limitless list of reasons. He says that he feels sympathy for the poor, but wants to see the CSA take steps to break that cycle of poverty.

"Edelstein and Kansas officials say that the new, consolidated program will go into effect on January 1. Other states are expected to follow suit. In the meantime, the monthly cash assistance benefits will remain untouched, but churches and food banks will be deluged, because there will be no Food Stamp program effective December 1, and the agencies administering those various, assorted other programs, are already putting signs on their doors, notifying the public that they are now out of business. This is Megan Howard, reporting from Emporia, Kansas."

Congressman John Perkins stood at a podium in the spin room outside the United States House of Representatives, adjusting the microphone to his short stature. He gazed at the assembly of twenty reporters and correspondents facing him, then began his statement: "I want to thank all of you in the media for coming here this morning. I would like to take this opportunity to inform the citizens of the United States that I plan to offer a bill to Congress to take the steps I feel are necessary to halt the crisis we are facing in our debt administration, and preserve investor confidence in the bond market.

"It is critically important for the citizens of the United States to understand that our economy is in imminent danger of collapse. We have simply spent much more money than we could afford to. Now the payment has come due.

"We have no choice but to do away with many costly programs and mandates to avoid the economic failure of our government, a tragedy that would send us into a depression. Therefore, today I am introducing a bill in the United States House of Representatives that will repeal over four hundred eighty-five pieces of legislation and administrative mandates I have identified as being nonessential to the security, safety and well-being of our citizens.

"All of these identified items were enacted or put into effect on or after January 1, 1986. Passage of my bill would result in an immediate reduction in federal expenditures by an amount of twenty-five percent. The bill also contains a provision limiting the size of the non-defense federal workforce to the level as of January 1, 2008 for a period of five years from today.

"Passage of this bill will avert the catastrophe we are facing. It will save us from plunging into a depression, and perhaps even permanent economic ruin.

"I ask you to think back to America at the end of 1985, or ask your parents what it was like. Was America not a vibrant, safe and secure nation then? Were the needs of Americans not met? Did opportunity not abound? Thank you. And I must get to the House chamber right away, to file this bill." As a chorus of questions were shouted out, Perkins turned and walked slowly to the chamber of the House of Representatives.

"Thank you for tuning into America in Real Time. My name is Ben Stirling, and I hope that you are having a good evening. We are going to dispense with our regular format this evening, so that we can bring you some updates on the significant events that have taken place over the past three days.

"A just released report of the office of the Texas Rangers says that the semi-truck trailer used in the bombing of the Magnum Oil headquarters was leased two months ago, and had been reported missing by the leasing company. Houston police acknowledge having received a report of the missing truck and trailer, but had been unable to come up with any solid leads in the case.

"Forensic investigators examining the remains of the trailer have concluded that one side and both ends of the interior of the truck had been modified by the welding of steel plates to the interior frame. As a result, the force of the explosion was directed through the unreinforced side, the one facing the Magnum building. Investigators said that this significantly concentrated the force of the explosion to maximize the damage and casualties. As a result of these revelations, it appears that the crime may fall within the category of eco-terrorism rather than a protest over secession.

"And in what may or may not be a related story, Austin police have released information from the county medical examiner on autopsies performed on the bodies of Charles Cushman, and several of the other protesters believed to have been among the gunmen. Cushman's body was among several having traces of a variety of hallucinogenic drugs in their system. Investigators continue a detailed search of Cushman's rented home for further clues.

"The Texas Rangers have also announced that they are conducting interviews with a wide ranging list of individuals who have been linked to Cushman over the years. They have concerns over the possibility that associates of the deceased radical could be planning similar actions.

"In Boston today, the City Hall continues to be the focal point of protests over plans by the state of Massachusetts to reduce welfare benefits effective December 1. A representative from the office of Governor Helen Gibraltar journeyed to the city building to speak with protesters who occupied the lobby of the building by laying on the floor and refusing to move. The representative also met with a delegation of neighborhood grocers and convenience store operators who explained that their businesses will be significantly harmed by the reductions in income for their customers.

"Virginia Congressman John Perkins today filed a bill in the United States House of Representatives that would repeal a list of four hundred eighty-five acts of legislation and administrative mandates put into effect after January 1, 1986. Perkins maintains that the elimination of those laws and rules would reduce federal expenditures by twenty-five percent without substantially affecting our citizens.

"The administration of President Bryce Hamilton and the Congress of the Constitutional States of America are now operating out of a large, sprawling convention complex near Omaha, Nebraska. Today, the Congress of the new heartland nation spent its first full day in session.

"The new government faces a daunting list of work to be done. It must structure an economy, decide upon a military structure, contemplate its role among the nations of the world and decide how it will respond to further acts of sabotage, terrorism and insurrection.

"However, not every moment of the day was taken up by grappling with headache inducing pressure and stress. Gwen Munro of our Omaha Bureau had the opportunity earlier this evening to speak with Congresswoman Colleen McBride of Oklahoma.

"McBride was the surprise selection to be the first Speaker of the House of Representatives of the Constitutional States of America. Just two days ago, McBride was selected to replace a retiring Representative, after having held no office beyond the county level.. And an interview with McBride produced some surprising comments and ideas, as you will see now in this previously recorded exclusive interview with Gwen Munro."

The image on the television screen was of the petite bureau chief sitting on a couch next to the new Speaker, again dressed in a Western style. "Madam Speaker... I have to ask you how that title sounds."

"Well... I am flattered and honored. The last twenty-four hours has been a whirlwind of surprises and activity. I just hope to serve the people of the CSA in an efficient and honorable fashion."

"I know that you are not well known outside of Oklahoma. However, among those who are familiar with you, you have quickly developed a reputation of being outspoken and forceful. Does that just come natural to you?"

The Speaker laughed. "I have read a lot about the British Prime Minister Margaret Thatcher. I wish that I could have had the opportunity to meet her, because she has become a hero to me. I understand the comments about my style, but Margaret Thatcher one time said something to the effect that, consensus meant that there was an absence of leadership.

"That same principle applies whether you're making decisions for the good of the public at the county level, the state level or a national level. Compromise can be a wonderful thing, but if you feel that one choice is much more advantageous to those you serve than another, it is your obligation as a public official to be firm and clear in expressing your preferences and policy and the expenditure of other people's money."

"I heard a rumor that you are considering a rather creative proposal for a special development in the CSA that would involve transportation, industrial development and recreation. Could you speak to that?"

The Speaker seemed surprised at the question. "Okay... I had not planned on speaking of this publicly for some time. After all... this falls into the category of a pipe dream. But here goes...

"I think that everyone understands by now that energy development and exploration will be a major focus of the economy of our new nation. Oil and gas pipelines and railroads can share a right-of-way, a common path if you will.

"I am not a surveyor, and I'm certainly not an engineer. But I have what you could probably call a fantasy project bouncing around in my head. And mind you, I would not propose using any public funds to do this. It would have to be done totally through private investment.

"Imagine a high-speed rail system, from the Gulf of Mexico north to the Canadian border. Perhaps it would be three tracks, and alongside them oil and natural gas pipelines. When a right-of-way would go through environmentally sensitive areas, it could go underground.

"It would be routed to pass by surface mining projects, that can someday be reclaimed by becoming lakes and nature areas, and passenger spurs could take people to ski resorts. Along the way, passengers could arrive at lodges, resorts with premier restaurants and golfing complexes. Not only would it provide a boost to the energy industry, it could become one of the world's major recreational tourist attractions.

"It may never happen, but in the CSA we will be free to dream big. We will spend our time and energy focusing on what we as a people want to do, not sitting around deciding what we want to restrict and regulate and tax next. We want people to achieve. We want people to enjoy their lives, and if people earn a lot of money in the process, all the better. I hope that a whole lot of people get rich because of our policies. We are not here to put limits on achievement, to put restraints on the accumulation of wealth or to lay a guilt trip on those who were smart and energetic enough to accumulate more money than others."

"As a county commissioner, you were known for being exceptionally frugal. In general, how would you explain your philosophy regarding public expenditures?"

"It's very simple. We live on a ranch, and when I would come home from a day working in the clinic, I would change clothes and head out to the barns to feed the horses, or even clean the stalls. All day long, my husband did that kind of work, or he was training horses and enduring a lot of bone jarring laps around a corral breaking in a new horse that had never been ridden.

"Bags of horse feed are heavy, and after you have filled a wheelbarrow with horse manure and have to push it out the barn door, your bones and muscles ache at night. And most of the people who live in my county work very hard, even if it's behind a desk.

"I considered taking the earnings of another person to be a necessary but radical act of government. And when you take something that someone worked hard to earn, you have a serious obligation to ensure that it's not wasted or used on frivolous things. If you want to waste money, waste your own money. But don't waste mine."

"Thank you, House Speaker Colleen McBride. I know you're winding down from a long and exhausting day following a short night. This is Gwen Munro for NewsNet."

NewsNet viewers once again saw Ben Stirling. "Now we want to get some feedback on the proposal by Virginia Congressman John Perkins to sharply and immediately reduce federal spending by, in essence, going back in time to the end of 1985. For comments on the Perkins proposal, we have with us Democratic Representative Sandra Boyle of Ohio. So, Representative Boyle, what is your impression of your colleague's proposal?"

A middle-aged woman with dark red hair appeared on camera. "Thank you for having me on, Ben, because it's important that everyone understand that what John Perkins is proposing is a nonstarter. It takes into account none of the crushing needs of those who depend upon the government to maintain even a meager existence.

"It would do away with many valuable and critical improvements we have made in protecting our environment, it would obliterate strides we have made in workers' rights and improvements in labor -management relations. But more than anything else, it will hurt the poor, especially the children. And at the bottom line, such a proposal shows a grotesque insensitivity to minorities."

"But is it not true that most United States residents benefiting from government programs are white?"

"That is true, but a higher percentage of members of minority populations receive government assistance, so they are disproportionately adversely affected by such a proposal."

"But we understand that your own state of Ohio is now perhaps three to four months away from facing the same crisis in welfare benefits as is now occurring in Massachusetts, and then Illinois and New Jersey. Do you consider it to be a possibility that failure to act on Mister Perkins' proposal now could result in more drastic cutbacks for people in your district a few months down the road?"

"Ben, there is so much wealth in this nation, that there is no reason for us to be considering reducing the income we are providing to what are, in effect helpless families."

"So are you proposing that we enact some kind of steep, emergency tax on the wealthy?"

"Absolutely, because once you become a millionaire, for what reason would it be necessary for you to have any more than that? If someone has several million dollars more than that, that one person's bank account or investment portfolio could provide for so many families month after month after month. And we have a lot of people in our nation who have tens of millions of dollars."

"So you would, in effect, enact a tax on wealth? Do I understand you right?"

"I think that as a nation with so much wealth, that is exactly what we have an obligation to do."

"So how much of a wealthy person's assets do you think the government should claim through taxation?"

"First of all, let me say that I agree with my colleague Congressman Perkins, that we are in an emergency. So I would tax 100% of all individual wealth in excess of one million dollars. That would alleviate our immediate crisis in providing for the poor."

"And what would you do about the rest of our deficit? We still face red ink in Medicare, and Social Security will soon be in trouble."

"First of all, we have to stay out of costly, unnecessary and unjust wars. Then, we have to be willing to increase the tax rates on high earners on an ongoing basis."

"One last question, Congresswoman. Do you have any concern that the wealthy or just average business owners listening to what you have to say may simply decide to move to the CSA to escape the possibility of ideas like yours becoming law?"

"Nothing can be done about individuals who move to the CSA. But I believe that we should prohibit the purchase by United States citizens and businesses of any goods or services produced in or provided by companies who have moved to the CSA after the secession."

"Thank you, Congresswoman Boyle of Ohio. I appreciate your candor, and I hope to have you on the program again. And when we return, a state senator from Florida will join me to discuss the possibility that the United States may scrap the Constitution. This is America in Real Time, and we will be back in a couple of minutes."

"This is Marcia Bentley, and welcome to another edition of American Morning, broadcasting this morning from Washington. Throughout this morning we'll be having updates on many topics, but overnight there was a startling development regarding the Houston bombing of the Magnum Oil headquarters.

"The Texas Rangers went to a home in the north side of Austin at around 2:00 A.M. local time to bring a suspect in for questioning. The suspect, Michael Winston, refused to open the door of his small, rented home. Rangers began a process of breaking down the door so that they could apprehend Winston, and when they entered the home Winston opened fire with a small caliber revolver. Winston was immediately shot and killed, and no Rangers were injured.

"The Rangers had identified Winston as a suspect through the use of photos of environmental extremists thought to be capable of violence. The photos were shown to the rental agent who had leased a truck to a man who identified himself, even with backup documentation, as Walter Harold. Texas officials have now verified that Winston, age sixty, had been living under that assumed name for some time.

"Ranger officials are also searching a barn on a farm west of Austin, supposedly as a result of rental receipts found in Winston's home. Officials have confirmed that packing crates in the barn indicate that dynamite was stored there, and tire tracks indicate that a semi tractor-trailer was housed in that barn.

"Officials are also backtracking on previous statements dismissing a connection between the Houston bombing and the attack on the Texas Capitol. It has been confirmed that the banking records of Charles Cushman are being examined for any link to Winston.

"As we assemble information on Winston and his past activities, we will bring them to you. In the meantime, funerals are beginning to be held throughout the entire Houston area for the nearly three thousand victims of that bombing.

"In Massachusetts this morning, public assistance recipients are bracing for the expected reduction in aid to take place on December 1. Governor Helen Gibraltar confirmed this morning in a press release that the typical Massachusetts family receiving public assistance will experience a twenty – five percent cut in monthly cash assistance, and a member of the governor's staff indicated that federal officials are projecting a fifteen percent reduction in the Food Stamp allocations.

"A large rally is expected to take place at 5:00 P.M. outside the Boston City Hall. Organizers have obtained a permit to do so, and several very prominent civil rights leaders are expected to be speaking at the event.

"Over at the Governor's office, a steady stream of spokespersons for concerned interest groups have been making their concerns known. Aside from the expected advocates for low income families, there have been objections filed by groups of landlords, grocers and convenience store owners.

"Other states are facing challenges as well. Illinois officials are hinting that they are one month behind Massachusetts in terms of having to limit welfare benefits. But not much attention has been paid to the effects that the state budget crisis, coupled with the lack of means for the federal government to provide assistance, will have on public employees.

"In Illinois, public employees ranging from welfare policy analysts to public school teachers will be holding their breath at the prospect of receiving pink slips. The Massachusetts Department of Transitional Assistance may be laying off up to seventy percent of administrative and policy staff, and forty percent of Massachusetts' welfare caseworkers may be furloughed.

"Unions representing Massachusetts public school teachers, as well as the union representing the welfare caseworkers are threatening to strike over the proposed layoffs. And student organizations at the University of Massachusetts and other state – funded universities and community colleges are threatening to conduct student strikes to express their solidarity with the public employees.

"Of course, at the root of all this financial chaos lies the debt crisis intertwined with a sudden worldwide loss of confidence in the bond market. In addition to some states facing welfare cutbacks and the layoffs of employees, a new wave of cities may default on their bond obligations, and that could wreak havoc in terms of providing police and fire protection, and even such services as trash pickup. Leaders in a number of cities warn that metropolitan areas could be plunged into chaos if the problem is not quickly resolved.

"One person who is trying to do something about the financial crisis is Virginia Congressman John Perkins, who yesterday filed a piece of legislation in the United States House of Representatives that would do away with decades of laws and regulations he has identified as extremely costly, but unnecessary for the everyday needs of Americans. Although Perkins claims that his legislation would immediately bring the United States into fiscal solvency, there have been very few expressions of support from members of Congress of either party. Nonetheless, Perkins states that he is resolute and pressing for the passage of his bill, and he says it is imperative that it be passed within two weeks in order to save the U.S. economy.

"And when we return in a moment, our Omaha Bureau Chief Gwen Munro will be bringing us some information on how the new Constitutional States of America will be handling matters of revenue. Please stay with us, and we will be back after this break. This is NewsNet".

"This is Gwen Munro reporting from the operational headquarters of the government of the CSA, here at the Great Plains Conference Center. Here within the sprawling complex of two hotels, several restaurants and a maze of meeting rooms of all sizes, the entire government of the CSA is establishing not only how the new nation will operate, but how it will differentiate itself from the United States.

"One notable departure will be the tax code. Secretary of the Treasury Tom Edelstein told me last night that the Congress of the Constitutional States of America will likely today adopt a tax code that will probably not exceed three pages in length. There will be an income tax for all CSA residents at a flat rate of 12%. That will apply to all income, from any source, and there will be no such thing as a deduction. There will be no corporate taxes, and Edelstein explains that most corporate taxes are just passed onto the consumer anyway.

"States and municipalities will have the right of home rule to decide at what levels they wish to establish income tax rates, if they even wish to have such a tax. Edelstein clarifies that states can choose to have sales taxes or income taxes, or a combination of both, depending upon what state residents and their legislatures decide.

"States will have the authority to establish an inheritance tax, but there will be no such tax at the national level. There will also be no capital gains taxation at the national level as well. This is Gwen Munro reporting from Omaha, and now we go back to Marcia Bentley in Washington with American Morning."

Viewers once again saw Marcia Bentley at the news desk in Washington, and setting next to her was NewsNet analyst Mason Howell. "Mason, I understand you have some information on some tensions that have been bubbling just below the surface in Ohio since the sixteen states seceded."

"That's right, Marcia. As we have mentioned before here on NewsNet, Ohio provides an example of a state with markedly divided loyalties, much as is the case in Missouri. But unlike Missouri, Ohio did not vote to secede. A resolution to secede was introduced in the Ohio General Assembly, but never made it out of the House of Representatives committee."

"So Mason, does that mean that there is really no significant sentiment in Ohio for sympathy with the states that did secede and form the CSA?"

"Well, Marcia... Ohio is a complex state in that regard. Ohio voted twice for Barack Obama, and went for John Malcolm by the narrowest margin. Still, large areas of the state are very conservative and hold very traditional values.

"In terms of population, Northeast Ohio, anchored by Cleveland, now regularly dominates Presidential elections in the Buckeye State. In contrast, most state offices are held by Republicans, and they also hold both houses of the state legislature. So what you have in Ohio are regions of the state in which most people still do not comprehend how America came to elect such liberal Presidents.

"In some parts of the state, gun ownership is simply assumed. And we are receiving feedback to the effect that this talk of abandoning the Constitution is being met with nothing short of disbelief throughout the state, outside the largest urban areas.

"Organizations dedicated to wise use of the taxpayers' money, and the desire to preserve the Second Amendment are widespread and fervent in Ohio. The state is hardly unique in that respect among the states remaining in the United States. But Ohio has a large population, and should the CSA prosper economically, and succeed in providing an environment that conservative residents of the United States feel was taken away from them, the bitterness could be significant.

"There was one incident two days ago on the Statehouse grounds in Columbus, where a group of between forty and fifty members of a pro-Constitution... pro-Second Amendment organization was rallying to ask the Governor of Ohio and the General Assembly to bring state policies in line with some of the tenants of the CSA. Some were even carrying Gadsden flags, the one that shows a coiled snake and the phrase Don't Tread on Me.

"A member of the group who lives in the small town of Coshocton was struck over the head when he was accosted by a member of an anti-gun group that was on hand to counter protest. That man was charged with assault.

"There are also letters to the editor showing up in such newspapers as the Cleveland Plain Dealer and Columbus Dispatch written by anti-tax groups, asking the General Assembly to not cave in to liberal special interest groups should Ohio soon face the same financial challenges such as we are seeing in Massachusetts, Illinois and New Jersey.

"While Ohio has never been known for having a lot more militia activity than other states, that appears to be changing. Since the secession became recognized as being imminent, there have been several militia – style groups formed in Ohio, and they are largely operating under the radar of the media.

"These new militia groups are trying to walk a fine line of recruiting members, while at the same time, refraining from becoming so visible as to make themselves vulnerable to what they see as a real chance that the federal government may take action against them. I understand that much of the information distribution and recruitment takes place at the many gun shows in that state.

"To conservatives who follow the media closely, it will come as no surprise that self-proclaimed hate group monitoring organizations are now paying a lot of attention to these groups springing up in Ohio. Of course, I should add that informally affiliated groups have been forming in Indiana, Kentucky and Michigan. So Marcia, we will be keeping an eye on those developments."

Marcia Bentley raised her eyebrows in response to the report. "Thank you, Mason for your work on that story. And when we return in a moment, we are going to find out about a major economic announcement coming out of the CSA."

"Thank you for coming back for our last segment of American Morning here on NewsNet. I am Marcia Bentley reporting this morning from Washington. But we are now going to switch to our favorite NewsNet Business Channel correspondent, Simone Dickerson, reporting from the floor of the New York Stock Exchange. So Simone, what is this new development?"

Suddenly viewers were seeing the smiling correspondent at her familiar post in front of a bank of television monitors. "Well, Marcia if you live in the CSA, you may be excited to learn that Alpine Motors, the increasingly popular joint venture between

Germany and Italy, has announced that it will build a very large manufacturing and assembly facility near Lincoln, Nebraska.

"Alpine has just purchased several hundred acres of land near Lincoln, and they are expecting to hire over twenty thousand assembly workers for the main plant, not including maintenance, janitorial and security staff.

"It is also expected that this new plant will generate thousands of additional jobs in nearby smaller manufacturing endeavors that will supply parts. It is also likely that several thousand additional jobs will be created in the general area of the Alpine facility in the form of food service, restaurants, gasoline stations and convenience stores.

"Nebraska officials have also acknowledged that a number of housing developers and contractors have notified them that they will be visiting the area over the next several days. In addition, two corporations that design and construct golf courses will be visiting as well.

"Alpine Motor executives state that the new facility will be used to manufacture a new line of sport cars, including a new roadster that will have a decidedly European flair. And in a section of the announcement that many will find ironic, Alpine announced that one of its new sports cars will be an electric model, one that they had hoped to produce two years ago in the United States, but environmental regulations made production of the batteries too expensive. Those batteries will now be manufactured at a plant near Abilene, Kansas."

Bryce Hamilton had never seen such a welcome vision in his long and eventful life. He also found it amusing to see his wife of decades decked out in a flight suit, but that was part of being treated to a National Guard helicopter ride from Lincoln so that her identity would not be so obvious.

As Bryce walked briskly toward the lobby of the Conference Center to greet her and thank the crew who had brought her to him safely, he was followed by several reporters, and he did not mind it one bit. And when she came to the door and the President of the

Constitutional States of America wrapped his arms around and kissed the First Lady, even members of the media who resented all that he had done over the past two years joined with his aides and assorted members of the new Congress in cheering and applauding.

The President had promised an interview to a reporter from a British tabloid, so a concierge, accompanied by an Oklahoma State Police officer, escorted her to their room so that she could change. Bryce Hamilton tried to do his best for his first interview with a foreign correspondent, but all that he could think about was having dinner with his wife, to be joined by Colleen McBride and her rancher husband. Those arrangements had been insisted upon by the First Lady after seeing the new Speaker's first nationally televised interview.

Having the love of his life with him seemed to take the stress and burdens of leadership off the mind of the President. As they sat in the elegant restaurant, Bryce took a rare moment to display some humor when a somewhat contentious reporter strolled by, and Bryce held up his credit card and announced… "No public funds paying for these fine steaks".

The two women soon paired off in their own conversation, while the President listened with fascination as the Speaker's tall and wide shouldered husband talked of the business of breeding fine horses. The mood was quite lighthearted, until the Speaker took a deep breath and turned toward Hamilton.

"Mister President… I hope you will not be greatly concerned by this. About an hour ago I got a phone call inviting me to appear Sunday on Policy Matters… I accepted. I hope you're not displeased by that."

The President appeared stunned at first, but quickly a smile developed beneath his arched eyebrows. "Wow… starting off at the top of the ratings heap, aren't we? And I couldn't be more pleased. In fact, I can't wait to see that." The President leaned closer. "And I'm sure that you understand… just how unfairly you're going to be treated. You will not get a single objective question during that appearance."

The Speaker replied in a near – whisper. "But you really have no objections? Because if you do, I will cancel."

"No, I truly don't. I must say, that I appreciate and respect that you asked, even though you didn't have to. I cherish the separation of powers. But, I have every confidence that you understand you will be representing the CSA." The President smiled once again. "And part of representing the CSA proudly means that you won't be bullied. And I don't think I have to worry about that with you."

"I may be way out of bounds in saying this. Tom and I had a long talk about this yesterday". She glanced with a smile at her husband, who nodded in encouragement. "But I am a big believer in what we are doing. In fact, I believe in it so much that I would like to be instrumental in guiding our new nation through its first, difficult years... I mean very instrumental."

The President held up his martini as if in a toast. "I get your meaning. And now, it all begins."

"Welcome to this busy Saturday morning on NewsNet. I am Mike Silver, and we wish to bring you some updates on some stories we've all been following.

"A spokesperson for the Texas Rangers has confirmed that the agency has uncovered a large wire transfer from a bank account held by the late radical activist Charles Cushman, to an account at a regional bank in Odessa, Texas. That account in the Odessa bank was opened under a false name, but has been traced to Michael Winston, believed to be the lone suspect in the Magnum Oil headquarters bombing in Houston. Winston died two nights ago when he fired at authorities attempting to take him into custody for questioning.

"Although there is no substantial evidence of any other plots against energy production assets, energy related facilities throughout the CSA are increasing security. Experts in financial forensics are continuing to examine banking records for any accounts that can be linked to Cushman, to determine if any other such payments were sent to other parties who may be planning more acts of violence.

"Analysts are said to be pouring over email and cell phone records of both Cushman and Winston. Computers taken from both residences are also being analyzed. Detectives are also said to be trying to determine if Cushman had any ties to the violent protests that took place in Austin and Omaha prior to the effective date of the secession. We will keep you posted on any findings.

"The United States Congress is planning to meet in a special Saturday session to discuss the debt and bond crisis. Virginia Congressman John Perkins has introduced a controversial proposal to immediately eliminate and repeal hundreds of pieces of legislation and administrative mandates to rapidly and dramatically reduce spending.

"The Democratic leadership in the House was indicating as late as last evening that the Perkins bill would not be allowed to come to a vote, deeming it to be too radical and disadvantageous to women and children. However, due to intense pressure from some Republicans and even a couple of Democrats, the Perkins bill will now be discussed on the House floor.

"An aide to a Democratic member of Congress from Pennsylvania who spoke on condition of anonymity, disclosed to one of our correspondents that members of Congress from both parties have been deluged with emails and phone calls from voters demanding consideration of the Perkins bill. Pressure is said to be most intense on Republican lawmakers who had initially shown relative indifference to the Perkins proposal.

"However, there are rumors that even Democratic Senators and Representatives are facing unanticipated pressure from their constituents over the bill. It is alleged that Democratic Senators are exerting significant pressure on their House counterparts to kill the bill in that chamber and not allow it to come to the Senate for a vote.

"There are unconfirmed reports that at least four state Republican Party Chairmen have threatened sitting House members with future primary challenges if they fail to support the Perkins proposal.

"On a lighter note, Benjamin Wallace, owner of Prestige Publishing, a conglomerate of more than a dozen newspapers in the United States and CSA, announced today the intention of his company to establish a brand-new daily newspaper geared toward readers in the new CSA. Wallace says that he intends to headquarter the newspaper in Fort Worth, Texas.

"The announcement comes on the heels of public statements by several existing newspapers and most of the major television networks and news channels to the effect that they are going to re-examine their operations in light of the secession.

"An example of the complications presented by the secession will be evident tomorrow morning on the most – watched Sunday news program in the two Americas. That is when the new Speaker of the House of the Constitutional States of America, Colleen McBride, makes an appearance on Policy Matters.

"Network executives state that McBride's appearance will be of interest to all Americans, and should provide valuable insight into the future of the new heartland nation. McBride is not widely known outside of Oklahoma, but has a reputation for her outspokenness and her conviction that secession and establishment of the CSA was clearly defensible."

Congressman John Perkins could still hear derisive muttering as he approached the microphone on the floor of the United States House of Representatives. "Thank you, Madam Speaker... I have just one motive by introducing this bill. And in spite of some of the more interesting comments that have been heard over the past day, my proposal is nothing more than an attempt to prevent the end of the United States of America as we know it.

"Literally days ago, this body rejected a proposal that was labeled the Last Chance Bill, a bill that provided one final opportunity to prevent the fracture of the United States. Unfortunately, sixteen states seceded, and formed a new nation.

"I would understand if someone would label my bill the Last Chance Bill, rather than Point in Time. I say that, because lacking another feasible proposal, the failure of this bill to pass will result in the final, financial downfall of the United States.

"I don't know how to state this in more stark terms. Our borrowing capacity has been zeroed out. The debt instruments issued by our government are no longer in favor by investors at home or abroad, and corporate bonds are being downgraded.

"We could spend the morning debating whether the secession brought this upon us. However, doing so would do nothing to address this crisis.

"We are spending far more than we take in, and our credit card has been revoked. Let me say that once more... we no longer have a mechanism to spend more than our income allows. Our deficit is far beyond any amount we could conceivably seize from the bank accounts and retirement savings of the wealthy. We could wave a magic wand, bring home all offshore money and take it, and we would still not be at the middle rung of our ladder of debt.

"Those of you trying to maintain the status quo of expenditures are attempting to do something that is mathematically impossible. We have just days to come to a common agreement that drastic measures must be taken.

"You all have a copy of the bill, and you have the list of the programs and mandates that would be eliminated. As you consider this bill over the next several days, I invite you to sit down with me over a cup of coffee and tell me what alternatives we have."

The Speaker pounded the gavel. "The gentlewoman from Maryland, Congresswoman Yancy is recognized." She continued pounding the gavel to quiet the chamber as the tall, elderly veteran Democratic lawmaker made her way to the microphone.

"Thank you, Madam Speaker. My distinguished colleague Mister Perkins has presented us with a novel approach to budget management: simply climb into a time machine, and make decades of progress evaporate into thin air. Critical aid to women and children... poof... it never happened. Environmental regulations needed to make our air and water clean, and stop the rising of the oceans... bingo... it's gone. Advances in civil rights... gone. Funding to educate our children... vaporized.

"My colleague dismisses the level of debt relief that could be achieved by simply asking the very wealthy to contribute more to the nation that has provided them with the opportunity to accumulate immense wealth. He does not even seem to consider the moral obligation we have in our nation to provide for those who have not benefited equally from the financial resources contained in our nation.

"My colleague would protect the large accumulations of retirement funds, much of which will be passed on to the lucky offspring of those who were privileged to put their excess money into the hands of their friends on Wall Street, rather than pay bus fare to transport them to a minimum wage job... to struggle to keep their rent paid and heat turned on.

"He would defend the corporations that stashed away its profits rather than pay a living wage to employees, or bargain in good faith with them. Then he would defend their hiding that

124

money from taxation by parking it in other nations, another step in evading their responsibilities to those who were not so fortunate and lucky in life.

"My colleague simply sees a different America than I do. He sees an America in which our treatment of our fellow man is governed by survival of the fittest. I see an America in which we all must share in the bounty America has always known. And when this bill comes to vote in the next several days, all citizens of the United States will be watching to see where each and every one of us stands on the matter of our humanity."

Colleen McBride would have preferred having more sleep before premiering as a guest on such a popular broadcast network news program. Her flight from Omaha to Washington on Saturday evening had included a longer than anticipated stop in Chicago as a storm containing some freezing rain passed through. She had spent a restless night in the hotel near the New York studio, finding the environment of a large city more than a little uncomfortable and alien. She may have had a reputation as a person with an extra dose of fortitude, but she was ready to begin an interview with a talking head who is fancied by himself and his producer, as well as much of the media, as being able to shape much of American public opinion.

The Speaker did not know if her interviewer and much of the audience would see her as a novelty, or a representative of a new republic. In any case, she knew the reputation of program host Wyatt Branson. She knew her tendencies as well, and hoped that her President had meant what he said regarding her maintaining her normal and direct manner of speaking.

She had been sitting in the green room of the studio for fifteen minutes after the culture shock of her first New York taxi ride. In spite of her emerging persona as a newly discovered firebrand, she began to eye the nearby trashcan in the event that she felt vomiting was imminent.

She was startled by a knock on the door, and then forced herself to smile as she rose to follow an assistant producer. While making small talk on the way to the studio, she managed to mentally recite the 23rd Psalm to herself, simultaneously chiding herself for feeling that she was being a little too dramatic.

She and the assistant producer arrived at the interview desk just as Wyatt Branson arrived. Branson shook her hand and thanked her for agreeing to be on the program. As Colleen was being seated and her microphone attached to her lapel, Branson turned away and reviewed some notes with the producer.

In the last thirty seconds before going live, Colleen McBride had never felt so lonely as she did amidst a handful of people paying virtually no attention to her. She finally found it calming when Branson turned to face the camera as the last five seconds counted down.

"Welcome to Policy Matters. My name is Wyatt Branson, and in our selection of our special guest today, we come to grips with reality, that there are now two Americas. Today, we have as our first guest a special person in the news, an elected official with a position of national power, but not within the United States of America. Today's program will contain a minimum of commercial interruptions.

"Colleen McBride, Speaker of the House of Representatives of the Constitutional States of America... welcome to our program."

"Thank you Wyatt... it is my pleasure."

"Speaker... you are now third in line in secession of the Presidency, of a nation of sixteen states that had been part of the United States for many generations. All of a sudden, you are the leader of the House of Representatives of a new nation that has emerged almost overnight, but ranks as the world's ninth largest economy.

"Still, you were just appointed to a Congressional seat just days ago, and you had never held elective office above the county level. What qualifies you to hold such a position of power?"

"First of all, Wyatt I want to take issue with the opening to your question. The withdrawal of states was not an impulsive, overnight act. Planning for the eventuality of withdrawal had taken place for over two...".

Branson interrupted her. "I would like for you to respond to my question about your qualifications...".

"But first of all, your initial premise is incorrect and implies to viewers that the CSA is in the midst of some form of amateur hour. What has taken place has occurred after exhaustive planning, the nature of which would serve the United States Congress well. Now as for my qualifications, I was chosen by my peers to lead the House. The twelve years I spent as a county commissioner yielded solid results, and obviously my peers find my philosophies and policies to their liking. I know of no further qualifications being required."

"But twelve years as a county commissioner is all that you have on your resume in regard to government?"

"Wyatt... I anticipated that question, so I took some time to review transcripts of your program around the time that Barack Obama became a serious contender for the Democratic nomination for President. I saw no comments from you questioning whether a rookie United States Senator with a meager record as a State Senator was qualified to serve as the President of a nation of fifty states. I see this as rank hypocrisy on your part."

Branson's face turned noticeably pink. "But you are a virtual unknown...".

"And to this day... how much can you tell me about Barack Obama's life before he became a Senator from Illinois?"

"Well, we are obviously not going to get anywhere on that topic, so let me turn to a question of national stability. The CSA has seemed to have gotten off to a rocky start. There has been a great deal of violence, and much has been said about the plight of minorities in the new nation, with the situation in Saint Louis becoming symbolic of your problems. How does the Hamilton administration, including you as the House Speaker, plan to address these issues?"

"First of all, Wyatt, the violence in Houston and Austin consisted of attacks on our new nation by some who felt that death and destruction was a proper way of expressing disagreement. Coming under attack is hardly a failure of policy.

"As for this so-called plight of minorities you speak of, there is no plight. Further, I know of no statements made by any of the elected leaders of the CSA that could be taken as expressing any intent to discriminate against minorities. Where are you getting that?"

"Speaker... don't you understand that the policy statements of the CSA, and the Council for a Free America before it, expressed little sympathy toward the poor and disadvantaged?"

"No. Give me an example. Give me one example of a statement by an office holder in the CSA or a member of the national Executive Committee of the Counsel for a Free America that was racist, or implied that minorities would not be welcome in our nation. Provide me with that, and I will demand that person's immediate resignation from office."

"Speaker... time and time again we have heard about the intent of the CSA and its states to pull very far back on funding for programs that help low income citizens."

"And Wyatt ... you are willing to imply today on national television that when one refers to low income citizens, they mean minorities? Have you looked at the demographics of recipients of those programs? Most are white. And are you saying that minorities don't want to work and need to be treated differently from other citizens?"

"Speaker, come on... is it not true that using code words like self-sufficiency, economic opportunity... self-reliance... aren't such words just another way of saying that you're not welcome if you need a helping hand? And statistics aside, don't most conservatives identify social programs with minorities?"

"Wyatt... it is liberals like you who identify minorities with welfare... Medicaid... Food Stamps. It is the CSA that offers everyone a chance to prosper. The United States is in a crisis partially because it has paved the road to Hell with good intentions it could not afford."

"And now we're going to take a brief break, and we will return with CSA Speaker of the House Colleen McBride."

As soon as the network cut to its commercial break, Wyatt Branson slammed his hand onto the desk and brusquely rolled his chair away. An impatient voice called out to him, and the Speaker saw the producer waving his hand for the host to come to him. Branson stood up, and without a word to his guest, stalked away to converse.

Colleen McBride sat alone as the host, the producer and other crew members on the set looked at her as if she were naked.

She could not understand the words being exchanged in the intense meeting, but the animated gestures told her that she had not complied with their expectations. Out of the corner of her eye, she could see another assistant producer counting down as the host scurried back to the interview desk and greeted the returning television audience with a smile.

"Welcome back to Policy Matters. I am Wyatt Branson, and we are now continuing with the Speaker of the House of the Constitutional States of America, Colleen McBride. Madam Speaker, there have been a number of industries announce that they are moving to the CSA. What do you say to the United States residents losing their jobs in such a manner?"

"I would say that you have two choices: either move to the CSA, or convince your elected officials to change policies to make the United States more friendly to business."

"In addition to business migration, there have already been significant developments in terms of energy exploration and production that had previously been banned when those same projects were under the jurisdiction of the United States. Do you feel that you are endangering the environmental well-being of all of North America by pursuing these projects?"

"I don't believe that we are. I think that we all know what has happened in the past when proper care was not taken when drilling for oil or natural gas, or mining for coal and metals. We certainly would not want to damage the air we breathe and the water we drink."

"Madam Speaker... I understand that the CSA will have a very low tax rate for your national income tax, and that the code will be so limited in its scope that it will fit on four printed pages. Do you really think that it is fair for people at the highest and lowest income levels to pay the same percentage?"

"One principle of our founding is that we do not want to penalize success. It seems contradictory to me to speak of equality of opportunity, but then turn around and make increased success less profitable. Further, if everyone pays into our national treasury, then they have a stake in seeing that the money is used wisely.

"If you are not paying any income tax, what is your incentive to be knowledgeable on how it is spent? Exempting low income individuals from taxation only further alienates them from the government. You may not care if someone else's money is being wasted, but you sure as hell do care if yours is."

"But Speaker... is there no acknowledgment on your part that one's lot in life can result in great disparities in income?"

"Let's take the disabled out of the mix. We have a moral and Christian obligation to help them. Now, as for the rest... I wholeheartedly agree with you that one's lot in life does indeed result in great disparities in income.

"However, Wyatt... I believe that one largely determines one's own lot in life. For example, if a person sets out to become a doctor, they have to be willing to study very hard beginning in high school. Then they must commit themselves to spending many years sacrificing any free time they would have otherwise, and then likely be willing to pay off many thousands of dollars in college debts upon graduation. Then they will work very long hours under a lot of stress.

"But that person is almost certainly going to end up much more wealthy than someone who makes a different choice. The same can be said for other professions. When I look at the financially successful... the wealthy... or simply the comfortable... they are the people who have made decisions that were success – friendly. They avoided the mistakes that brought about frustration and failure.

"I am not saying that luck plays no role in life... I am saying that there are certain elements in life that bring a higher likelihood of success. Get an education... work hard... take employment seriously... don't have children you can't support. You do those things, and you are likely to succeed. But if you don't take advantage of our free education system... treat your job with casual indifference... get a police record... shoot yourself in the foot by having children you can't support... then expect failure, because that's what you have set yourself up for.

131

"I am trained to be a physician's assistant, and I have several years experience in that field. It was my choice to not become a surgeon. I chose to not go to school that many years, or to sacrifice that much of my life to the training and schooling required. Similarly, I did not decide to enter the role of business, and I had no desire to become the CEO of a large corporation, although I would've been much more wealthy had I done so.

"I've made my choices, and I am happy with them. However, I do not envy that CEO or surgeon, or feel that I have some right to take earnings from them so that our incomes are more equivalent. Perhaps someday, I will decide that I made a mistake to my own detriment."

"But even for those people who have made mistakes to their own detriment... don't we still owe them enough assistance to sustain them?"

"What we owe them is the chance to salvage the rest of their life. We owe them the opportunity to take employment and try to overcome their self – inflicted wounds. We all know people who have overcome all kinds of adversity, including past mistakes such as criminal records, substance abuse and having children they could in no way afford to raise. I respect such people.

"I think that everyone should be given a chance for a new start. That does not mean that everyone is to expect an equal outcome."

"But Speaker... you seem to be spouting a form of social Darwinism. The strong survive, and the rest are to survive on the crumbs dropped on the floor?"

"I will admit that I'm going off on a bit of a tangent here... Hollywood and the entertainment community tend to support liberal causes. So when...".

Branson interrupted her. "This has nothing to do with Hollywood, so would you...".

"In Hollywood and show business, these bastions of liberalism... some actors and musicians and other performers make much more money than others. We see celebrities sitting in the stands at NBA games in which some athletes are paid many times more than others. Still, you don't see Hollywood celebrities demanding a sharing of the immense wealth in their own industry. If Hollywood is not an example of Darwinism, then I don't know what is."

"But, Madam Speaker, I think it's safe to say that all professional athletes live comfortably. "

The Speaker leaned forward. "I certainly agree with that. But what about all the struggling actors who would die for spot in a commercial for a dishwasher detergent? What about all the struggling and unknown musicians who would give anything to be one of the anonymous band members on one of the late-night variety programs? They have to succeed by talent and perseverance. And yes, a dash of luck thrown in for good measure.

"But professional athletes negotiate their contracts based upon how valuable their performance has been, and how they stand out from their teammates and rivals. The same principle applies among actors and musicians of all kinds of entertainers.

"But tell a factory worker after a hard day standing on a concrete shop floor that he or she is supposed to give up more of his or her income so that there is less of a gap in disposable income between himself and someone who is not working? That's a concept that does not work well in the general society, and is certainly not an example set by those who so visibly and vocally champion all of these social programs."

"Speaker... are you saying that people living on public assistance programs are enjoying some type of carefree lifestyle?"

"No, but let's look at reality. Let's take a look at Massachusetts, since it has been in the news about its problems with funding public assistance programs. First of all, a family can only receive cash assistance for twenty-four months in one five-year period, unless there is no exemption from that rule because of, for instance, there may be a disabled child in the family. So we do need to acknowledge that, receipt of welfare assistance does not necessarily mean that you enroll for a lifetime.

"But let's say that this Massachusetts welfare family is composed of four people. They are likely to get $731 in cash and as much as $668 in Food Stamps. At first glance, that total of $1399 would calculate to just $8.10 per hour based upon working one hundred seventy-two hours in a month.

"But that is all free and clear of taxes, and then one must consider that such a family would receive total medical coverage, likely worth some hundreds of dollars per month. Then, in Massachusetts, if you receive Food Stamps, you also receive discounts on utility and phone bills. None of this takes into account free school lunches. Finally, if you're not working, you do not have those daily transportation costs or the expense of work clothing."

"But we cannot lose sight of the manner in which children are caught up in these ideological exercises. So what do we do when a parent fails to meet these impassioned ideals that you outline? Do we take the children away from their parents and put them in foster homes, or put them up for adoption?"

The Speaker leaned in once again and smiled. "I have an older friend who used to be a welfare caseworker in another state. She told me how the state had these regulations on the books... if the adults refused to look for work or accept a job, they could take the welfare check away, then directly pay the landlord for the rent, make the utility payments for the family, then give them a credit voucher to buy groceries. If anything was left over out of their welfare grant for the month, they were given a check for the remaining cash. That caseworker told me that the best penalty for welfare parents who did not want to work was to take the money out of their control.

"She told me that the problem was that the state never allowed the county office to actually do that. People would ask for an appeal to the state, and it was never put into effect.

"I would never say that some situations would not call for the children to be removed. Sometimes situations like that fall into the category of neglect. But the more you remove the distinction between those who work for their money, and those who simply receive money, the more society deteriorates."

"So Speaker... you are willing to use a lack of income as a punishment for being poor?"

"Let me say this in my own words, without your heinous little twist on them. When hard-working people see little difference in disposable income when compared to those receiving government aid, all that keeps them working is their own sense of pride. Or it could be that they want their children to see them as self-sufficient."

"Onto another matter... President Hamilton has made it clear that some of the more prominent social issues such as abortion and gay rights are far down the list of priorities in terms of national policy. Why would that be the case?"

"Our priority is personal freedom and economic opportunity. The states are likely to enact their own policies on abortion and gay rights. We don't think that a national government should set such policies. Our immediate and main priority is to make sure that people can have jobs and business can flourish. I'm not saying that these other issues may not gain more of our attention later on, but as for now, such decisions will rest with the states.

"We believe in a minimum of interference in civil policy by the national government in general. That is why we put so much emphasis on the 10th Amendment to the Constitution. I cannot say that over the course of time we will not grapple with some of the same issues that consumed so much of our time when we were part of the United States.

"I suppose that the matter of abortion will end up going to our Supreme Court, for we are adopting the Constitution of the United States in its entirety, at least through the first ten amendments. This is my own personal bias... I can't understand how you can have liberty or the pursuit of happiness if you are not first given life. So I am unabashedly opposed to abortion. That is my own opinion, and I don't speak for any other officials in the CSA."

"But you are the Speaker of your House of Representatives, and your word carries some weight. I expect you will be asked this question later. What about abortion in cases of rape or incest?"

"I don't think that a baby should be killed because its conception took place in an act of violence. And yes, I am willing to take all the slings and arrows that come my way for saying that. As for cases of incest, that does not make the baby some instrument of evil, something to be destroyed because our societal mores frown upon it. I I am speaking in terms of a sibling relationship. Along with that, I think that the rape of a minor should bring the death penalty. I believe in life for the innocent, but not for the rapist of someone who is not yet even an adult."

The host arched his eyebrows and leaned back in his chair. "Do you understand how extreme your point of view sounds?"

"I give honest answers to questions. I could give you another answer you may find more to your liking, but it would not be an honest one. Political correctness is the mark of weakness."

"Speaker, I would now like to ask you about the revenue the CSA will operate on. I understand that you will have a rather low, flat rate for income tax that is already in effect, and no corporate taxes and no inheritance taxes. How in the world do you plan to operate a national government on what appears to be such a low level of revenue?"

"It is simple. We are not going to create the federal government of the United States all over again. We're going to have no more than a handful of federal agencies, and states are going to operate their own social programs absent all of the multiplication of programs and the resulting explosion of bureaucrats.

"Since we will be taking less away from employees, they will be allowed to put the amount of money they were paying as individuals into Social Security into self-directed accounts. People will be expected to take the money they have been paying into Medicare to be put away into an account for the future. They will then be able to purchase health insurance, and we are encouraging fierce competition among insurance companies across state lines to provide those policies.

"For people in their retirement, or nearing it, we will be contracting with the United States for Social Security and Medicare. We have an obvious problem there of course, for people younger than fifty-five. We will have to assist with the accounts for people that age down to age thirty. That will be a strain for a couple of decades, but will benefit future generations.

"We believe that having such a free market economy, largely unencumbered by federal regulations and hindrances will result in enough revenue for us to accomplish our goals."

"One final question, Speaker McBride... I would assume that you have heard the criticism from some elected officials and political analysts, contending that the CSA has displayed a collective arrogance, and seems to refuse to consider the possibility of economic failure. Would you please comment on that?"

"The United States is on the brink of economic collapse. The deficit can hardly be conceived of by the human mind, and many states are facing everything from cutting back welfare benefits to massive teacher layoffs. So, if someone feels that we are being arrogant because we feel that we have a superior plan, then I can only reply that we are not having to meet a very high bar."

"Speaker of the House of the Constitutional States of America, Colleen McBride... thank you for being here today."

"Welcome to Weekend Roundup. I am Catherine Litton bringing you the latest from NewsNet. We just received some breaking news out of Boston. Massachusetts Governor Helen Gibraltar has just announced that due to the perilous financial situation facing the Commonwealth, after public schools enter the long weekend break for Thanksgiving, they will remain closed until at least February 1.

"The Governor further stated that Massachusetts officials have notified all public teacher unions of their intention to enter into emergency negotiations for the purpose of amending contracts and instituting teacher layoffs. Spokespersons for the unions have already issued scathing statements critical of the Governor's announcement.

"The Governor also announced that funding to all Massachusetts public universities will be slashed by thirty-five percent effective January 1. The Governor intends to speak with all state university presidents in a conference call tomorrow to inform them that they will need to greatly reduce the ranks of faculty and administrators.

"Governor Gibraltar has also announced that the state police will face a ten percent reduction and all departments overseeing natural resources and public recreation will be slashed by forty percent, effectively closing all state parks and recreational areas.

"Naturally, while some of these actions can be taken by executive order, others will have to meet the approval of the Massachusetts state legislature. While a handful of Republican legislative leaders have already expressed their support for her actions, many members of her own party are stating their unwillingness to support her proposals.

"In Saint Louis today, an altercation broke out when marchers protesting the secession of Missouri from the United States were taunted by a group of about a dozen men, all dressed in khaki and shouting racial slurs at the largely black and Hispanic crowd. Police made several arrests of men known to belong to a white supremacist group from Southern Illinois.

"The supremacist group is believed to be linked to those who had attempted to intimidate Saint Louis minority residents from moving into East Saint Louis, Illinois. No serious injuries were reported, but authorities vowed to maintain a strong police presence in the city.

"Also this afternoon, similar marches took place in Dallas, Houston, Austin and El Paso, Texas. All of the Texas protests took place without incident.

"In Columbus, Ohio today, members of organizations favoring policies being implemented within the CSA, braved a cold brisk day to rally on the grounds of the state Capitol. As happened with a previous rally of that nature, counterdemonstrators were on hand. There were a handful of minor altercations, but no severe injuries were reported.

"Today was just the latest political skirmish in the Buckeye State between groups sympathetic to the principles stated by the founders of the CSA, and a coalition of progressive organizations and unions who oppose such philosophies. Jim Brand, a spokesman for the conservative Ohio Founders' Coalition, stated that his group does not seek for Ohio to secede from the United States, but rather to adopt policies more favorable to business and economic development, and place a greater emphasis on individual liberty.

"Brand states that his organization's goal is to educate Ohioans on the benefits to be derived from reducing government interference in business and industry, and encouraging people to exercise their rights outlined in the Constitution of the United States. Brand states that recent talk of abandoning the Constitution is treasonous, and adds that such a move would plunge the United States into a crisis.

"Brand and his organization have held rallies in Cleveland and Cincinnati as well. Typically, they are met by counter – demonstrators, and while there have been no serious injuries, scuffles have been common. However, the discussion of scrapping the Constitution is being taken seriously by Brand.

"While Brand disavows any link to the Lexington Regiment, the militia – style group is said to be rapidly growing throughout much of Ohio. Attempts to find anyone to go on the record on behalf of the Lexington Regiment have been unsuccessful so far. However, Ohio law enforcement officials are said to be examining cryptic social media references that hint at armed resistance should the state of Ohio ceased to honor the Constitution. Progressive groups in Ohio have made so far unsubstantiated claims that Brand is involved with the militia organization.

"In an interview with a reporter from the Columbus Dispatch, Brand went on to state that the Ohio Founders' Coalition is assisting residents and other states to organize, and has been in frequent contact with the movement in the Michigan Upper Peninsula exploring the possibility of becoming a separate state and joining the CSA. The office of the Michigan Secretary of State confirmed Friday that a meeting is being held next week with a delegation from the Upper Peninsula who will present petitions to provide for a vote by residents there to express their desire.

"All individual Americans and businesses must decide how to adjust to the reality of a divided nation. So this evening, we are announcing that NewsNet is leading the way in serving our viewers in the face of these monumental changes.

"NewsNet owner Belinda Milton is announcing that Ben Stirling, familiar to all of you as the host of America in Real Time, will be the first president of NewsNet Heartland. NewsNet Heartland will be dedicated to providing the finest of news coverage to residents of the Constitutional States of America. And to tell you a little bit more about our new channel, is the man himself, Ben Stirling."

The camera scanned to the imposing figure of Stirling, sitting at the same desk. "Thank you, Catherine. First of all, I want to say that I am greatly honored to be given the opportunity to take part in such a groundbreaking effort. I am looking forward to ensuring that objective and relevant coverage of events regarding the Constitutional States of America is made available, not only to the residents of those sixteen states, but to any Americans who want quality of coverage and honesty in the content of reporting.

"Although our primary focus will be related to life, work and government in the CSA, we will not seek favor with the leadership of the new nation by providing unduly favorable coverage. Just as important, we are not going to join other news outlets in purposely casting the CSA, its leadership and residents in an unfavorable light.

"America has suffered a tremendous trauma. Not that many years ago, it would have seemed unthinkable that states would secede and form a new nation. My pledge to you is that NewsNet Heartland will provide all sides of the issues relevant to the progress and problems encountered by the CSA.

"And whenever developments and issues in the United States are relevant to the CSA, as will often be the case, policies and events will be covered without bias. Americans of both nations have a right to expect that, and they will find it, if nowhere else.

"Much of the coverage of the CSA and its leadership on other networks has been derisive and belittling in its nature. At NewsNet, we have attempted to provide a comprehensive set of voices and analysts as events took their course.

"Information on program scheduling and availability will be released tomorrow. To the residents of the sixteen states of the CSA, we look forward to serving you. This is NewsNet."

President Calista Meyers rubbed her temples to try to alleviate a throbbing Monday morning headache. Across the desk in the Oval Office, Vice President Eli Skinner ran his fingertips across his gray mustache, an old habit the tall and elderly veteran politician resorted to when he was stumped for an answer.

Skinner shook his head: "As difficult as it may seem to believe, I think that we have some governors and members of state legislatures who refuse to acknowledge the reality of mathematics. Helen Gibraltar may have walked into class a little late, but she can add and subtract. She's one of the few real men we have in the party.

"Illinois is really on the brink. It's not been made public, but the House leaders there are telling the Governor that they have to lay off twenty percent of the entire state workforce immediately. Their own budget commission is saying that pension payments have to be cut by twenty-eight percent effective December 1, and current and retired state employees are going to face health insurance premium increases of several hundred dollars per month.

"They are looking at mass consolidation of schools, and layoffs of at least thirty percent of the public school teachers in the state. That is not going to sit well with anyone. One of my old Republican friends in the leadership of their House says that you can't take the toughest job in the public sector and increase class sizes like that."

The President rose and gazed at the thick glass block window behind her desk. "Reality is a funny thing... it makes all of your ideals seem rather meaningless at times."

"Madam President... we all have to take our share of the collective blame for this. Can any of us really say with a straight face that we did not know for several years that we were living in a house of cards?"

The President turned to face him. "We always thought that we could put everything off until the next term. The next

President... the next Congressional election in two years... it was always a matter of just getting by for a little longer. Put it off... hope for a way to place the blame on someone else... at some later time of course. Now, it's not a pretty scene I see out there."

The Vice President shook his head. "Losing our ability to borrow money... to print money. Now the loudest mouths out there do not have the slightest grasp of what that means. They just don't understand that this is immediate... this is the moment of crisis." He turned to face the wall. "It's 2017. Are we too far down the road to blame George Bush?"

President Meyers laughed. "Yesterday... a pundit actually said that...".

The Vice President leaned back in his chair and placed his hands over his face. "They just don't understand that we are at the wall. When our bonds went wobbly... recess was over. But they still want to stay outside and play. Helen Gibraltar confided to me in confidence that she has plans drawn up for bringing the National Guard into the cities... as if she can handle that added expense. But she's very worried about violence."

"Eli... that's a real possibility, isn't it?"

"Well... in any state with any sizable population, when you dramatically and suddenly cut benefits to the poor, you're going to have hundreds of thousands of people very upset and angry. Some are going to feel very desperate.

"For a certain percentage, living on such benefits is a generational thing. It is easy for us to forget that there are young adults with children on welfare who have never really had a job, and never saw a parent going off to work either. For that more narrow portion of the population who receive those benefits, this is going to generate some serious feelings of fear and hopelessness.

"I fear a vicious circle, mainly in the metropolitan areas. You could have some civil disorder generated by fearful and angry people who have had their income reduced. Then their neighbors could begin to feel under siege because of their fear of real or imagined violence.

"It could spread to other parts of the city... everyone goes into a bunker mentality. Or worse, people could begin to feel threatened and begin to confront each other in public. People who have been receiving these benefits and are seen complaining publicly about a reduction could feel some backlash from resentful taxpayers. The possibilities are endless... and unsettling."

The President pulled a pack of cigarettes and an ashtray from her purse, and proceeded to light up. "Helen called me early this morning. There are hints that things are heating up. She told me that she would give anything for a blizzard to keep everybody inside, but this week it's going to be unseasonably warm for late October.

"She's very concerned about some of the more vocal characters assuming the role of spokespersons for the poor. Some of them have been very instrumental in turning out the vote for her, but now they are holding her feet to the fire. She told me about how a couple of her aides had warned her about a primary challenge for her next term. She was just aghast that they did not realize that the last thing they needed to worry about was another term."

Skinner moaned loudly. "That's a perfect example of what I was just saying. Our entire power structure has a widespread refusal to look at the numbers. If it were only gubernatorial aides... the same thing is true of our Congress. That's why I'm so pessimistic today."

The President sat back down and leaned toward Skinner. "What do you see as the bottom line?"

The Vice President shook his head and looked down. "This is so unpredictable. But I see chaos, perhaps riots. We have to be worried about mass looting."

"Eli... do you think that we are vulnerable to the total breakdown of some cities?"

"Yes... at the very least."

Congressman John Perkins took a place at the back of the group of several United States Representatives and Senators as they posed for the press photo. In front of them was President Calista Meyers, symbolically signing the bill the group had cosponsored, granting additional tax credits to foster parents.

The bill signed, the photo taken, Perkins stopped to admire a painting on the wall of the Oval Office while the rest were ushered away. When the door closed, he took a seat in a guest chair across the desk from the President. The President laughed, and then nodded toward the door. "That was smooth, Congressman... I don't think they realize you stayed behind. Now let's talk...

"Congressman... I want you to understand how much appreciation I have for what you are trying to accomplish. I find all of this very frustrating, because I have no doubt that if your bill were to be adopted, we would avert a catastrophe beyond comprehension."

The Congressman slowly nodded his head. "But...?"

"But... I have heard the catcalls. It is described as too... forgive me... simpleminded. It is criticized for painting with too broad a brush. Never mind that it would work and rescue us. It lacks... let's see... sophistication... nuance. I'm certain I am forgetting many of the criticisms. You see, Congressman... it is simply not complex enough to result in the high-minded debates we all cherish so."

"Madam President, your party has an overwhelming majority now in both houses of Congress. Even if you would come out and publicly support my bill... you are certain that it has no chance?"

"Of course not, Congressman. And there is no doubt in my mind that you already knew that? I think I know the answer to this question... why have you presented it anyway?"

"Because, if I hadn't... I could never have lived with myself. As we both have acknowledged, it would work. Therefore, I had no moral choice but to propose it."

The President sighed. "And it will not pass, and I will forgive you if in the spring you stand on the steps of the Capitol and scream out loud, 'I told you so'."

"This is going to get ugly. We're going to crash."

The President nodded silently, and then looked down at the desk, where her gaze remained fixed. The Congressman rose slowly from his chair and left the room. As he walked down the hallway nodding to the Secret Service agents on hand, he recalled wistfully how, until that day, that storied room had served as the office of the most powerful person in the world.

Calista Meyers felt as if she were having an identity crisis. She had been President of the United States for several days, but upon waking that morning her first thought was that she needed to get to work in her office at the Department of State. Now she was facing her first press conference in her new capacity.

She stood just out of sight behind a curtain on the stage of the White House press briefing room, until she heard the announcement: "Ladies and gentlemen... The President of the United States." She stepped out onto the stage, and felt as if her lunch was rising in her throat.

The legendary White House Press Corps was seated as the President walked to the microphone and began to speak, although her mouth felt as if it were filled with cotton. "As you are aware by now, the recent secession of now sixteen states has precipitated the most serious financial crisis in the United States since the Great Depression. The fact that our bond market has been placed in peril means that our ability to enter into the process of borrowing that has long been established as a routine function of the United States Treasury is in a virtual state of suspension.

"As a result, the federal government must operate on a cash basis for paying its obligations, and deferring excess payments until sufficient revenue arrives. In other words, we have no capacity for operating in excess of available funds.

"Through Executive Order, I am suspending operations of all national parks, all military activities of a ceremonial or entertainment nature and all foreign travel not related to our national security. There is a total freeze on federal hiring, consulting

146

contracts and domestic travel by federal employees for training and seminars.

"Tomorrow I will ask Congress to authorize a freeze on all Social Security benefits for current recipients, and a reduction by 20 percent in benefit levels for recipients scheduled to begin receipt on or after December 1.

"I will also ask Congress to enact significant but progressive increases in Federal income tax rates for wage earners above the Federal Poverty Level, just as soon as possible. I will now take some questions."

The trembling President did not at first know how to decide upon whom to recognize out of the loud and rancorous group, then pointed to a reporter from the Associated Press. "Madam President... do you have any mechanism at all to provide relief to the handful of states unable to meet their obligations under federally mandated benefit programs?"

"At this time, we are unable to provide any additional funds whatsoever. However, we will continue to work closely with the states to potentially provide relief from some federal mandates."

The President pointed to a reporter from Fox News. "Madam President... you stated in your opening remarks that the debt crisis can be attributed to the secession. Did the secession actually cause the debt crisis, or was the federal financial status already one of a near emergency?"

"I am of the belief that, given a little more time and some revenue increases through adjustments in tax rates, we would have been able to get back on the road to financial stability. The secession took away that opportunity."

The President pointed to a reporter from NBC. "Madam President... one of the proposals in the Last Chance proposal that failed in the Congress prior to the secession called for giving social program funds to the states in block grants. Is that idea being considered by your administration?"

The President hesitated for a moment. "We're going to have to consider many options. Right now, no possible solutions are off the table."

A correspondent from CBS shouted over the crowd. "What about the proposal from Congressman Perkins?"

Calista Meyers began to find it difficult to speak. "As you are probably aware... the idea floated by Congressman Perkins has not picked up significant support within the Congress. We are looking at other ideas."

She pointed toward a reporter from the Washington Times. "Could you speak to your reaction to the proposal being presented in the Senate tomorrow by Senator Ford of Pennsylvania, to evaluate support for abandoning the Constitution?"

"I would... I think... perhaps that is a topic that should be put on hold. For right now, the situation with our economy is more than enough to occupy the time and attention of everyone on Capitol Hill."

The same reporter shouted out again: "But what are you going to do if Senator Ford pushes the matter in the Senate as planned?"

The President stared at the crowd for a moment. "I am not in favor of what she is proposing. I did not want the secession to happen. I am known for being a liberal, but I believe in America and its traditions, including its founding."

The President's expression changed dramatically. "I wanted to stop the secession. Doing away with the Constitution would provide perhaps the death knell of the United States of America. But first we have to get through a financial disaster that provides an existential threat to our nation.

"I have long been an adherent to the philosophies and causes championed by my party, the Democratic Party. I do not want my call for higher taxes to be misinterpreted. I did not do so out of some generic liberal reflex. I do so because we may not otherwise survive.

"But what am I hearing out of my own party when we are going under? I am hearing calls to seize the wealth others have saved, or even expansion of programs we already cannot afford. I want everyone to understand... political affiliation notwithstanding... we are facing a crisis that will leave no one in the United States untouched.

"Much of the media attention in the past three days has concentrated on the plight of those dependent upon government assistance. Those concerns are dear to my heart, but our economic situation is a threat to everyone currently working or employing others.

"Within our very heartland, we now have an economic rival. I may not agree with or believe in many of their philosophies, but we are now in competition. We cannot cripple our remaining job providers by threatening their capital. We cannot ask struggling, but working families to contribute more to the national treasury, only to see that money used to hold harmless the incomes of those on welfare."

The President wiped her brow and nodded toward a correspondent for CNN. "Madam President... when do you expect Congress to take up your proposed actions?"

Calista Meyers exhaled deeply. "I would recommend tomorrow." She waved her hands. "Thank you." The President walked off the stage as shouted questions went unanswered.

"This is Ben Stirling, and I want to welcome you back to this evening's broadcast of America in Real Time. Today we caught up with Virginia Congressman John Perkins to ask him... I am being told that we are going to be interrupted by a breaking development... we are going to be joining Deanna Ambrose of our Columbus, Ohio affiliate. Deanna... what is going on in the Buckeye State?"

Viewers suddenly saw a tall black woman in front of the scene of flashing blue and red lights. "I am now on the scene in Musgrove, Ohio where there has been an explosion at a building that served as a headquarters for the Ohio Public Service Union. The union hall in the small East Central Ohio town served members of unions representing not only public employees, but some service industry unions as well.

"The residents of the town of Musgrove are in total shock after hearing initial but unconfirmed reports that this explosion was a result of a deliberate act. According to the local fire department, at around 6:15 PM, or around ninety minutes ago, the building was virtually leveled as a large gathering of union members and families gathered for a potluck dinner that was serving as a fundraiser for a State Senate candidate.

"Tom Parcells is the only Democratic candidate to file for a special election to be held in March to replace a Senator who resigned abruptly last month due to health. Parcells has been outspoken in his criticism of some of the patriotic conservative groups that have been blossoming in eastern Ohio, and has been very vocal in his support for increased gun control.

"Union officials have been cautious when asked about how many people were in the hall at the time of the explosion, but one organizer of the event told me that seating had been arranged for as many as five hundred people, and that he saw event volunteers setting up additional chairs.

"That same union official broke down in tears as he related to me that he saw a large number of children being brought into the union hall. It is feared that the death toll could be quite high.

"A handful of FBI and ATF officials are already on hand from offices in Columbus and Cleveland. Considering that a high casualty count is likely, solving this case will no doubt be a high priority for federal authorities. This is Deanna Ambrose, for NewsNet Columbus."

"Welcome to another edition of American Morning on NewsNet. I am Cynthia Warren, and we have a lot to report to you this morning, including this tragic story out of eastern Ohio. Yesterday evening in the small town of Musgrove, one hundred ninety-four people were killed when a bomb went off in a crowded union hall where a potluck dinner was being held to raise funds for State Senate candidate Tom Parcells.

"A spokesperson for the FBI states that it appears that a dynamite bomb had been concealed in a large cooler, and investigators are pursuing the possibility that an attendee at the gathering could have been tricked into bringing the bomb to the hall. Due to the cool early evening temperatures, the doors were closed, and the force of the blast wreaked havoc in the crowded building.

"Nearly three dozen additional victims are in critical condition in a variety of hospitals, and nearly one hundred seventy-five others were injured seriously enough to need medical treatment, and many of them are still hospitalized. One deputy sheriff who was outside the building watching for traffic problems, but who asked to not be identified, stated that the blast was so intense in the confined space that many injuries were caused by bone fragments from the victims closest to the point of the explosion. The county coroner has also announced that everything from shotgun shells to ball bearings to several pounds of assorted nuts bolts and screws and nails was probably packed around the dynamite.

"Investigators fear that if one of the attendees brought the cooler to the event, whether on purpose or through being tricked into doing so, it is a distinct possibility that such a person could have been among the casualties, making it even more difficult to solve this case.

"Senate candidate Tom Parcells arrived on the scene just minutes after the explosion, and spent the entire evening helping in the rescue and recovery efforts. Parcells declined to be interviewed about the explosion, shouting to reporters that he preferred to help the victims.

"Law enforcement authorities refused to speculate as to whether the bombing could be tied to the increasingly bitter verbal sparring taking place over the past two weeks between Parcells and leaders of some of the conservative activist groups opposing his election. We will have more information on the Musgrove tragedy as it becomes available.

"In news from Washington, President Calista Meyers is asking Congressional leaders to spend much of today considering her proposals for immediate and dramatic spending cuts. The United States is suddenly unable to incur any debt through bond issuance, even as states plead for federal assistance to help fund a number of social programs. Public aid recipients in several states face income reductions on December 1 unless a solution is found.

"While the situations in Massachusetts, Illinois and New Jersey have been in the news for several days, President Meyers is finding that the situation has just gotten much worse. It has been revealed that California, the largest state in population, is now in a similar situation to Massachusetts. Last evening, Governor Michael Ellington announced that he was informed late yesterday that state officials have concluded that by mid-December, California will reach the point of insolvency.

"Last night at an emergency meeting in Sacramento, Ellington told leaders of the California Assembly that austerity measures mirroring those planned for Massachusetts would be required. Ellington, a Democrat, was only half way through his talk when the Democrats in attendance walked out in protest.

"The situation in California is greatly complicated by the fact that several large cities are individually facing bankruptcy. Ellington had already been consulting his advisers to determine how to maintain order in such cities if there was no way for the municipalities to pay police and fire forces.

"Ellington also vowed to provide the public with an explanation as to why financial data indicating such a deep crisis

152

had not been brought to him sooner. Several public employee union officials charged that Ellington had been aware of the situation, but was manufacturing a crisis for the purpose of pressing union members to more willingly accept cuts in pay and benefits.

"Today in the United States Senate, Pennsylvania Senator Elaine Ford is expected to attempt to bolster support for her proposal to do away with United States Constitution. But that may not be all that Senator Ford has on her mind today. For a special report, we now go to our sister channel NewsNet Heartland, where Megan Howard brings us a special report from Omaha."

"I'm Megan Howard, reporting from the Great Plains Conference Center near Omaha. Over the past several days, our investigative staff has been looking into the past of the late radical activist Charles Cushman, believed to be behind the bombing of the Magnum Oil headquarters in Houston and the Austin shoot out.

"A disillusioned former associate of Cushman's informed a member of our staff that when Cushman was living in a small commune in New Mexico in 1970 he was spending much of his time with a woman who identified herself as a follower of Karl Marx. His former friend identified that woman as one Elaine Glassner, and was adamant that this woman is the same person now better known as Senator Elaine Ford of Pennsylvania.

"Senator Ford refused to comment on our inquiries. And now back to NewsNet studios in New York."

"Thank you, Megan. On the other side of the world yesterday, several Chinese naval vessels appeared in the area of the Reed Bank. That area of the South China Sea contains significant potential for retrieval of underwater reserves of natural gas, with the Philippines also laying claim to the right to those resources. The island nation placed its naval forces on alert, and its ambassador to the United Nations is requesting a special session of the Security Council as a result of the Chinese actions.

"In another exercise of muscle flexing yesterday, two Chinese fighter bombers reportedly violated Taiwanese airspace, prompting the small nation to scramble several fighters. The White House summoned the Chinese ambassador to the United States to a meeting at the State Department this afternoon. Defense Secretary Leonard Albertson issued a statement cautioning China that the United States remains strong and alert, and ready to meet any challenges. Please stay with us for more coverage of America's news. When we come back, we will have more on the scene coverage from the union hall bombing in Musgrove, Ohio. This is NewsNet."

Governor Helen Gibraltar sat behind her desk, across from her Chief of Staff, Melvin Bartlett. "When do they plan to walk out?"

The forty-year-old staffer ran his fingers through his dark black hair. "They plan to go on strike tomorrow."

The Governor closed her eyes and shook her head. "Just the teachers, or everybody... janitors... building maintenance staff?"

"To our knowledge, it's just the teachers. With a lot of winter still ahead, we will have a lot of facility problems if there is no one around to take care of the buildings."

"I don't know what part of 'We have no money' they don't understand. It looks like the children are going to get a very long break. Do we have to pay them if they walk out?"

"The Attorney General is reviewing the contracts right now. In any case, any decision will go at least to our state Supreme Court."

The Governor stared at her desk. "Even if we had to pay them unemployment compensation, it would be a big savings. I hate to put it in those terms... I just want to be realistic right now."

"Governor... they put out a press release a few minutes ago. It's all about fighting the layoffs. But there are other concerns as well, and it goes beyond the schools. Boston and the other cities are already facing major cutbacks in police protection, and now they may be faced with kids on the streets for at least a couple of months."

The Governor leaned back in her chair. "And what is the latest blowback on the welfare cuts?"

"Some of the local offices around the state, not just in Boston, are reporting incidents. Some consist of nothing more than just angry exchanges, but there have been a few threats against caseworkers and receptionists, and an office in Braintree reported a staff member being assaulted in a parking lot.

"We are getting requests for extra security, but we hardly have the money for that. There are rumors of staff in the local offices going to work armed, with security staff and administrators looking the other way.

"As of thirty minutes ago, about a dozen offices reported picketing. Some of the civil rights leaders are on their way, too. State police are also investigating a rumor of a supposed sit – in being planned inside the legislative chambers."

The Governor pointed to a printed out email on her desk. "And now some minor window smashing and looting?"

"In a number of cities, yes. All around the state, there has been an increase in everything from robberies at convenience stores to shoplifting at malls over the past several days.

"My fear is that we are seeing a glimpse of what we may be in for, only growing exponentially in magnitude as days go by. In spite of our gun laws, police are seeing store clerks and even pharmacists being willing to carry guns. And I hate to tell you this, Governor, but the reactions from law enforcement would best be described as mixed and confusing."

The Governor leaned back in her chair and closed her eyes. "What else do I need to know?"

"The state police headquarters has announced a suspension in hiring, and new recruits in the Academy have been sent home. Nearly all the National Guard units are maintaining activation procedures, but canceling weekend drills to save money.

"Jim Broaddrick called me this morning from the Medicaid division... all the bills are already backing up. They were a week behind in cash flow before everything crashed. Doctors are calling in, threatening to stop serving Medicaid patients if the state does not make an immediate and public declaration that the payment will eventually come.

"Transportation officials are suspending highway maintenance projects, and health departments all around the state are starting to lay off staff."

The Governor stood up and began to stare out the window behind her desk. "And just how bad do you think this is going to get?"

The Chief of Staff laughed. "Last night, I bought a gun for the first time in my life. From an old friend… off the books."

"This is Simone Dickerson, with your midday update from the NewsNet Business Channel.

"About thirty minutes ago, Wall Street was shaken to its core by a convergence of news reports. Within the first ninety minutes of trading, the Dow Jones Industrial Average had lost another one thousand seven hundred eighty-seven points. Automated trading curbs immediately went into effect.

"On the domestic front, the CEO of the Atlantic Mutual Fund company announced that investors holding shares of bond funds issued by Atlantic would experience a fifty percent reduction of management fees.

"Van West explains that Atlantic hopes that the fee reduction will encourage investors to curtail the dramatic and massive redemptions of bond funds that began nearly thirty-six hours ago by thousands of online investors. Overall, the net asset value of municipal bonds has fallen by sixty-five percent to ninety percent.

"Overall, the Mutual Fund Institute announced this morning that approximately forty-five percent of holdings of municipal bond funds have been redeemed during the past twenty-four hours. Nearly all cities and states in the United States have suspended and canceled the issuance of bonds.

"Bond fund managers are now concentrating on bonds issued by government and business entities in the CSA. Those bonds have suffered net asset losses to a lesser extent, and some analysts are speculating that bonds originating in the CSA may become the focus of bond investors.

"One side effect of this tandem drop in the net asset value for stocks and bonds is that nearly all public employee pensions are heavily invested in the markets. States that are already facing financial crises, are going to find it mathematically impossible to meet obligations to pensioners at current levels of payment.

"Further rattling the markets this morning was a threat from the Chinese military that the island of Taiwan could face a blockade should the island nation continue to support the claims of other nations to underwater resources in the South China Sea. China is claiming ownership of and rights to any natural resources in that region.

"Pentagon officials asked to comment stated skepticism that China has a naval capability for such a blockade.

"This is Simone Dickerson, for NewsNet Business Channel."

"This is Judy Radley for Afternoon Report here on the American News Network. Just a little while ago, Pennsylvania Senator Elaine Ford responded to questions raised by a reporter from NewsNet about her past connections with the late political and environmental activist Charles Cushman. In a press release, Ford stated, quote: 'It is true that I knew Charles Cushman in the early 1970's. I met him at a seminar for environmental volunteers that was held at the University of Indiana.

'Mister Cushman and I were familiar to each other, and I did encounter him at a New Mexico project devoted to studying desert ecology.

'I was startled to hear of Mister Cushman's death in the unfortunate violence that took place in Austin, Texas. If the allegations of Mister Cushman's planning violent activities turn out to be true, I will be among those individuals shocked and saddened by such a revelation. Nothing that I ever heard him say, and nothing that I ever saw him do would have indicated that sometime in the future, he would be capable of such acts'."

The news anchor continued. "A news director for NewsNet maintains that the network stands by its reporting on the link between Ford and Cushman, including a statement that NewsNet is following up on other leads that would indicate a much more extensive relationship than is being characterized by Ford.

"I am now being joined by our Washington chief correspondent Clinton Marshall. Clinton, what are you hearing within the Beltway about this Ford – Cushman story?"

Viewers now saw a split screen, with the middle-aged and silver- haired reporter on the right. "Judy, as might be expected, Democrats are forming a protective cocoon around Ford, stating that any such relationships from so many years ago are irrelevant today.

"One Senator who asked not to be named, said that an allegation of being in the company of a person such as Cushman decades ago, in no way reflects upon her capability to serve as a United States Senator in the year 2017. The same Senator went on to compare such revelations to confessions of drug usage three decades ago.

"On the other side of the aisle, Senator Simon Brewster of Indiana says that the United States Senate must take seriously any allegations that a member has had ties to a violent radical. Brewster is also calling for investigations into rumors that Ford was aided in her political rise by laundered money supplied by Cushman, and that Cushman and other associates were instrumental in encouraging Ford to give up her seat in the Pennsylvania House of Representatives and run for the United States Senate.

"Brewster is also pointing at so far unsubstantiated rumors that Ford, in her younger days, was an ardent student of Marxism. He points to her call to do away with the Constitution as a reason to question her motivation.

"That proposal by Ford is said to be gaining unofficial expressions of support from Senate members. A spokesperson for the Senator indicated that it was not out of the question that a nonbinding Sense of the Senate vote could be taken late this week.

"Another dramatic moment expected to take place in the halls of Congress this week, will be a vote on a proposal by Virginia Congressman John Perkins to adopt what is being referred to as the Point in Time proposal. That measure would eliminate most major legislation enacted after 1986, and deeply cut federal spending immediately. Judy…"

"Clinton… does anyone in Washington give the Perkins proposal any chance of passage?"

The reporter laughed and shook his head. "No one of any consequence. And the bottom line, Judy, is that the only vocal support for such a measure is coming from the most extreme and reactionary Republican members of Congress. It may be summed up by a cartoon ran in several newspapers in the United States: it showed Perkins, wearing a Superman costume, and flying through space to go back in time. Upon his arrival in the past, Perkins is portrayed standing with a smile on his face while watching an overseer marching slaves along a road while holding a whip. Now, back to you Judy."

President Bryce Hamilton had just walked into his office after a meeting with his Cabinet and Vice President Chiles. He had just sat down at his desk when his phone buzzed: "Sir, it's Governor Ellington calling from California."

Hamilton shook his head in surprise before answering. "Governor… how can I help you?"

In Sacramento, a redhaired and balding middle-aged man in a high-backed leather chair sat with his eyes closed and rubbing his temples. "President Hamilton… I want to make you aware of something, and ask how you may respond to it."

"Go ahead, Governor."

"I would ask that this conversation not go beyond your closest advisers. I need to let you know, we are two weeks behind Massachusetts as far as fiscal emergency goes. I know that you are probably aware of that."

"For all practical purposes, yes."

159

"Some things are just starting to hit local media now, and by early this evening it will be common knowledge. The crisis in law enforcement cutbacks is going to be much more dramatic, and will happen sooner than the public were being led to believe or... that I was being led to believe for that matter. Nonetheless, some of the cities with our highest crime rates and most explosive potential for violence are going to be the most disadvantaged in terms of police protection.

"You know that the sheriffs' departments and our National Guard will also be restricted by finances from offering any meaningful assistance. Are you catching my drift?"

President Hamilton pondered his response for a moment. "Governor... I hope that you are not joining the chorus of those blaming the secession and the establishment of the CSA for this financial collapse of the United States that is taking place."

"No, Mister President. I may not agree with what you did, but I understand basic economics well enough to know that this pot has been simmering for quite some time. Rather, I am wanting to make you aware that it is quite possible there could be a significant migration of people, including many undocumented workers, to the CSA states. I wanted to clarify my understanding of how the CSA would approach such an event."

Hamilton hesitated, deciding to choose his words carefully. "As we speak, a joint committee of members of our House and Senate are working on the final points of our statutes on immigration and citizenship that would be applicable to all of our states.

"I know that you are quite busy, but this meeting was televised, so what I am telling you is public knowledge: states are likely to set their own limits on how many people will be granted residence status but were not citizens of the United States of America as of the moment of the formation of the CSA.

"Residents of the United States who were citizens as of that moment, should not face any restrictions on immigration to the CSA, at least at this time.

"We do not have plans to round up people who came here illegally, and send them to nation of origin, unless they pose some type of risk or have a police record. However, anyone who came to the United States, or subsequently the CSA as an adult illegal alien, will never be allowed to be given citizenship in the CSA, but those who were minors brought here by adults will be allowed to apply for citizenship.

"In the CSA, birth will not mean citizenship, and we will not be allowing family members to serve as a means for relatives to be allowed to come here."

The Governor nodded as he listened, although he was alone. "I want to clarify something... those undocumented residents who come to the CSA, or are already in the CSA who have bad records...".

"Depending upon their individual circumstances, they will be imprisoned or deported."

"I want you to know that in some sections of our state, there is a possibility that criminal and gang elements could try to migrate...".

"Our Congress has taken up that very topic. A current citizen of the United States who comes to the Constitutional States of America with the intent of committing a crime, to engage in organized crime, or who is a member of any organization or group whose activities are primarily criminal in nature will be considered to be entering our nation with hostile intent, and will be treated accordingly. We have no desire nor immediate intention to patrol or close our borders. But you can quote me on this Governor... if that becomes necessary, anyone caught trying to cross our border will pay a stiff penalty, and their safety will not be guaranteed."

"I understand... I was not expecting to hear anything different. But let me go on for a moment... I do want to make you aware that this fiscal crisis, and the prospect of the chaos that could come along with it, is causing a schism among officials in our state. Believe it or not, there are portions of California that more closely resemble Texas in philosophy and attitude, than Hollywood. There are some parts of the state that resent Southern California, feeling that it is bringing economic ruin to the rest of the state.

"Mister President, I want you to know that so that you will understand that if this situation unravels further, I may not always be responsive to your communications, especially if I have a section or sections of the states spiraling out of control, with other regions feeling that they have been taken advantage of as a source of tax revenue to do things they did not believe in."

"Governor... I think that what you're saying is that, California can be described as a microcosm of America in that regard. Some states never saw a social program or a pet project they didn't like, while others wanted spending to be reduced and brought under control. What America had state-by-state, it seems that California has region by region."

"Mister President, I think we understand each other. I will admit to being very fearful about the next several weeks. If the United States currency and treasury fails...".

"Then, Governor, you have no way to support a myriad of obligations and promises that everyone already knew was mathematically impossible. Do I have that right?"

"Yes, Mister President. Best of luck to you."

"And to you, Governor."

"This is Wallace Carpenter for NewsNet Evening Roundup. It is 10:00 PM Eastern Standard Time, and 9:00 PM Central Time in Omaha, Nebraska, where today a committee of House and Senate members of the Constitutional States of America agreed to a legalization, citizenship and immigration policy. It will be one of few laws passed by the CSA Congress that will be imposed upon all states in that new nation.

"The CSA policies will be very different from those in effect in the United States. Although it will not ban undocumented citizens from remaining in the CSA unless they are considered to be threats to public safety, it will restrict prospects for gaining citizenship of anyone who immigrated unlawfully. You can see the entire text of the bill on our website, and you can even view a video of congressional discussion there too. That measure is expected to pass both chambers of the CSA Congress tomorrow.

"Troubling news reports are coming in from the South China Sea. Taiwanese government officials stated two hours ago that Chinese fighter – bombers fired upon and sank a ship that was just one hundred miles off the coast of Taiwan. The ship was described as a destroyer, and initial reports indicate that over seven hundred Taiwanese sailors and officers were killed in the attack.

"The Philippine Ambassador to the United Nations, on behalf of Taiwan, has requested a special meeting of the Security Council, but with China being a permanent member with veto rights, it is not known whether the island country will receive a hearing among the body of nations.

"Just days ago, tensions between China and the Philippines escalated over a disputed territory known to hold valuable natural resources. This evening, the Philippines, South Korea and Japan have placed their military forces on higher alert, along with Taiwan.

"Pentagon officials say that they are watching the situation carefully, and that the United States supports the independence and sovereignty of Taiwan. China, on the other hand, views Taiwan as a rightful part of the mainland nation.

"In other news today, an official of the Chinese central banking system hinted that China, the largest holder of United States Treasury Bonds, is suffering great losses because of the reduction in the net asset value of those debt instruments. United States Treasury officials would not comment on concerns held by many financial analysts that China may decide to declare their investment a loss, and cease making interest payments on those bonds.

"Some conservative economists are saying that China would have a defensible position in front of any international arbitration panels, based upon a failure of good faith of the United States Government to preserve the integrity and value of treasury bonds.

"Today in the states of Massachusetts, Illinois and California, coalitions representing the poor threatened to begin a series of acts of civil disobedience aimed at disrupting government and businesses in those states. The threats are a response to announcements made by state and federal officials of an intention to reduce public assistance, Food Stamp and Medicaid benefits.

"This comes on the heels of an announcement by President Calista Meyers this afternoon that all other federal programs providing assistance to low income families or individuals would be going into a state of suspension due to the bond and debt crisis. This includes all rent, housing and utility assistance programs, as well as supplemental assistance to families with children, such as the Women, Infants and Children program that assisted low-income families with young children in buying things such as formula.

"The announcement by President Meyers was on live television on this network, and included a dramatic moment at which the President broke down crying in making the announcement. Seeing the President's distress did not dissuade her critics from attacking her announcement. Members of her own party were quick to savage the President for taking such measures, calling instead for tax increases on the wealthy to fund such programs.

"Today in Ft. Wayne, Indiana, a member of our NewsNet staff was able to conduct an interview with a woman who is said to have been part of the circle of friends of Senator Elaine Ford and the late radical activist Charles Cushman at a commune in New Mexico in 1970.

"NewsNet investigative staff members are still trying to verify the veracity of the woman's statements. It should be noted that her name came up during the investigation, and she did not at first speak willingly with NewsNet staff. She did state that she would have fear for her safety, because of some of the remaining members of Cushman's inner circle, who she considers capable of violence.

"However, it has been determined that this still unnamed individual was adamant about hearing Ford praise the prospect of a Marxist America, and castigated the Constitution for the Bill of Rights, because she felt that it allowed arms to be held by civilians, and protected dangerous speech that was counterproductive to instituting a collective society.

"After we return from a break, we will look at how progressive and liberal officials and residents of the CSA are attempting to tamper the growing popularity of the CSA Speaker of the House, Colleen McBride. This is NewsNet."

"This is Margaret Lipton, and welcome to American Morning here on NewsNet. We have breaking news coming out of Boston this morning, and we are hoping to soon bring you live coverage of the demonstrations taking place at both Boston City Hall and the office of Governor Helen Gibraltar.

"Early this morning, demonstrators overpowered security guards at both locations and are occupying the Governor's office and the entire lower level of the City Hall. The demonstrations are assumed to be in response to announcements by Massachusetts officials that the state is cutting back on public assistance and Food Stamp benefits, and several federal programs that requires staffing by state and local employees.

"Several Boston streets in the vicinity of the City Hall have been closed down due to protesters laying down in the streets. A number of arrests have been made, and some scuffles have broken out between police and protesters, and even protesters and bystanders.

"The demonstrations this morning came on the heels of over a dozen incidents of arson and looting in the city of Boston. Several convenience stores or the subject of looting by large groups of individuals who also commended much property damage. In addition, two electronic stores were ransacked, one being burned to the ground in spite of efforts by firefighters.

"Mayor Edward Tomlin has so far turned down pleas to establish a curfew in the city, but it is reported that a request has been made to Governor Gibraltar for National Guard troops to be put on standby. There has been no commitment or denial for National Guard assistance forthcoming from the Governor's office, but a spokesperson stated that everyone had to remember that state funding is in a crisis situation right now, including funds for the National Guard.

"In Los Angeles, California last evening, Lieutenant Governor Maria Pennington appeared at a public forum at the Staples Center to address mounting concerns that California may soon follow in the footsteps of Massachusetts and other states planning to reduce public assistance benefits.

"The hastily arranged forum came about after an unidentified Democratic State Senator told some constituents in South Central Los Angeles that cutbacks were a possibility. The atmosphere grew tense during the meeting at the Staples Center, and Pennington was often shouted down when trying to explain the budget situation being addressed by officials in Sacramento.

"Nearly thirty individuals were removed from the meeting, and several were charged with disorderly conduct. The gathering had been scheduled to last for two hours, but Pennington and local police made a joint decision to shut the meeting down after ninety minutes due to the raucous atmosphere.

"After the meeting, there were a number of altercations that took place between the police and angry citizens. In addition, there was one reported instance of violence breaking out between members of two gangs, one composed of black members, and the other Hispanic.

"Local police increased their presence during the night in areas known to be prone to gang activity, hoping to avert outbreaks of more street violence in a time of budget problems.

"In Ohio last night, a member of a militia organization was wounded by an unknown assailant outside his Jackson, Ohio farmhouse. Edgar Waterman, is in serious condition in a Columbus hospital, being treated for a gunshot wound to his chest. Waterman is an outspoken member, and one of the leaders of the Ohio Lexington Brigade. The Ohio State Highway Patrol is assisting local authorities in the investigation.

"And overnight, tensions ratcheted up between China and some other Southeast Asian nations over conflicts centering around support expressed by the government of Taiwan for rival claims by regional nations to underwater resources in the South China sea over which China seeks dominance. Just yesterday, Chinese fighter-bombers sank a Taiwanese naval vessel, resulting in the loss of over seven hundred lives. A press release from the Chinese government claims that the Taiwanese vessel had fired two antiaircraft missiles at the Chinese planes in international waters, and that the two aircraft crews were defending themselves.

"Overnight, Taiwanese officials claimed that a Chinese destroyer entered their territorial waters off the east end of the island. Taiwan has placed its military on a state of high alert, while China is claiming that the destroyer was following what they believed to be a Taiwanese submarine that had approached the Chinese ship in a threatening manner.

The Pentagon announced early this morning that American forces stationed around the Pacific Rim are also in a higher state of readiness.

"When we return after a break, we will speak to two Ohio officials about the growing discord in that state since the establishment of the CSA. This is NewsNet."

"This is Marcia Bentley, and we are interrupting this morning's presentation of American Morning to bring you this special update from our Boston affiliate. We take you now to Roger Lippmann, on the scene in downtown Boston. Roger...".

Viewers suddenly saw a young black man in a trench coat looking anxiously back and forth between the camera and the scene taking place behind him as he stood just outside an area cordoned off by yellow police tape. "Marcia... I am standing just a little more than a block away from the City Hall here in Boston, where chaos has erupted.

"The morning began with the lower floor of City Hall having been taken over by demonstrators, while the office of the Governor was the site of a sit – in demonstration. In both locations, police have responded by simply arresting and carrying away protesters who had gone limp. Several police vehicles were filled with protesters, and it appeared for a while that the demonstration was going to remain peaceful.

"Unfortunately, if the camera can pan over to the scene behind me, you can see that a cloud of tear gas is still hanging low

168

on the streets. Less than an hour ago, some of the demonstrators who were out on the street attempted to charge into City Hall to prevent the arrests inside. Police, who were vastly outnumbered, began to employ tasers and stun guns, along with their batons. We are being told that the protest at the state office building housing the Governor's office has also deteriorated into a violent situation.

"You may also be able to see down the street behind me that there is smoke rising from a burning building. We're also getting reports that nearly all the windows at ground level for several blocks around have been broken, and that sidewalks for several square blocks are covered with broken glass.

"I am standing about thirty yards from a triage center that has been set up by emergency medical personnel, because there have been reports that some ambulances have experienced difficulty getting injured people out of the immediate area. There have been several police officers treated for cuts, and our cameraman was told that some of the broken glass had been turned into crude weapons by demonstrators.

"Earlier this morning...". Suddenly, viewers were only seeing the grate of a storm sewer next to the curb. "Marcia... I think I just heard gunfire... that's why we ducked down. There was some more right now... I know that was gunfire. Now the police... I'm being waved back by the police. It looks like we're going to have to move farther away because some shooting is going on...".

Viewers watched the scene of the street going up and down as the camera man retreated and the sound of gunfire and people screaming was all that could be heard. Several seconds later, the camera was once again steady, and focused on the shaken and breathless reporter.

"Marcia... I have no idea as to who is shooting at who... I think that you can see on your screen that people have scattered and taken cover. Now we hear more sirens approaching... I think we have to move out of the way... I'm being told that we have to make way for... there they are... two fire trucks are coming. We're going to get out of the way right now...".

The voice of the reporter was drowned out by the shrill sirens and roar of the diesel engines that viewers could see passing through the intersection. Finally, Roger Lippmann came back on the screen. "Marcia... I am being told... now I see the smoke. The back portion of the City Hall building is on fire. And now, somewhat reminiscent of the coverage we saw at the Omaha protest, the firefighters are facing resistance... a large number of demonstrators have succeeded in halting the progress of the fire trucks... there are demonstrators surrounding the fire trucks.

"Marcia... I hope our video feed is working because this is simply unbelievable. In case you can't see what is happening, firefighters are being physically restrained by demonstrators... they cannot get to their equipment on the trucks... they cannot get to the hoses. I just saw a pair of firemen knocked down. Now demonstrators are dragging the two firemen away from their truck so that they cannot put out this fire.

"As you can see, some police officers are now arriving at the back of City Hall. Marcia... there are just too many demonstrators for the police to handle. I don't know if you could hear that... I hope that wasn't very clear on the screen... a police officer just shot two demonstrators who were attempting to overpower the officers.

"Marcia... I'm not even going to ask if you could hear this latest burst of gunfire. We're going to have to get a little farther back...". Although viewers could only hear volleys of gunfire, the cameraman managed to keep the lens focused as he and the reporter moved back in caution and took positions behind a trash dumpster.

"Marcia, we are now about forty yards away from where police have taken cover behind a handful of cars parked behind City Hall. They are virtually pinned down themselves by gunfire. And this is getting bad, Marcia... firefighters cannot get near the building, and the smoke is billowing out in much greater amounts... I can now see flames coming out through the roof of the building. Now the entire back of the building is engulfed in the fire. Marcia, this building is visually dominated by rows of windows on the top three floors, but due to the smoke and flames, we cannot see in. Now

170

some windows are breaking, but we don't know if that is being caused by people inside trying to get oxygen or looking for a way out, or by some effect of the fire itself. And that shooting is sporadic, but it is continuing.

"So now we... Okay... Marcia, I am being told by a producer on the scene here that protesters have so badly outnumbered the police that they have placed everything from newspaper vending machines and trash receptacles, to a motorcycle to block the doors around the building to prevent anyone from getting out. A reminder, police had succeeded in clearing the building of demonstrators, so everyone left inside would either be city employees, or members of the public there on business.

"I'm going to move around very carefully here so I can see the front of the building, because we are being told... Jim, can you adjust your lens to pick up what's happening there?

"Marcia, some police in riot gear just tried to rush the main entrance of the City Hall to remove the items the protesters had moved there to keep people from exiting the building... those police were overwhelmed by several dozen demonstrators. There was some gunfire, I see two police on the ground in front of the building... can you hear that? A loud cheer just went up from the crowd of demonstrators.

"Now there are... Marcia, two police vans just pulled up to our right. There are now another dozen or so police in riot gear. Marcia... these guys are carrying some serious weaponry. Let me look around to see... I just saw another police van arrive and another right behind it... Marcia, these are firefighters getting out of the last two vans.

"They are hanging back for the moment... I see these newly arrived riot police... Marcia, those police are carrying assault rifles. The police are moving toward the fire trucks... I am now hearing a lot of gunfire.

"Now some of the police are ducking down and taking cover, but they're still moving forward. I can hear what sounds like pistol fire along with the sounds of the police weapons. It appears that the police are close to eliminating the armed protesters who were keeping the firemen from fighting this blaze that we assume now is threatening the lives of hundreds of people trapped inside this building.

"Now we see some firefighters reappearing, and now the police are waving the newly arrived firefighters forward. It appears that the fire department can now get to work on this blaze, and we can only hope that there have not already been many injuries or even deaths inside.

"It appears now that the police are in total control of this area behind City Hall, and we now see some paramedics coming to the scene. We have no way of knowing how many demonstrators could have been wounded or killed in that exchange.

"And Marcia... I think that we're going to move over to the left a little, as long as we can stay covered... I want to see what's going on at the front of the building again... I see riot police once again approaching the front of that building. Demonstrators have reassembled by the hundreds and are swarming in front of the building to keep them away... not only do they want to get the front door open to evacuate people inside, but there are at least two police officers down...".

The reporter went silent as gunfire again erupted, and viewers watched in horror as the camera captured the scene of demonstrators falling to the pavement, while others charged at the police, and others fled the scene.

"Marcia... we apologize to our audience for that. We do not have our coverage on a delay. Nonetheless, now you can see that the police are reaching the front of the building, and are moving the debris away from the door. Several officers are moving the downed officers away... I can see now that they have the door open... now police have formed a protective human barrier around the front of the building to protect at least the initial wave of people attempting to reach safety.

"We can now just barely see that there are people coming out of the building, but the police are having them get down on the pavement. Unfortunately, we can see that the police are exchanging fire with some of the protesters who have backed away from the City Hall, and it is going to be very difficult for them to expand this safe zone to make room for the rest of the people attempting to flee this fire.

"Marcia, we now see windows being broken out by people apparently trapped on the second floor. After that first window was broken, flames just flew out. Now we see the rest of that window pane being broken out by what looks like someone hitting it with a fire extinguisher. Marcia... I just saw a man leap from the second floor, but he is rolling around on the pavement in pain, but at least he is alive.

"Now more officers in riot gear are coming on the scene, and a couple of them are rushing to the man who just escaped the fire. And we... Marcia... I don't know if our camera caught that. A woman just jumped out the same window, but she does not appear to be moving. Apparently some people in the building are not aware that the police have been able to open that front door.

"A bus is coming up behind us... I think it is a city transit bus. This must have been on standby for when the people inside that building were freed.

"The bus is moving slowly toward the front of City Hall... I can see now that there are several officers in the bus. As the bus is approaching the front of the building, quite a few protesters are now throwing a variety of objects at the bus... I see police now firing tear gas at what must be several thousand protesters still ringing this area.

"Now the police have formed a protective corridor and are helping people get on the bus. It looks like they are going to squeeze as many people into the bus as possible. We cannot tell how many people are boarding, but now the door has closed.

"Now the bus is beginning to back very slowly away from the City Hall. There are four or five police officers walking on each side of the bus and carrying assault rifles.

"The teargas is beginning to dissipate, and the protesters are trying to once again close in on the front of the building. Now we can see more people coming out the front door into that protective barrier of police officers. At the same time, we are catching glimpses of what we are assuming to be the bodies of some of the demonstrators who were shot by police as they refused to move away from the front of the building so that people inside this burning structure could be brought to safety.

"As I look back to my right and watch the bus full of rescued people make its way slowly to safety, we see a lot of steamy smoke billowing from the back of City Hall. Marcia, I can say this from having covered many major fires... I think this type of smoke indicates that firefighters have gained the upper hand in attempting to put out the flames, but we have no way of knowing how many people inside have been hurt or killed, and how much damage has been done to the functioning of the city government of Boston.

"Now, in the distance, I can see plumes of smoke coming from what must be several different fires throughout the downtown area. There is now a constant wail of sirens in the distance as well as nearby, as ambulances keep arriving on the scene.

"Our producer has gone back to where people are disembarking from the bus, apparently so that more people can be brought out of the City Hall. Just a minute, Marcia... I am now hearing from my producer that many of those who had been taken to safety on this bus are suffering from burns of various degrees of severity.

"Those in the building who were not injured, apparently saw to it that those who had been hurt were put at the head of the line for evacuation. We do not... Marcia, please hang on, I'm getting another message from our producer... I am being told that there are a number of fatalities, several of which occurred in a side exit that we were apparently not aware of... I am being told that several people were trying to leave the building through that door that had been blocked by protesters, and are assumed to have died by way of smoke inhalation.

"That bus is now making its way back to the front of City Hall, and now behind me more police vehicles are arriving... I cannot see the markings on the vehicles to see where they are from. All of a sudden, there is a tremendous show of force taking place, as many of these officers arriving are either carrying assault weapons or are moving onto the scene with handguns drawn.

"Police are arriving by the dozen, many moving up near the front of City Hall to greatly expand the protective perimeter so that larger numbers of civilians caught inside can be brought to safety. The ring of police is expanding, and officers are facing the protesters with weapons drawn and pointed.

"I cannot tell how many hundreds of heavily armed riot police are now on the scene, and how many thousands of demonstrators they are facing. Now a couple of dozen police officers just walked past us, and they are carrying what I think were teargas launchers. We may need to take cover in a moment if the teargas cloud we are expecting to see momentarily comes our way.

"I see two men I take to be in command of police activities who appear to be checking the direction of the wind. Now they have motioned to this brigade of police officers who just passed us. And now... I hope this stuff does not drift our way. I have never seen such a barrage of teargas canisters in my life, and I have covered several incidents where it has been used. But we now have probably as many as thirty officers launching teargas into this large crowd of protesters.

"Oh, wow... there goes another volley, probably another thirty canisters of teargas into the crowd. And now... we're going to hit the deck again. Gunfire has broken out once again in this smoky chaos, and there suddenly seems to be a lot of guns among the protesters, and I... I just saw two protesters fall... The police have stopped bringing people out of the building.

"Marcia... I just saw a police officer go down, and now police are firing down the street at where they must think some of the gunfire has been coming from... I just saw another police officer hit the pavement, and he is obviously in pain but just wounded. Now there are... Several protesters holding handguns have just stepped forward out of the crowd, and their firing at tires on that bus.

"Oh... I just saw two of those armed men fall to the pavement. This is getting very bloody, Marcia. How the police appear to be changing their tactics... Marcia, another massive volley

175

of teargas was just launched into that crowd... I now see that probably forty or fifty police with gas masks in place are now heading toward this massive crowd of protesters.

"If anything, the situation is getting more out of control, and there are some protesters refusing to back away from the police who are advancing on them. Even with his heavy cloud of teargas, the protesters are refusing to break away from this... I have to call riot. It was a protest and now this is nothing but a riot.

"Now there are... I think these are National Guardsmen running past us toward the crowd. They are also wearing gas masks, and some are carrying rifles and others have teargas launchers. The soldiers with the teargas launchers are running up to meet the police, and they appear to be setting up for another massive teargas assault.

"Marcia... I don't know if you and the audience saw that. I hope not. It appears that several of the soldiers were just hit by gunfire... I don't think that they were wearing the same kind of bullet resistant body armor that police have. I can see better now... yes there are several National Guard soldiers laying wounded on the street.

"Now the Guardsmen are firing back toward the crowd... I don't know if they can tell for certain who fired the shots. But several people have just fallen, and the scene is now one of carnage, and people are running and screaming in every direction.

"I hope you can hear me now Marcia... the sound of gunfire and sirens is deafening. Police and National Guardsmen are now under heavy fire while trying to keep the people on this bus safe, let alone evacuate more, but the fire appears to be under control.

"Some of the soldiers are trying to tend to their wounded, and the rest are engaged in a pitched gun battle with armed protesters, and for the life of me, I can't imagine how they can tell which individuals are firing at them.

"Now about forty to fifty soldiers and police are moving toward the protesters. Finally, the protesters are retreating... I don't know if you can see this, Marcia... I want the camera to move away from the scene. Suffice it to say that as the crowd retreats, there are several dozen dead and wounded protesters being left behind on the street and sidewalk.

"There's going to be a terrible loss of life, but the protesters are finally moving back, and police are resuming the evacuation of City Hall. But Marcia, the farther the protesters retreat, it becomes more obvious that we are going to be shocked and saddened by the number of casualties, among the protesters as well as police and National Guard Troops."

Viewers once again saw the image of Marcia Bentley in the NewsNet studio in New York. "Thank you, Roger Lippmann, for that compelling and dramatic coverage. Please stay safe.

"And while all that violence and bloodshed was taking place in the vicinity of Boston City Hall, we are getting word from a source at the Boston Herald that demonstrators have been cleared from the office of the Governor, but that Governor Helen Gibraltar was injured by a shard of glass when a bullet fractured a window pane several feet from where she was standing. We understand that the Governor received only a very minor cut.

"As Boston plunges into violence today, a coalition of civil rights leaders in Chicago have issued an ultimatum to the Illinois state government demanding a pledge that no assistance to low income families will be reduced. A communiqué from the coalition pledges that, absent such an assurance, the city of Chicago will become quote: Ground Zero: unquote, for protests. A member of the Mayor's staff speaking on condition of anonymity, confirmed that leaders of the threatened protest are vowing to shut the city of Chicago down if necessary.

"Similar threats of civil disorder are coming from advocacy groups and civil rights leaders in California, another state facing a stark budget emergency. And overnight, there were a number of clashes between various ethnic gangs operating in the Los Angeles area, as well as Compton, San Jose, Stockton, Oakland and San Francisco. Police around the state of California are speculating that gangs are jockeying for positions of power should police protection and presence be deeply downgraded through budget cuts.

177

"When we return, we will bring you back to our regular program of American Morning. And of course, all through the day we will keep you updated on the developments in Boston, Chicago, Los Angeles and Ohio, where tensions are rising among various regions of the state. This is NewsNet."

Ohio Governor Michael Hillerman took a deep breath as he looked out over the assembled media in the lobby of the James A. Rhodes State Office Tower, across the street from the Capitol Building on Broad Street in downtown Columbus. Hillerman attempted to look calm and assured, in spite of the raging migraine headache.

The Governor glanced at his watch, then to his Chief of Staff who nodded to signal that it was time to begin. The tall, blonde haired fifty-year-old former bank executive leaned toward the microphone.

"I want to thank you for coming here today on short notice. I felt that it was important to address the citizens of Ohio regarding the rift that has developed among some Ohioans, since the recent secession of states.

"First of all, I join all of you in mourning the more than three hundred innocent people, many of them children, who died in the senseless and cowardly bombing of the union hall at Musgrove. Our hearts break for all these families and their friends.

"There is no cause, no ideology, no fear of consequences that can justify such a brutal act. We cannot allow our differences to allow us to abandon our basic humanity.

"We cannot allow acts of reprisal to force our citizens to live in fear, and alter the course of their lives. I know that there is much speculation that the shooting near Jackson was in retaliation for the Musgrove bombing. The point I wish to make is that, even police investigators have not yet determined who may be guilty of that heinous act. And we are without proof that the shooting near Jackson is related.

"We must allow law enforcement and investigative authorities to do their work. We must show patience and rely on our confidence in their abilities to resolve these crimes. Given time, and the cooperation of the citizens of Ohio, those charged with investigating what has happened will provide us with the answers we so badly want and need.

"I understand that Ohioans of different political ideologies are feeling great levels of frustration right now. Many of our citizens feel that the secession movement in other states was based upon principles totally incompatible with their beliefs and desires.

"And I understand that there are perhaps just as many Ohioans who feel that the principles under which the Constitutional States of America was founded most closely adhere to their own vision of what America should stand for.

"I want all Ohioans to remember, there is no place you can live in either of the Americas, where some citizens will not be living under a government that operates contrary to their wishes. It has always been that way, and it will always be that way. But Ohio was never one of the states seriously considering secession. Whether as an individual one finds that to be a positive or negative fact, it is fact nonetheless.

"It is our heritage as citizens of the United States of America, that minds are to be changed through reason and debate. All that changes when a bomb explodes, or a rifle is fired, is that more people feel restrained from exercising the rights and freedoms we all hold dear. We do not reap more freedom or liberty: we only attend more funerals, shed more tears and find ourselves further removed from our ideals. Now I will take your questions."

A reporter from CNN shouted above the rest: "Governor, one thing that you did not address in your remarks is the specter of the United States abandoning the Constitution, although it is that proposal that has energized groups such as militias, and the Ohio Lexington brigade in particular.

"What do you think would be the impact on Ohio, should the Congress of the United States adopt such a measure?"

The Governor cleared his throat before speaking. "I have joined with my fellow Ohio Republicans in adamant opposition to such a concept. The Constitution is sacred to most Ohio residents, and removing the Constitution as our core document would unnecessarily elevate the tensions we are experiencing."

The Governor called on a reporter from the Dayton Daily News. "Governor, are any criminal investigations being directed at the activities of the Lexington Brigade?"

"To my knowledge, there are no investigations being directed against any organization. It is our goal to determine what individual, including any accomplices, are responsible for any crimes. To my knowledge, in connection with the recent events I just addressed, there are no indications of organized criminal activity."

A reporter from the Cleveland Plain Dealer was the next to be recognized. "We hear various comments from community leaders in the Democrat – leaning metropolitan areas of the state feeling frustrated that conservative candidates tend to win statewide elections. At the same time, many residents of the rural portions of the state have felt overwhelmed by the influence of the large cities during Presidential elections.

"There is great fear among conservative Ohioans, especially in the rural areas, but they will find themselves soon living in an Ohio that is part of a nation without the Constitution. There are seminars being held on how to minimize financial losses when selling homes and farms and businesses in advance of migrating to the CSA.

"Can Ohio prosper in the wake of abandoning the Constitution? How are such stark and divided loyalties to be resolved?"

Governor Hillerman hesitated for a moment: "What you just described about Ohio could be said about many states. But I do recognize that over the course of the past several Presidential elections, Ohioans have probably felt an elevated sense of pressure in being considered the key swing state.

"I assure you, I am not attempting to dodge your questions when I say that, regardless of what happens, I hope that Ohioans will exhibit patience and tolerance, and attempt to adjust to what has already changed, what is changing as we speak, and what may change in the future."

A reporter from the Akron Beacon Journal shouted above the rest: "Governor, do you see any possibility of Ohio seceding and joining the CSA?"

"As we all know, there was one attempt made to bring a bill to the floor of the House to initiate secession, and to my own relief, that bill did not make it out of committee. I really see no reasonable prospect that Ohioans in general would desire to leave the United States. However, I do see a continuation of movements to encourage adoption of some of the basic guiding principles that drove the establishment of the CSA."

"This is Robert Carter with you on NewsNet Midday Update. The demonstrations which started this morning in Boston to protest planned cuts in various welfare – type benefits have so far resulted in over sixty deaths, and dozens of injuries.

"City Hall was badly damaged when a large fire resulted from an incendiary device being thrown through a broken window at the back of the building. Firefighters retrieved the bodies of seven fire victims who apparently were overcome by smoke inhalation when trying to exit the building through a door that had been blocked by protesters. Law enforcement officials in Boston are examining surveillance videos from the area to try to identify the individuals who blocked doors.

"There are now pockets of rioting around the city, and more National Guard units have been activated. There are reports of scattered gun battles in progress between police and National Guard, and the rioters. Massachusetts Governor Helen Gibraltar received a minor injury from broken glass this morning, and has declared a state of emergency in Boston and the surrounding area.

"The city of Los Angeles was the scene of a night of the highest level of gang violence the city has ever known. Throughout the night, gun battles erupted throughout the city, as the cash strapped Los Angeles Police Department and Los Angeles County Sheriff's Department were not able to respond with additional patrols, in spite of requests from community leaders for a show of strength.

"The violence follows an appearance two nights ago by the California Lieutenant Governor to address concerns that California will soon move to reduce welfare and Food Stamp benefits in a similar manner to Massachusetts. Law enforcement officials theorize that gangs are staking out expanded territories in advance of a predicted decreased police presence and possible increased dependency by residents on gang revenues and protection.

"Several community leaders have accused city officials of not giving a high enough priority to the sudden upturn in gang violence. Several ministers of churches in the city state that there are pockets of Los Angeles in which gangs now hold more control over neighborhoods than the police or the city government.

"And in Chicago this morning, poverty advocates and civil rights leaders are continuing to pressure Illinois state officials to call off any possible cuts that would be disadvantageous to low income families and individuals. A rally is scheduled for this evening at the Chicago City Hall, and several speakers are expected to encourage Chicago and Illinois residents to make it clear to the state government that cutbacks are unacceptable, and will be met with civil disobedience if all else fails.

"In Columbus, Ohio today Governor Michael Hillerman called upon residents of his state to not allow differences over political ideology to bring about further disunity. The state of Ohio is reeling from a bombing at a political fundraiser being held at a union hall in Musgrove. Over three hundred people, many of them children, were killed in the blast that is still under investigation. Law enforcement officials are also investigating the shooting of an outspoken member of the Ohio Lexington Brigade, a militia – style organization that has been growing in membership and influence. Police state that they are unable at this time to determine if the incidents are related. Please stay tuned to NewsNet, for continuing coverage of all of these stories."

Marine General Byron Zeller had been Chairman of the Joint Chiefs of Staff for less than twenty-four hours when he made his first trip to the White House to meet with the President who barely had any more experience in her own position. His appointment had been made in haste, to remedy a crisis in a cauldron of crises. He assumed that his selection had been based primarily upon experience and seniority.

He was actually running behind schedule, but he knew he would be forgiven for wanting to carefully read a number of bulletins that had arrived over the preceding two hours. In addition to President Meyers, he would be meeting with her successor James Florentine as Secretary of State and Secretary of Defense Lawrence Spencer. Spencer, having been on the job since January, was the only one of the expected participants in the meeting who had not played musical chairs as the result of the sudden death by suicide of President John Malcolm. At the same time, Vice President Eli Skinner was flying from state to state, trying to troubleshoot the budget crisis.

Upon his arrival at the Oval Office, the General was quickly ushered in, and a round of quick introductions followed before the President took charge: "General... I understand that you have some troubling news to share with us."

The General opened his briefcase and handed folders to everyone in the room. "These are copies of the dispatches that have just come in. In brief, a lot has happened over the past few hours.

"A pair of Chinese destroyers started flirting with Taiwanese territorial waters. The Taiwanese responded by sending a battleship and a missile cruiser to the area. Once their GPS technology confirmed that the Chinese ships were in Taiwanese water, they fired upon the Chinese with ship to ship missiles.

"One of the Chinese destroyers was sunk, and the other was badly damaged. One of our surveillance satellites is tracking it – it is limping back toward the mainland, but there still appears to be a fire on the ship."

The Secretary of Defense spoke up: "When all of this becomes known, the Chinese are going to want to save face. I wonder if they are going to send one or two of their new carriers to the area. Recently, they have been keeping at least one carrier within a hundred miles of the Taiwanese territorial waters."

The General nodded: "You're right. And we are not picking up any indication of any movement of troops on the mainland. China has been putting its resources into carriers and ships specifically designed to take out our own carriers.

"They really do not have watercraft that would be advantageous for an actual invasion of Taiwan. What they do have the capability for is blackmail. And they do now have the capability to implement a naval and air blockade of the island."

The President leaned toward the General. "What are our capabilities for a response?"

The General shook his head. "Madam President... we simply do not have the Navy we had just several years ago. On the water, we can no longer stare them down. Our Air Force still has great capability... once the fighting breaks out, that is. Of course, we have a vastly superior nuclear arsenal in comparison to China. But that has no meaning unless we are actually willing to use nukes to defend Taiwan. But we could use nukes to take out their navy."

The President stood and began to pace the floor. "But what about conventional missiles?"

The Secretary of Defense interjected: "Madam President, those missiles are very expensive, and what we have in our stockpile is barely enough to protect our own forces and installations. The number that would be needed to protect Taiwan would exceed what we have. And for that matter... even if our defense contractors could turn them out quickly, could we pay for them?"

President Meyers continued to pace the floor. "And the United Nations will side with a Security Council member over Taiwan." She hesitated for a moment. "Thank you, everyone. General... stay in close touch."

"This is Cynthia Warren, and we are interrupting our regularly scheduled programming here on NewsNet to bring you several updates on breaking stories. The conflict between China and America's ally Taiwan continues to escalate.

"Over the past forty-eight hours, each nation has lost a naval vessel in this so far limited skirmish. In addition, one other Chinese ship is reported to have received major damage, but was able to return to its base. Taiwan now has its military on a war footing, and additional Chinese war ships are being relocated to the waters between the two nations.

"Just hours ago, three Chinese fighters reportedly entered Taiwanese airspace, and were warned away by Taiwanese aircraft. The Philippine military remains on a level of elevated alert because of a recent arrival of Chinese warships in a section of the South China Sea to which both nations have staked claims to the right to harvest natural resources.

"The city of Boston has declared a curfew and the mayor is speaking with advisers regarding the possibility of declaring martial law as rioting continues over announced cuts in benefits to low income families and individuals. This morning, thousands of protesters surrounded and temporarily blockaded City Hall, even as a fire raged inside the building. Several government buildings, including the Governor's office were the scenes of protest and sit – ins. Three community offices where welfare benefits are administered were taken over and occupied.

"There have been numerous exchanges of gunfire between protesters and police officers and National Guard troops. So far, one hundred twelve protesters have reportedly died, along with two police officers, seven National Guard soldiers, and nine individuals who were in the City Hall when it caught fire.

"Meanwhile, in Chicago this afternoon, the center of the city is in chaos as demonstrators objecting to upcoming welfare benefit reductions there have managed to shut down traffic and businesses. Thousands of protesters have staged a mass sit – in on downtown streets and sidewalks, and thousands of downtown workers and apartment residents are unable to leave the downtown area.

"We are also getting word that police and firefighters are attempting to respond to reports of arson and looting. A number of assaults have also been reported.

"And in California, Los Angeles authorities have confirmed that there have been nearly thirty deaths reported over the past twenty-four hours as a result of raging gang violence. Also, throughout Los Angeles County demonstrators have been rallying outside local welfare agencies to protest the fact that discussions are being held at the state level to reduce welfare benefits there as California joins other states struggling with the debt and bond crisis.

"The Los Angeles area is among several metropolitan areas of California coping with increased violence and protests. And in the capital city of Sacramento, thousands of protesters were on hand in response to a proposal by Republicans in the state Senate to initiate immediate and dramatic cutbacks in retirement benefits for public employees. A spokesperson for a coalition of retiree organizations vowed to file a court injunction against such a move, contending that retirement benefits are a vested interest, making such reductions unconstitutional.

"In Ohio this afternoon, violence broke out on the Statehouse grounds in Columbus, when altercations broke out between those rallying in support of having Ohio adopt the operating principles of the CSA, and opposed to scrapping the Constitution, and a group of several hundred who were on hand to try to shout down speakers addressing the conservative rally.

"Police in riot gear had to be brought in to break up the dozens of fights that broke out, and the Statehouse grounds were eventually cleared by use of tear gas. More than fifty individuals are reported to have been injured, with nearly two dozen being taken to various Columbus hospitals. Stay tuned for the latest and breaking news.

"And in Lansing, Michigan today, the Secretary of State announced that voters in the counties of Michigan's Upper Peninsula will not have the opportunity to vote on breaking away from Michigan to join the CSA as the state of Superior. The Attorney General of Michigan has advised the Secretary of State that Michigan's Constitution does not allow for such a move. In a recent poll, more than 75% of Upper Peninsula residents of voting age favor secession.

"And standing on the steps of the Capitol Building just thirty minutes ago, Pennsylvania Senator Elaine Ford acknowledged that in her college years, she did establish a personal relationship with the late Charles Cushman. Cushman was recently determined to be the mastermind behind the bombing of the Magnum Oil Company headquarters in Houston and the armed insurrection at the Texas Capitol Building in Austin.

"Flanked by a group of nearly twenty Senate Democrats, Ford acknowledged not only the relationship but her former Marxist leanings. She stated that that part of her life is far in the past, and that we all should be allowed to move on as we mature. Ford went on to vow that her Marxist past is in no way related to her actions in voiding the Constitution of the United States. This is NewsNet."

President Calista Meyers sat on a sofa in the White House Library next to Senator Yvette Coleraine from New Jersey. The Senator was in her first term, but she and the President had been sorority sisters at Yale and close friends ever since.

The President leaned back with her coffee and closed her eyes. "Tomorrow, already?"

The Senator sighed deeply. "Yeah... the Sense of the Senate vote takes place tomorrow morning. And Elaine easily has the votes. Not mine, of course, but she has enough. Late tomorrow afternoon, she will introduce the actual bill. It will pass, and I think it will narrowly pass in the House. It seems to be an inevitability."

The President began to tear up. "Let's see... North Carolina will leave first in this next round. Kentucky, too... I think the only southern states left will be Florida and Georgia. But Indiana will be gone, and it's kind of hard to say what will happen in Utah and Arizona."

The Senator nodded in agreement. "I'm afraid we may end up with the Ohio Syndrome in other places. I mean states like Iowa, Georgia... New Mexico."

"I have been thinking about what Governor Hillerman said in Ohio today. He pointed out that every state has that situation to some degree. But this is different. I mean, of course, the secession changed everything.

"But prior to the secession, the bitterness and acrimony... all fed by the twenty-four hour news networks. They all have to fill their time up with talking heads and pundits entering into debates. And those debates became more strident so that every program and every pundit and talking head could stand out from the rest.

"Every political belief now, and every disagreement... well, it's taken personally now. I think the compulsion to try to put the other side down has overrun us. I'm just not very optimistic about reconciliation."

"Good evening... I am Ben Stirling, and on this evening's edition of America in Real Time, we are going to dispense with our usual format and discuss what did and did not happen today in the halls of Congress.

"Joining us from the Capitol Building in Washington is Virginia Congressman John Perkins. Thank you for joining us, Congressman. So today your Point in Time proposal was rejected in the House of Representatives, with less than 50% of Democrats in favor, and just 60% of Republicans voting for the proposal. To what do you attribute the failure of your bill to pass?"

The Congressman stood beneath the dome inside the large building. "Well, Ben... I suppose that reality is not always a guiding force. For more than two hours today, the government of the United States of America had to suspend writing checks because our cash level had zeroed out. The same thing happened for over an hour yesterday.

"Bondholders, including the Chinese, are making their interest payments. However, we are unable to sell any more Treasury Bonds, and the emergency spending reductions the

188

President has put in place by executive order are simply not large enough to get things under control. We have to be much more aggressive, and that must happen right now. We are probably just days away from disaster."

"Now Congressman… disaster is a very strong word. Really, isn't the worst that can happen is that we just drastically cut back on spending as you propose".

The Congressman threw up his hands in exasperation. "Ben… that is the point. Congress has refused to take that simple step. They keep talking about taxes… we could take every dime of income away from the high earners, and we would still be heading to bankruptcy. But we seem to be unable to get away from that.

"We keep hearing these cries to tax the wealthy even more. But we have to be willing to tell people to do without and cut out the nonsense. Now no one wants to buy corporate bonds from companies domiciled in the United States. That means that businesses and industries cannot borrow money for expansion, improvements or job creation.

"That also means a reduction in money being paid into the federal and state treasuries who are already without enough income to pay for basic necessities, let alone the frills."

"Thank you Congressman… at least you're trying. And perhaps of equal importance was the non—binding vote taken in the Senate today to do away with the Constitution. Now joining us from Washington, also from the rotunda of the Capitol is the sponsor of that measure, Senator Elaine Ford of Pennsylvania. So Senator, I understand that the Senate will take a formal vote on this measure tomorrow, is that correct?"

"That's right, Ben. Myself and my seven co – sponsors were very gratified in receiving a comfortable majority today, so the formal vote will be taken tomorrow morning, and the House of Representatives will hold a similar vote early tomorrow afternoon."

"Senator, after your non-binding vote today passed so easily, leaders of the state legislatures in North Carolina, Indiana and Utah indicated that adoption of your measure by both houses of Congress is likely to result in their secession. Could you comment on that please?"

"Actually, Ben... I think it was only a matter of time anyway before those states seceded. They tend to be rather conservative states, especially North Carolina, and the CSA is nothing more than a refuge for those who have resisted progress in such areas as civil rights, in terms of both race and sexual identity, women's rights, the rights of workers and protecting our children from the danger of guns. These are also the states that have tended to favor the squirreling away of wealth by the fortunate at the expense of the unmet needs of the less fortunate."

"So you are willing to do away with the entire Constitution... including the Bill of Rights, correct?"

"Ben, the public sends us to Washington to operate our nation in a modern and progressive manner. Through statute, we can see to it that the rights we feel are necessary can become the law of the land through our votes in Congress."

"And am I to understand that the definition of rights through the votes of Congress may not mirror the rights emphasized by our Founding Fathers?"

"This is 2017. That old piece of parchment written by white men so many generations ago, simply needs to be replaced. As to whether those gentlemen got our nation off to a good start, that question will be debated by historians. But as a modern people, we can decide our own destiny."

"And could you clarify the role of the Supreme Court in a post – Constitution United States?"

The Supreme Court will still play a vital role. Instead of trying to read the minds and intent of men who lived in the 1700's, the Court can determine whether a federal or state statute is being correctly applied. Another vital role of the Court will be to determine if laws and statutes and their application are being carried out in a fair and equitable manner."

"To shift gears, Senator, the United States has long supported Taiwan in its opposition to being annexed by China. It has also been understood that our military might was always available if necessary.

"Now that there have been military clashes between China and Taiwan, how do you expect the government of the United States to respond?"

"I know that the matter will be taken up in the United Nations. I have every bit of faith in President Meyers that she will be able to reason with both sides, and avert the outbreak of any more hostilities. Such a situation calls for the use of words, not missiles."

"Thank you, Senator Elaine Ford of Pennsylvania. And when we come back from our break, we're going to get you caught up on the other big stories of the day. This is NewsNet."

"Thank you for staying with us on this special edition of America in Real Time. Now for the latest news out of a very chaotic Boston, is our own Carol Rogers now on the scene there. Carol, can you hear me?"

Viewers could now see the correspondent in front of the police barricade, while the darkness was illuminated by many blue and red flashing lights. "Ben, I am standing just a block from the campus of Boston University. Late this afternoon, students here and at Boston College began student strikes, saying that they will not return to class until the Commonwealth of Massachusetts pledges that no benefits to the poor will be cut.

"Students have also occupied the administration building at Boston College, and are pledging to stay there until the budget issues are resolved in favor of the needy. There were several arrests at both universities today, primarily for disorderly conduct, but no serious injuries were reported on either campus.

"Unfortunately, that is not the case for the rest of Boston. The city is now under a curfew and a state of emergency, although martial law has not yet been declared. The Mayor has called upon all citizens to voluntarily surrender their guns to their closest police precinct, but if what we are hearing through anecdote is correct,

Boston residents have been attempting to obtain even more weapons for self-defense.

"This morning there was a massive demonstration at City Hall, and a smaller one near the building where the office of the Governor is located. As you probably know by now, City Hall was on fire when demonstrators blocked exit doors. Police now have leads from surveillance cameras, and vow that those who barricaded the doors are subject to being charged with attempted manslaughter. Several people died in City Hall as a result of that fire.

"Throughout the entire day, demonstrators have been exchanging gun fire with police and National Guard troops. We are now being told that as many as two hundred twelve demonstrators have died, along with four police officers and eleven National Guardsmen. We also found out just a little while ago, that one of the first firefighters to arrive to fight the flames in City Hall has died. We were aware that at least one firefighter was dragged to the ground and assaulted, and that firefighter died from his injuries.

"The Mayor of Boston and the Governor have asked residents to go inside their homes and lock their doors. But it is evident that, even with police officers from area cities coming in to help alongside the National Guard, the sheer number of protesters on the street, especially those who are armed, means that Boston is in danger of spiraling totally out of control.

"At last count, we were aware of eighty-two fires currently burning, far exceeding the capabilities of Boston and surrounding fire departments under the best of circumstances. But these are not the best of circumstances: in at least eleven cases, fire units had to halt their approach to fires because of either having shots fired at them, or being warned away by armed protesters. In several cases, fire units had to simply back away and return to their firehouses.

"For the residents of Boston, there is much fear. And that fear is very understandable, considering what happened earlier this evening in South Boston. There, a police precinct came under attack when reportedly several hundred protesters launched a barrage of rocks and chunks of mortar and broken bricks at the building and police and civilian cars parked in the area. Three police cruisers were reportedly destroyed, and thirty-two city and civilian vehicles were badly damaged, some being turned over and set afire. This is Carol Rogers, reporting live from the scene in Boston."

Ben Stirling again greeted viewers. "And now we go to Chicago for a report from our own Robert Carter."

The reporter was standing in an area outside Wrigley Field illuminated by police lights. "Thank you, Ben. No, I'm not standing in line months in advance for Cubs tickets. But this is as close as media are allowed to get right now to downtown Chicago, where a large and loud rally is taking place at City Hall.

"To say the least, we were hoping to be broadcasting from the site of that rally, but just as we were getting ready to leave to go there, we were turned back by police who said that the area was being cordoned off, and that no more people were being allowed inside that perimeter, even the press.

"About forty-five minutes ago, I got a phone call from my contact within the coalition that organized the rally, and those organizers are not at all happy that press cannot cover the rally as a live event. As is the case with any such event, organizers wanted press coverage in hopes of placing more pressure on the government of Illinois to find ways to avert cutbacks in welfare benefits.

"We are being told that a traffic reporter who was able to see the crowd assembled by way of helicopter, is estimating that as many as twenty thousand people may be at the rally itself, but also observed that the streets are full of people who are in the immediate vicinity, but do not appear to be part of the rally audience.

"All over the city, and in some of the suburbs of Chicago, there were crowds demonstrating and chanting outside nearly every welfare or Food Stamp office. There were several incidents of employees being accosted or even assaulted in those buildings, or when leaving those buildings. In several cases, police and Cook County Sheriff's Department officers arrive to escort caseworkers and other staff to their cars.

"A spokesperson for the union representing caseworkers in Illinois announced that should sufficient security not be provided, the caseworkers and support staff will exercise their right to not report to work. A member of the coalition that organized this evening's demonstration responded that such a threat is symbolic of a welfare system that tolerates, but does not care about, people in need.

"Also in Chicago today, local officials met to determine in what order other services may be curtailed due to lack of funding. Administrators from agencies that provide assistance for things such as utility bills, housing costs and supplemental assistance to families with young children, announced that it may be a matter of just days before their agencies cease operation.

"Although he would not speak on the record and allow us to use his name, a member of the Chicago Police Department, quite high in the level of command, told me a little while ago that demonstrators, especially those who are armed, should not count on unlimited restraint from police officers.

"He went on to express his concern that vastly outnumbered police officers finding themselves in danger will defend themselves, and defend the lives of innocent bystanders.

"He would not say anything more, but we can only guess that anxieties are running high at the prospect of this demonstration ending this evening, with so many thousands of people being challenged by the speakers to resist the intentions of Illinois officials. This is Robert Carter, reporting live from Chicago."

"In California today, state officials in Sacramento met with legal aid attorneys and advocates for the poor to discuss the possibility that California will, within weeks, reduce public assistance and Food Stamp grants to low income families and individuals. Lieutenant Governor Maria Pennington says that the purpose of the meeting was to provide information, but noted that the attorneys and advocates are threatening to sue the state over any reductions.

"Lawsuits are also being threatened over comments made by Republican members of the California state legislature regarding the possibility of reductions in pension payments to retired public employees.

"In fact, across the United States, cutbacks in federal expenditures are happening everywhere. The Pentagon acknowledges that military recruitment has been temporarily suspended. Training flights are being cut back for Air Force, Navy and Army aviators. In addition, the Navy has announced that several ships have had routine cruises canceled.

"National parks have been closed by Executive Order, non-emergency domestic and overseas travel by federal employees has been put in suspension, and a federal hiring freeze has been put into effect.

"Farm subsidy payments have been suspended, federal food inspection will be halted tomorrow, and federal funding for school lunch programs, Head Start and housing and utility assistance programs will all be closed down next Monday.

"Also by way of Executive Order from President Meyers, federal funding for highway and bridge repair and construction will be canceled for work not yet started.

"Also being halted are inspections by the Environmental Protection Agency, and forty-two smaller airports will cease operations for commercial flights due to federal cutbacks.

"In response to this list of cutbacks, twenty-three Democratic members of the United States Senate and House of Representatives have demanded in writing the resignation of President Meyers. The letter goes on to state that the United States must demand that the very wealthy pay their fair share in taxes rather than literally take food out of the mouths of children. Please stay with us, and after this break we will take a look at what may be ahead for California, our most populous state. This is NewsNet."

It was nearly 10:00 PM as the speaker was winding up his address to the Eastern Ohio Freedom Alliance. The guest for the evening had traveled from Indiana to talk to the militia group about maintaining a low public profile, while still being effective at recruiting and screening new members. Beforehand, there had been a wide – ranging discussion of the ramifications of losing the Constitution.

The Freedom Alliance had largely avoided any mention in even local newspapers. Fifty-seven members strong, they were able to fit inside the class room where the public would come to take instruction to have a concealed gun permit at the Paragon Gun & Archery Shop on the outskirts of Zanesville, Ohio.

Paragon had become one of the leading gun dealers in eastern Ohio, and was more than willing to allow the Freedom Alliance to hold monthly meetings there, as many of the members were already frequent customers at the store that had a large inventory of guns and ammunition, as well as supplies related to the art of survival in an emergency.

Paragon had even become the target of some picketing by Columbus residents and college students. Some had taken offense to Paragon's television and radio advertisements, which had extolled the virtues of being armed and prepared to preserve freedom.

As for the Freedom Alliance, they had found no better friend than Ron Fridley, the large and gregarious man who owned the store, and understood their point of view. The group had come into existence just a year earlier, its founders gaining new members through conversations at the many gun shows throughout Ohio.

The Freedom Alliance actually did not exist on paper anywhere. There was no treasury, no property, no dues or anything else that would make the group subject to an audit or inquiry from the Internal Revenue Service or Ohio Secretary of State.

Just as the speaker from Indiana invited the attendees to ask questions, the floor rose up in a ball of flames that most in the room never saw or even sensed as half the structure was immediately leveled by the explosion.

Fridley himself was virtually vaporized by the blast, for he was in the archery department in the basement beneath the meeting room at the moment of the explosion. Two other employees in the store, one his son and the other his son-in-law were thrown into the parking lot behind the store, already dead before they hit the pavement.

Paragon was now part gaping hole in the ground, and part inferno in which rounds of ammunition were exploding by the hundreds at a time. A dozen of the members of the Freedom Alliance survived the blast in spite of being thrown outside or against crumbling walls, but two met their death by way of bullets being propelled by the fire.

The spectacular explosion and fire lit the night sky near the town, and residents nearby were confused as to what had happened and shaken their houses. As local fire crews arrived on the scene, they initially had to take cover because of the bullets in random flight.

Once again, Ohioans rushed through a scene of horror, fear and grief. Hearing the news through phone calls and text messages, family members and friends arrived one at a time, parking behind a cluster of emergency vehicles, and running toward the smoldering debris.

"This is Marcia Bentley for American Morning here on NewsNet, and we have a lot of important stories to get to.

"Today in Washington, both houses of Congress are expected to hold a vote on a proposal to abandon the Constitution of the United States. There is much argument as to the legality of such a move, and several states have threatened to secede the moment the Constitution is done away with. We will report related developments as they occur.

"We will now continue with the coverage that began just before midnight of the most recent violence in Ohio. Last night, an explosion at a Zanesville, Ohio gun store resulted in the deaths of forty-one individuals, most of whom were members of a militia group called the Eastern Ohio Freedom Alliance.

"The meeting was being held at the Paragon Gun & Archery Shop near Zanesville. Among the dead were store owner Ron Fridley and two family members who worked with him.

"The authorities have so far refrained from releasing the identities of any members of the public killed in the explosion, and it is not known how many killed were random customers.

"Local authorities are declining to answer questions about whether the Zanesville explosion is related to the deadly bombing at a political fundraising event in Musgrove, or the recent wounding of a member of another militia at his home near Jackson. Soon after the rural Musgrove bombing, there were accusations made that the bombing took place due to the fact that the event was being held on behalf of a liberal candidate for the Ohio Senate.

"Federal authorities and investigators arrived on the scene in Zanesville soon after midnight, and the Ohio State Highway Patrol and county sheriffs' departments are increasing patrols in rural sections of eastern and western Ohio, where most of the militia activity is taking place. Authorities assure that the patrols are to keep everyone safe, and that the militias are not being singled out for any special scrutiny. We will continue to keep you updated on developments in Ohio.

"The city of Boston has been placed under martial law as rioting and violence continued through the night and into this morning. Gun battles, arson and looting remained rampant throughout the night. Dozens of intersections have been blocked off by police and National Guard troops.

"Also during the night, four hundred additional National Guard troops arrived in the downtown area. In South Boston, one company of troops was fired upon from a vacant building as the soldiers began to exit their troop carrier. The soldiers entered the building, and automatic rifle fire could be heard. A while later the bodies of four men were brought out.

"Police and National Guard troops frequently found themselves under fire by armed protesters in vacant buildings and waiting behind dumpsters and vehicles to ambush the police and soldiers. This has caused a much more aggressive response as the hours have gone by. The death toll among the demonstrators and rioters now stands at three hundred twenty-one.

"And in Chicago, a rally attended by nearly twenty thousand people opposed to possible welfare cuts turned violent when the rally ended. Among the people who had attended the rally, and the several thousand additional people who were milling around the area, were several hundred who began to break windows and engage in looting stores and businesses in the area near Chicago City Hall.

"When police moved in with force, hundreds and hundreds of protesters joined in the destruction and confrontations with police. It took several hours and nearly two hundred arrests for police to get the area under control. For blocks around City Hall, windows have been smashed and hundreds of businesses lost property through looting, general theft and arson.

"Finally, Los Angeles authorities are bracing for a wave of protests over proposed welfare and public employee pension cuts in the state of California. Other California cities are faced with similar situations.

"Complicating the situation in Los Angeles and its suburbs is a stark rise in gang violence over the past several days. In fact, Los Angeles is just one of several cities in California facing the prospect of seeing gangs gaining control of entire neighborhoods as funding for police protection spirals downward.

"Police authorities in Los Angeles and the other cities with large gang populations will not concede that some neighborhoods have been written off as too dangerous or beyond the point of ever becoming stable neighborhoods again. But reporters for several California newspapers have filed requests for police response and dispatch records to see if certain high – crime neighborhoods are being avoided.

"After the break, we will have more coverage of these stories, and the increasingly tense situation between China and Taiwan. This is NewsNet."

President Bryce Hamilton and Vice President Franklin Chiles relaxed in Hamilton's office with cups of coffee while sitting in a pair of high backed leather chairs. Hamilton took a sip, and then leaned back with his eyes closed. "These interviews with the media... the same questions over and over. Illegal immigration... gay rights... and abortion. They just don't get it."

The Vice President laughed. "I am shocked... shocked I tell you... that you don't get asked about economic freedom... the number of people finding jobs... projections about how much businesses will save by the reduction in regulations."

Hamilton rolled his eyes. "We are being castigated over our illegal immigration policy. No matter that we aren't sending anyone packing except for those who are dangerous. The vast, vast majority of illegals will get by just fine. But oh my... that clause about illegals having a lifetime ban from receiving welfare...".

The Vice President shook his head. "I understand that already Arizona and New Mexico are feeling the strain... people who were living in Texas and Oklahoma. That is unfortunate for the kids. That has to be rough on them.

"I agree. Still, every adult who crossed the border illegally, are assumed to have known what they were doing. We can only go so far in protecting people from the ramifications of their illegal actions." Hamilton arched his eyebrows and smiled. "There are likely people saying the same thing about us right now."

The Vice President sat his cup on a table. "Have you talked to Calista Meyers?"

"Yes... I told her that we were part of the United States when that commitment was made to Taiwan, and that we will do everything we can to help with the readiness of all the bases located in the CSA."

"And what about Fort Knox?"

"That did not go as well. But I made the offer, with the blessing of our Congressional leadership of course. We drop our claims to a portion of the bullion... but they have to adopt the measures they have already rejected twice. Our Congress is not going to go along with relinquishing our rights to our portion of the gold if it's only going to be used to continue bad habits."

"Do you think that she has caught on to the latest list of industries coming?"

The President managed to smile. "I think that she has so much on her plate, no one has bothered her with it. But two years from now, unemployment in downtown St. Louis should be almost nonexistent. First the construction companies get to rehab those empty industrial buildings, and then St. Louis becomes the ammunition manufacturing capitol of the world. I can't believe how many proposed international contracts are being negotiated."

"And what about the others?"

Hamilton looked down at an email that had been printed out "Also in the St. Louis area, two more international firms... one a motorcycle manufacturer... a new factory to be built by an American company to manufacture window air conditioners and dehumidifiers.

"Then there is that plastics manufacturing complex going into Nebraska... over two thousand jobs. Then the big one... the new auto parts megaplex in Kansas. That thing is going to turn into a small city of its own. The construction work from all of this is going to be... staggering. Even if some of these construction jobs are temporary, I think that success will draw more success, and there should be enough for all to go around."

"Welcome to Afternoon Report... my name is Marcia Bentley. Today will go down as one of the most crucial days in the history of the United States of America. Both houses of Congress have voted to invalidate the authority of the Constitution.

"Within thirty minutes of that vote in the House of Representatives, the state legislatures of North Carolina and Indiana voted for secession. We have also received word from Michigan that an assembly of county officials and the members of the state legislature representing the Upper Peninsula have just signed a declaration of separation, and establishment of the state of Superior. Officials representing the Upper Peninsula have been all but assured by the Congress of the CSA that they will be granted admission to the new nation.

"An informal group of Republican Senators and Representatives in the United States Congress have asked President Calista Meyers to do all that she can to preserve the Constitution, including asking the United States Supreme Court to declare this Congressional action invalid, and if necessary, employee use of the military to preserve the authority of the Constitution.

"Asked about the most recent votes of secession, CSA President Bryce Hamilton said that he will ask the Congress of the new heartland nation to stay in session so that admission votes can be taken before the day is out.

"Under any other circumstances, we would devote the entire day to discussing the congressional vote on the Constitution. However, in other urgent news, the city of Boston remains under martial law and a state of emergency. We are still getting reports of numerous gun battles taking place between protesters and police and Guardsmen.

"There are also now a number of reports of protesters being fired upon by private citizens when the protest activity and rioting neared their homes. In one blue-collar neighborhood, three men believed to be rioters were gunned down when they scaled a wrought iron fence and attempted to enter a private home. One more Boston police officer and one more Guardsman were killed today, and the latest comprehensive casualty count in Boston is six hundred and five dead, and seven hundred forty-three wounded or injured.

"In Chicago, rioting and looting continues there as well. The entire downtown of Chicago is paralyzed, with rioters and protesters clashing with police in a number of areas. There have also been reports of scattered gun battles between rioters and police.

"A spokesperson for the office of the Mayor says that Chicago police are doing all that they can to restore order while holding down the number of injuries. He added that the people of Chicago must be patient, because it could take a couple of days to quell the disturbance.

"And in California, protests continue in Los Angeles and Sacramento over the prospect of reduced welfare benefits. In addition, picketing took place in front of a hospital and a community health clinic that announced imminent closures due to insufficient funding and the costs of treating undocumented immigrants. We will have more news for you after the break. This is NewsNet."

President Calista Meyers attempted to appear calm and in control as she stepped to the podium in the White House Press Room. The reporters took their seats as the President glanced down at her written notes, as she wanted to have nothing to do with a Teleprompter during press conferences.

"Thank you for coming today. Before I begin to speak on financial issues, I want to address the matter of the votes taken earlier today in Congress to nullify the Constitution.

"I believe that doing away with the Constitution is a dangerous and impulsive act. The legality of the vote itself is in question, as is the status of authority of the United States Supreme

Court at this moment. In my opinion, this act violates our long-standing adherence to the concept of a Separation of Powers. In effect, Congress has just stripped the Judicial branch of our government of its authority and independence.

"As for this moment, as your President I will have no choice but to move ahead with the understanding that this act by Congress is in effect. However, I do call upon Congress to immediately rescind this action.

"Now I must address the immediate emergency we face with our national budget. As you know, we have lost our ability to encumber debt. Payment obligations are now being processed as revenue comes into our treasury.

"I think that everyone understands that for many years, we have been running a budget deficit. In other words, we have been spending more money than we receive in income, and have used borrowed money to fund payments in excess of our income. That is no longer possible, at least until our bond status is repaired.

"I do want to express my admiration for Virginia Congressman John Perkins for his work and effort to avert financial catastrophe. As you know, Congress did not adopt the Congressman's proposal, and no alternatives have been forthcoming. Right now, all that I can do as your President is to issue executive orders related to spending.

"Based upon information provided to me today by the Treasury of the United States and the staff of the Congressional Budget Office I have just issued the following executive orders:

"We will establish a set of priorities for use of cash deposited in our Treasury. There will be two co – equal spending areas given this priority status: the military and a grouping of expenditures consisting of Social Security payments, Medicare and Medicaid.

"As, and if, cash is available, funding to the states for public assistance and Food Stamps will continue, but at a reduction of 60%. Also by executive order, I have granted the states authority to reduce their own matching fund requirements for these programs by 60%.

"All federal funding to states and local government for supplemental assistance programs for low income families and individuals are immediately suspended. That includes programs for housing assistance, utility payment assistance and telephone services.

"All federal funding for public transit and Amtrak are suspended as well. In effect, virtually all federal spending not included in the high priority categories I just explained should be considered to be at high risk, if not totally unavailable. I now have time for a limited number of questions."

The President was subjected to a loud and rancorous chorus of nearly unintelligible questions, so she simply pointed to a reporter from the Associated Press.

"President Meyers, by executive order, are you not in effect implementing or even exceeding the proposal Congress just rejected?"

"I suppose you could say that. But math is math. The experts I spoke to today have told me that we simply cannot tax our way out of this. I have long been a believer in requiring the most wealthy to increase their contributions to the nation that has provided them the opportunity to become so wealthy. But the numbers are not there.

"If you don't have enough money to pay for what you would like, you pay for what you can afford. When you are unable to borrow, you have no other options but to live on your available funds."

The President pointed to a correspondent from CBS: "Madam President, between federal and state funding cuts, many low income families are going to lose hundreds of dollars per month. What do you say to them?"

"I am sorry."

The next question came from a reporter from Reuters News Service: "Are you concerned that these measures may result in more unrest of the nature we are seeing today in Boston and Chicago?"

"I am concerned about it... but I cannot make decisions based upon that concern. I can take one more question."

The President called upon a correspondent from NBC: "Would you comment on the situation involving China and Taiwan?"

"In spite of everything happening here in the United States, I am being kept up to date on that situation as well. We can only hope that reason and diplomacy will prevail, and prevent any further senseless loss of life. Thank you all for coming today."

As soon as the President exited the Press Room, she was joined by Vice President Eli Skinner, and they moved quickly down the hall, accompanied by Secret Service agents. Within a couple of minutes, they had made their way down to the Situation Room, where they were greeted once again by Defense Secretary Lawrence Spencer, Secretary of State James Florentine and General Byron Zeller.

Upon entering the room, they saw that the General had projected a map of the South China Sea onto a screen hanging on the wall. They dispensed with pleasantries and sat down so that the General could begin his briefing. "Our satellites have been picking up a lot of activity, and a couple of planes we have in the area are tracking some things with radar.

"Taiwan is patrolling its airspace with fighters, of course. But the Chinese keep poking at them with fighter – bombers, and they seem to be testing to see how far into that Taiwanese airspace they can go before they are warned away or even shot at.

"Two Chinese carriers are now hovering just outside the Taiwanese territorial waters, but about once every hour they will take a turn and cruise about a mile or two inside the boundaries."

The President spoke up. "Still no evidence of any preparations for an invasion?"

The General shook his head. "No... I think this confirms our long – held understanding that the Chinese simply do not possess the capability for an actual invasion. However, we are detecting a buildup of warplanes along that part of their coast.

"They have brought dozens of planes from other parts of the country to that region. I think they are looking at intimidation... blackmail if you will."

The Vice President shook his head. "Could you expand on that, General?"

"They may not have the type of amphibious landing craft needed for an invasion, although they certainly have the manpower. But they have these carriers, they now have a larger number of battleships, cruisers and missile frigates. And they have dramatically increased their inventory of fighters and bombers over the past three years.

"Add to that that they have nukes, and Taiwan is very close by. My fear is that China could effectively blockade Taiwan by sea and air, with that nuke factor hanging in the background, although they do not want to absorb a damaged Taiwan. They want to seize it.

"So they put into effect an air and naval blockade, then Taiwan is forced to agree to reconcile with the mainland. Then, a statement is issued that a compromise has been reached, and Taiwan becomes a part of China again, with a certain degree of autonomy similar to that granted to Hong Kong when it was reabsorbed."

The President began to nervously tap her pen on the desk. "General, do you see any new options for us?"

"The Chinese are smelling blood in the water. They see us in crisis and a weakened state. It still comes down to what I told you at our last meeting... we either move most of our Navy to the region, or we threaten to use nukes, and only if we mean it. Or... we stand down and let it happen."

The Vice President spoke next: "What will be the long term effect if we sit by and do nothing?"

The Secretary of Defense answered: "Of course, a democracy gets absorbed by a dictatorship. Then we lose the trust of all of our allies. China will know that they have a green light to bully everyone in that part of the world, especially when it comes to underwater resources. The Philippines will be the first to feel that affect.

"China will no longer feel any pressure to keep the North Koreans in line. And things will swiftly become much more dicey in the Middle East, because Israel and Lebanon will feel that we have become a paper tiger. They will feel much more strongly that they need to fend for themselves, and the sabers will start to rattle.

"Those problematic neighbors surrounding Israel will feel much more free to punch at them, because they will no longer view our pledges of support for allies to have as much meaning."

The Vice President spoke. "Of course, if you find yourself going to war with someone, I suppose you stop paying interest on their bonds. Then, our financial situation gets even more dire."

The President could be heard to moan. "And then Russia could assume a green light to try to bring Eastern Europe back under their control, and deal more violently with some of the dissident provinces."

The room went silent for a moment, before all eyes eventually turned toward the General who was obviously seething in anger.

The President gestured toward the Marine with four stars on his shoulders. "Please General... feel free."

The General shook his head then stood and pointed toward the projected image on the screen. "Is there anyone in the United States government with a beating heart who has not seen China as an emerging threat to our interests in the Pacific... all around the world, for that matter?

"But when we had to make a choice between living within our means and borrowing money so that we could spend extravagantly, what did we do? We just kept on spending by allowing that threat to loan us money, and we became dependent upon their generous willingness to hold our debt and our financial future in their hands.

"Now I can't afford to train pilots. I had to delay a shipment of fuel to San Diego this week. And why? Because over the years we were worried over things that may have been well intended, but only ended up making us weaker as a nation. But now I just need to know what you want me to do."

The President looked around at the uncomfortable group. "I don't think I can authorize a nuclear response. And from what you're saying, General, we would sacrifice a lot of people and treasure to do this with conventional weapons. Am I correct?" The General nodded.

"If you disagree with me, speak up. But I see that we have no choice but to try diplomacy and just hope that it works."

The rest slowly nodded in agreement one by one, except for the General, who continued to stare at a notepad in front of him.

The President stood and looked around once again. "So, General... you have your answer." The career Marine stood and nodded to the assembled group, then closed his briefcase and left the room.

"Welcome back to our NewsNet coverage of, frankly, almost too many stories to keep track of. My name is Mike Silver, and I am being joined by... I am getting a news update here on our screen.

"Boston authorities have requested that President Meyers send federal troops into the city to assist in quelling the rampant violence that is spreading throughout Boston and its suburbs. Hundreds of National Guard soldiers are assisting Boston and area police along with Massachusetts state police officers.

"The level of violence reached a frenzy this afternoon after President Meyers announced a cut off of federal funds that will reduce and eliminate much of the income received by low income families and individuals. Poverty advocates and civil rights leaders are demanding that federal and state authorities pledge to restore those benefits.

"Throughout Boston, police officers and troops have spent now over thirty-six hours being fired at and being confronted by angry citizens. The officers and soldiers seem to be growing less patient by the hour, and more quick to employ their superior firepower. The total death toll in Boston now stands at eight hundred twenty-one, with seven hundred and ninety-eight of those being protesters.

"Rioting in Chicago is also widespread, and is becoming more bloody. Authorities report that twenty – three protesters have died, and four police officers have been wounded by gunfire.

"Most of downtown Chicago is still inaccessible for traffic and business. Illinois National Guard troops have arrived in the city, and are being dispersed to problem areas.

"Large but peaceful demonstrations continue today in Los Angeles and Sacramento, California to protest that state's tentative plans to cut welfare benefits. There have been several arrests for disorderly conduct, but since the recent event at the Staples Center, there have so far been no new outbreaks of serious violence during demonstrations in those two California cities.

"At the same time, reports are coming out of California that in Los Angeles, San Francisco, Stockton, Oakland and Long Beach, gang influence is growing to the point of being in control of some neighborhoods.

"And this is just breaking... Atlanta, Georgia is also the scene of a large demonstration to protest federal cutbacks in aid to the poor. We are now learning that the Atlanta demonstration has turned violent, and what started out as a peaceful expression of disagreement has evolved into a riot. There are now reports of multiple clashes between police and rioters, and several people have been taken to various Atlanta hospitals.

"When we come back, we will try to resume our discussion on the vote taken in Congress to abandon the United States Constitution. Stay with us here on NewsNet."

President Bryce Hamilton strolled quickly to the microphone in the auditorium of the Great Plains Convention Center. He unfolded his notes as a large contingent of reporters and correspondents took their seats.

"First of all, on behalf of the Constitutional States of America, I wish to express sorrow at the senseless loss of life taking place in several United States cities. Most of all, I want to express condolences to the families and friends of those who have died while trying to protect and defend the citizens, and of those innocent citizens who have been victims of the violence.

"I wish to announce that as of ten minutes ago, Indiana, North Carolina and Superior are part of the CSA. We welcome the citizens of those states to our nation, and wish them all the best.

"If you look in the information packets that are being distributed to you as we speak, you will find the final draft of national tax rates and provisions passed by our Congress last evening. You will note that our entire tax code is four pages long. There will be no government body to oversee the collection of income taxes. Such taxes will be collected at the state level, and forwarded to our national treasury. Money forwarded to us from the states will be transmitted in lump sum fashion, with no breakdowns by individuals.

"Even while our new, temporary taxation system is in effect, we will continue to explore the best way to implement a permanent tax code that will be based upon expenditures and purchases only. It is our goal to completely eliminate any national income tax within twenty-four months of today.

"Also in your packet is a new list of industries that have agreed to either move to the CSA or create new businesses here. As you can see, in the past four days, three heavy manufacturing enterprises have announced moves to the CSA. In addition, twenty-one small and medium – sized industries have announced intent to relocate.

"You will also see that three overseas firms have announced plans to locate large manufacturing plants in the CSA, and so far fifteen new corporations will come into existence in our new nation.

"We have also provided for you our first report on revenue receipts by our treasury. We have also included projections for our first six months, as we really have only been in existence for a matter of days. Nonetheless, you'll see that we expect that our revenue will exceed our expenses of operating our government by roughly 18%.

"I am certain that you understand that such projections are very speculative in nature at this point. You will continue to receive such reports, and after a couple of years, should our revenues continue to exceed expenses at such a rate, we will consider how to adjust our possible consumption tax lower so that we are not asking our citizens to pay any more in taxes than absolutely necessary.

"We are no longer part of the United States, so I would have no reason to criticize our former nation. So, I say this just so that you understand how we intend to operate: we will have low taxes, because we're going to phase in a system through which citizens can put money away for retirement in self-directed accounts, rather than a government operated pension fund. We are not going to have a permanent Department of Commerce. The staff of our current Commerce Department will concentrate on economic development. We will not have a Department of Transportation, a Department of Education and on and on and on.

"Each state will provide environmental and worker safety oversight. Each state will be in charge of its own highways, bridges and speed limits. They can design their infrastructure as they wish, without oversight, regulation and hindrance from a national government. We will no longer be taking funds away from residents of each state to simply return it in the form of highway grants minus bureaucratic overhead at the national level.

"I hope that these examples help you to understand why we are confident that we can operate while taking so little money away from our citizens and businesses. Let me rephrase that... our businesses are our citizens, and vice versa.

"I apologize if I seem to be speaking with a tone of arrogance. But I am confident that the Constitutional States of America will be a success, and provide the opportunities that we would hope were sought and longed for by all Americans.

"I will now take your questions...".

Hamilton recognized a reporter from Fox News: "Mister President, soon after the CSA came into existence, a serious situation seems to have developed between China and Taiwan, a long – standing ally of the United States. I think that even you would agree that the breakup of the United States has weakened a collective America militarily. Would you please comment on that?"

"What you say is true, two separate Americas cannot be as strong militarily as one nation. And to be very candid, I am very troubled by that reality.

"Still, I feel that the states that seceded did so for the long-term good of their citizens. Every important action has unintended consequences, and I am deeply concerned that one of those consequences is a weakened military status. I will not insult anyone's intelligence by saying otherwise.

"It is a case of determining what is likely to be best for our future, and the future generations. I have assured President Meyers that the CSA will cooperate in a situation of joint interest and obligations."

The President called on a reporter from CNN: "We have heard from some advocates for the rights of undocumented immigrants that they are being made to feel unwelcome in the CSA. Could you address that?"

"Anyone who enters another nation knowing that they're doing so unlawfully, would by virtue of sheer logic feel unwelcome. But we're not telling illegal aliens that they have to leave unless they have a record that would make them appear to be dangerous.

"Further, they can stay here and work as long as they obey our laws. The only catch is, if they entered the United States illegally as an adult, they can never become citizens of the CSA. However, their children can apply for citizenship upon reaching the age of eighteen. I see that policy as humane and logical."

The President nodded toward a reporter from the Houston Chronicle: "Mister President, two members of the United States Senate have called on President Meyers to demand financial restitution from the CSA for the loss of federal lands. How do you respond to such a demand?"

"We have to remember that, first of all, it was the states that created the federal government, not the other way around. At some point, the federal government decided that it had the right to declare portions of states to belong to the federal government.

"I find it preposterous for a United States Senator to have such a narrow view of the relationship between states and the national government. What has happened is that the land has simply been returned to the states. The states can decide what kind of activities, be they commercial or recreational, will take place on those properties. Perhaps a state may want to auction off such land. But that really is a decision to be made by each state."

A reporter from NewsNet Heartland was called upon: "Mister President, an editorial in a St. Louis newspaper implied that industries were being directed to locate in St. Louis as a way of muffling the criticisms expressed by city residents who do not like the policies of the CSA, but do not want to move away. How do you reply to that?"

The President smiled before he answered: "Sometimes things happen in the most serendipitous manner. It is true that St. Louis came to the attention of many because of the high level of unhappiness expressed by those who did not like our approach to addressing needs of the low income and unemployed.

"In turn, those very protests made it evident that so many residents of the city are in need of good employment. Those people need jobs... new and relocating industries need employees. It can't get any better than that."

A correspondent from National Public Radio received a point and a nod: "President Hamilton, there has been speculation among energy investors that the CSA may attempt some sort of end – run around the global oil markets. Could you address that?"

"The Constitutional States of America have not entered into any treaties of any kind, including those regarding trade. It is my assumption that existing oil producers would honor contracts that were already in effect, except for any provisions that were mandated by the laws of the United States.

"An interesting situation comes about in terms of an oil producer coming into existence in the CSA now, or when existing contracts expire. There is much dust to settle on this matter, but an oil or gas company that emerges in this new nation will be able to sell gas or oil to whomever they wish. I do not foresee any federal

CSA laws being adopted that would require such an energy producer to enter into any formal global market. And due to a busy schedule, I will take one more question."

Hamilton pointed to a correspondent from MSNBC. "Thank you, Mr. President... I was wondering if you could respond to allegations that policy analysts and leaders of the Council for a Free America knew that a secession would derail the ability of both nations to maintain programs providing aid to the poor, with an end goal of reducing benefits to minorities."

The President shook his head. "Anyone making such allegations is incorrect. I would say that it would have been a logical conclusion to expect that there would be a narrower array of social programs in the CSA as compared to the United States. It has been no secret that an assumption behind the formation of the CSA was that a healthier and freer economy would provide better opportunity through employment, thereby reducing the need for publicly funded assistance. Of course, that has nothing to do with race.

"We are very aware of the fact that there are many residents of the new CSA who feel that new and unwanted policies have been thrust upon them. At the same time, there are millions of United States citizens who feel that their nation has abandoned the principles and ideals that made America as we used to know it the greatest nation the world had ever known. To be very honest with you, and I'm speaking only for myself, my sympathy lies more with them. Once again, I have to go now... I thank you for your time and attention."

"This is Harriet MacRae, and we interrupt our normal programming of Midnight News Roundup here on NewsNet, to report that the building conflict between China and Taiwan has taken a turn for the worse. Pentagon officials just confirmed that three hours ago a pitched naval battle broke out, with the loss of two Taiwanese battleships and one destroyer.

"In addition, United States and Japanese intelligence report that one of China's new aircraft carriers and two missile frigates were lost in the battle. The forces of Japan, the Philippines and South Korea have placed their forces on various levels of elevated readiness as a result.

"More information is coming in... Pentagon officials have just confirmed that a large number of Chinese naval vessels are nearing the island nation of Taiwan, and that squadrons of Chinese fighter – bombers are circling the perimeters of Taiwanese airspace. The Chinese embassy has notified our Department of State that China is exercising its right to defend its military forces in the region, and is instituting an air and naval blockade of Taiwan. It has long been an establish claimed by China that Taiwan is a renegade province that should rightly be reunited with the mainland nation.

"I'm now seeing another... announcement... on my screen... China has just announced that the United States of America has used money borrowed from the people of China to prop up the illegitimate government of Taiwan, while also failing to meet its fiduciary responsibilities to ensure that debt obligations sold on the global market are maintained in good faith.

"Therefore, the people of China are no longer under any obligation to make payments on debts issued under false precepts, and will offer the nation's holdings of United States government debt for sale on the global bond market."

The tall, blonde newsreader began to look to the side, several seconds of silence confirming to viewers that she and the NewsNet night staff had been taken by surprise.

"We are…". She attempted to force a smile while she once again glanced to her left. "We are going to try to get someone with some military expertise to come on the air to speak to the matter of this blockade… and we're going to try to find someone from the NewsNet Business Channel to try to come on and explain just what in the world the announcement about the Chinese dumping our debt means to a United States economy already on the ropes."

The anchor went silent for a few seconds once again, and then pressed her ear phone against her head. "We know that most of the eastern residents of the United States are either in bed, or were preparing to go to bed. But we now have on the line retired Air Force Colonel Simon Casters, one of our NewsNet military analysts. Colonel… I thank you for answering your phone late at night… I would like for you to explain to all of us the military and defense ramifications of a successful blockade of Taiwan by the government of China."

"Thank you Harriet… I hope that we have a good telephone connection. First of all, it is not a given that the United States military will not become involved at some point in this conflict. Several months ago, such a move by China would have been unthinkable. But the secession and the economic breakdown of the United States economy in its wake has presented a situation that the Chinese have likely found to be as confusing as it is tempting. "I want to clarify something… I am not blaming the secession states for this Asian conflict. The Chinese have known for some time that the integrity of our bonds was deteriorating.

"In any case, Taiwan is in a hopeless situation. They know that the United States military muscle is not what it was even three years ago. They are not an insignificant military power in their own right, but they cannot withstand what they are facing now.

"Then you factor in that they did some significant damage to the Chinese navy. Now the big bully in the region is going to puff out its chest. Within a matter of days, Taiwan will have capitulated and surrendered to mainland China.

"There may very well be some sugar – coating of reality… I can see Taiwan being given the same kind of status as Hong Kong when the British lease expired. After all, Taiwan is likely to surrender without any more meaningful bloodshed, and it will be one of the most progressive and economically profitable regions of China.

"But China will have dominion over the shipping lanes in the South China Sea. And they will control all those underwater resources, and the Philippines will be forced to sit by and watch China harvest everything off their coast that had been under dispute."

The anchor shook her head: "What about Japan and South Korea?"

"South Korea has the potential to become even more of a powder keg. And as for Japan, I expect that they will move rapidly to become a nuclear power. But don't forget India. They have also had conflicts in the past with China. They are a nuclear power, and I think we will see an arms race between China, Japan and India."

"Thank you, Colonel, for your insights. Best of luck in trying to go back to sleep. And now we are being joined... oh, I am welcoming Brandon Tillotson from NewsNet Business Network." Viewers saw a short, dark-haired man of forty sit down at the desk to join the anchor.

"So, Brandon, I know that you were about to go home, so I thank you for joining me. Perhaps you could address what is likely to be the result of the Chinese announcement that they will be making no more interest payments on their United States government bonds, and will be placing their holdings for sale on the global market."

"Harriet... I am speaking about this matter with some reluctance. I was uncertain as to whether I should even come on the air under the circumstances...".

"Could you explain?"

The economist took a deep breath before speaking again. "The Chinese have some good manners. About ninety minutes ago our State Department received a hand – delivered communiqué giving advance warning of the bond announcement.

"Thirty minutes ago, Cheryl Worthington, the president of the NewsNet Business Channel received a phone call from the Treasury Department. They were conveying the very strong desire from the White House that networks not comment on this development. However, Cheryl gave me the green light to come here and speak freely."

The anchor smiled grimly: "So what do we need to know about this action by China?"

"This is a two bladed dagger in our back. First of all, the United States Treasury could hardly stand to lose the revenue of the bond interest payments being paid by the Chinese. Now, they put their large bond holdings on the market. That means a fire sale of our bonds, and what had been the safest investment on earth just a few years ago will lose significant net asset value."

"So what is the bottom line?"

"United States government bonds have long been the 'safe' portion of investment portfolios. So all of those pensions for private systems, public employees… teachers. Well, yesterday people were marching and protesting over the likelihood of cuts. In the morning, when the global investors are done for the night, it's going to be much worse."

"My name is Mike Silver, and we thank you for joining us this morning at NewsNet, and we are once again dispensing with our regularly scheduled broadcasts to bring you up-to-date on a number of urgent developments.

"Late last evening, Chinese military forces imposed a naval and air blockade on the island nation of Taiwan. State Department officials speaking off the record are acknowledging that Chinese takeover of the island within days is all but inevitable.

"In a related matter, the Chinese government announced just after midnight Eastern Standard Time, that it is suspending all interest payments on United States Government bonds, and is placing its portfolio of United States bonds on the global market.

"Financial analysts fear that government bonds will now be categorized within investor sentiment as having a 'junk bond' status. It is feared that under any circumstances, pension, retirement and investment funds will have taken another major hit before the day is over.

"And while a conflict in the South China Sea was downgrading America's military influence, and our economy was being battered, there was more bad news on the domestic scene. As the city of Boston continued to be the scene of bitter conflict between authorities attempting to quell a virtual uprising and city residents protesting cutbacks in government programs, martial law was declared at 2:00 AM.

"The city was already under a state of emergency and a curfew, but armed protesters continued to engage the police and Guard troops. Just after midnight, a police spokesman confirmed that the civilian death toll had reached one thousand, and that there have been eight hundred fifteen police or National Guard soldiers injured.

"President Calista Myers is yet to announce a decision on a request for federal troops. Morgues in the city of Boston have been overwhelmed, and suburbs and surrounding cities have been receiving bodies for processing. In some cases, authorities have not been able to retrieve bodies due to the level of violence.

"Now the city is starting to feel the impact of the inability of delivery trucks to reach the grocery stores and carryouts that have not been burned or totally looted. Police and fire departments are beginning to receive calls from panicked residents virtually trapped in their homes by the violence. They are also receiving reports from individuals who were able to leave their houses and apartments, only to find the stores empty or abandoned.

"There have been dozens of reports of home invasions and robberies, as well as numerous carjackings as desperate residents begin to fight over food as well as a means for driving to it. There are unverified reports of casualties during these confrontations.

"The casualty figures from the unrest in Chicago is but a fraction of that in Boston, but the downtown area remains shut down. Virtually no one except police and fire personnel are able to get in or out of the center of the city.

"Thousands of downtown Chicago inhabitants are for all practical purposes stranded. They may have all the water that they need, but if they tried to venture out into an environment of questionable safety and security, they will find few stores open. As in Boston, most stores in the vast swaths of the city engulfed in the rioting and protests have either been destroyed or emptied out.

"And when we return from this break, we will have updates on the plans for very large protests to take place later today in the California cities of Los Angeles and Sacramento, where those who oppose planned cutbacks in assistance to low – income residents will be taking to the streets."

President Calista Myers sat at the large desk in the Oval Office across from Vice President Eli Skinner and Attorney General Mitchell Pryor. She peered warily at the Attorney General: "You don't have to tell me Mitchell... I shouldn't have had those calls placed to the media outlets last night. But regardless... we need to decide what we say to the nation this morning."

The Attorney General shook his head. "Madam President... I am flattered that you bring me into your confidence on such a matter. But why me, and not the Treasury Secretary?"

The Vice President spoke up. "It was my recommendation. You may not be an economist, but you have good judgment. And at this moment, we are an inch away from being in a state of total default and bankruptcy."

The President clasped her hands and placed them on the desk. "This is so damned confusing... Congress has voted to dispense with the Constitution. Now we have these other emergencies. So, Mitchell... I need for you to hear what I plan to do, and let me know if you think I should back off... I mean taking all of the current circumstances into account. And keep in mind, that I will make it clear that any of these policy changes can be rescinded should we be able to right our financial ship." The Attorney General nodded and watched as Calista Myers glanced down at a list in front of her.

"I'm going to ask the Congress to enact a one – time National Emergency Defense Contribution Tax. This will require all United States citizens to immediately contribute 20% of balances in IRA's, 401-K's, similar retirement plans and annuities. All such contributions will be absolutely and without exception designated for use by the United States military.

"I am ordering an immediate shutdown of all non—defense agencies of the United States government. The only exceptions will be in the Department of State, and those agencies dedicated to matters of immediate public safety, such as air traffic control operations and railway inspections.

"I'm also asking Congress to enact a 15% federal income tax increase on all households with a gross annual income of $75,000 and over. I'm also asking for a 5% tax increase on earned income for households below $75,000. I'm also asking for the elimination of the mortgage deduction for households with incomes in excess of $60,000. And I'm asking for the abolishment of the Earned Income Tax Credit. And I'm asking for Congress to make all these changes effective immediately.

"I plan to announce the closing of at least eighty percent of our foreign embassies. And all foreign aid will be immediately suspended.

"I plan to announce a suspension of all immigration. For those already here illegally, naturalization processes will continue.

"Further, I plan to ask Congress for its blessing of an opening of dialogue with Mexico for the purpose of asking for reimbursement for medical services and education costs for those who have crossed the border illegally."

The President looked up from her list. "All right now, gentlemen... I want to hear what you think."

Vice President Skinner broke the silence. "I think that we need to explain to the Attorney General, how you arrived at these decisions over the past several hours."

The President nodded: "During the night I worked with staff from the Congressional Budget Office. In light of the Chinese announcement, they calculated how much was needed in cash flow to maintain Social Security and Medicare, and a very pared – down military.

"The work was done quickly, but I have faith in it. If we want to avoid large cuts in Social Security benefits for current recipients, and maintain Medicare, then we had to announce drastic reductions in everything else. It is a simple matter of cash in – cash out.

"We have to do this to keep all of our systems from crashing. If we make these moves, we can maintain a military that will still be lethal. It comes too late for Taiwan. We were in simply too great a state of disarray. The Chinese saw their chance, and they took it. And the world will be forever changed because of it.

"Taking these moves, in their entirety I want to add, will still allow us to provide some funding to the states for financial assistance programs, although at a greatly – reduced rate. With what has happened to the bond and stock markets, states will have to make choices, all of which will be very uncomfortable. Some of those decisions will be made within the next few days, and in other states over the coming weeks.

"There are very many states that will be deciding whether to try to maintain programs for low – income residents while perhaps reducing pay for public employees and cutting pension benefits. They will have to shut down state parks and suspend maintenance of roads and streets. If this were simply a matter of academic speculation, it would be fascinating. But the reality is, gentlemen, states are going to have to swiftly decide whether they're going to protect and hold harmless those who receive the public largess at the expense of those who provide it.

"So there are unity… sympathy protests planned for today in most major California cities. The same thing for New York, Newark, Philadelphia, Cleveland, Tallahassee and Miami. The Tallahassee protest has a special twist to it – community activists are planning a sit – in at the Statehouse. The protesters are going to issue a demand that Florida enact a state income tax to make up for federal reductions in public aid benefits."

The Vice President rubbed his chin and laughed. "Now for some reality. We see what is happening in Boston, and to a less violent extent in Chicago. And we see that things are starting to get out of hand in different parts of California. But for the general public, they are going to see these demonstrations, protests and so forth as nothing but welfare riots."

The Attorney General spoke up. "What about the situation in Ohio?"

The President responded. "The staff is keeping me briefed on that. Fortunately, since the bombing at Zanesville, there have been no more major incidents. There are scattered reports of loud and boisterous confrontations at things such as community meetings and the demonstrations in Columbus. All of that could change at any moment." She glanced at her watch. "So late this afternoon, I put all this in front of Congress."

"This is Charlene Allen with your NewsNet Heartland Noon Report. Just moments ago, the governments of China and Taiwan issued a joint communiqué announcing their reunification.

"Taiwanese officials stated that reunification with the mainland will bring greater prosperity to what had been an American ally for decades. They cite benefits of reunification such as increased trade opportunities, the ability to scale back its massive defense costs and reintegration into one of the world's great and historic civilizations.

"The Chinese Ambassador to the United Nations announced that this reunification is a major step toward establishing an ongoing peace and era of cooperation among the family of nations in Southeast Asia.

"Officials of the United States government have collectively issued statements recognizing that further bloodshed has been avoided, but caution that the interests of the United States and nations in the Far East may face some troubling after effects of Taiwan being absorbed by the mainland nation.

"In the United States today, President Calista Myers will be addressing both houses of Congress in an emergency session. Although the White House has not officially released any information, anonymous sources are indicating that Myers will be proposing draconian measures to prevent the insolvency of the United States.

"Here in the CSA, a major economic event will take place later today in St. Louis. President Bryce Hamilton will be on hand for a joint announcement by three of the world's largest manufacturers of ammunition of their intent to establish operations in that city.

"The three armament firms will be collectively purchasing five abandoned factories within the city of St. Louis. Three of those factories will be retrofitted, while the other two will be demolished and new facilities built in their place. It is expected that the renovation and construction projects will generate several thousand jobs in a part of the city with the highest unemployment rates.

"Once the ammunition manufacturing facilities are finished, it is expected that as many as seven thousand permanent jobs will be created, when factoring in all of the support positions and new businesses that are expected to come into existence in the immediate vicinity. The joint announcement by the three ammunition manufacturers state that it is their intention to hire local residents to the extent possible.

"In addition, a separate company has announced that five hundred acres of land on the west side of the city has been purchased to be the site of a massive warehousing facility, much of which will be dedicated to the firearms and ammunition industry, including special security and environmental controls preferable for such products.

"It is expected that once the warehouse facility is completed, as many as two thousand employees will be needed. It is also expected that additional jobs will be available in trucking, and construction and maintenance of railroad spurs.

"You can go to the NewsNet Heartland website to see the various locations in downtown St. Louis where these new employers will begin accepting applications for employment as early as tomorrow.

"Several union and civil rights leaders in the area have announced that protests will be taking place outside of any locations where applications for employment in the firearms industry are being accepted. Union officials are accusing the companies relocating to St. Louis of simply dodging their responsibility to pay decent wages by moving to the CSA. At the same time, some local civil rights leaders and clergy are objecting to the recruitment by companies that they referred to as 'merchants of death'.

"President Hamilton stated earlier today that the economic development blossoming in St. Louis is an example of how a free people can prosper and find opportunity when government welcomes them, rather than building roadblocks in their way.

"There has been an immediate reaction from officials in those states from which the ammunition manufacturers are moving. One Connecticut State Senator told a meeting of business leaders this morning that these companies are doing nothing more than escaping an environment in which the rights of workers and their safety are held to be sacred.

"Overnight in Boston, the bodies of three men believed to have been among the protesters battling police and National Guard troops were found in the middle of the intersection of two residential streets in South Boston.

"Around midnight last night, the intersection was the scene of some exchanges of gunfire between protesters and some homeowners. Police say that they have no eye witnesses coming forward, but that all three of the deceased men had been shot with .22 Magnum and 20 gauge shotgun rounds.

"And Chicago authorities have issued a state of emergency in the third largest city in North America. Nearly all of the downtown area is now paralyzed by protests over planned reductions in public assistance benefits. Nearly all of the city's businesses are shut down, and many have been badly damaged by rioters.

"Many residents of the downtown area are virtual hostages in apartment buildings. As is the case in Boston, food shortages are becoming rampant. Most troubling to city officials is the uptick in violent encounters between protesters and police. In the last seventy-two hours, there have been one hundred seventy-five protesters and rioters reported killed, and three hundred eleven injured.

"At the same time, fourteen police officers have been killed, and forty-seven others injured. Illinois National Guard troops are now patrolling the perimeters of the downtown area, checking identifications of those wishing to enter the downtown. Several legal rights organizations have filed for a court injunction, contending that being required to prove identity is an unreasonable restriction of free movement.

"And when we return after break, we are going to have an exclusive interview with Jim Brand, leader of the Ohio Founders' Coalition. This is NewsNet Heartland."

"Thank you for returning to NewsNet Heartland. Yesterday correspondent Melinda Sedgwick journeyed to the Ohio home of Jim Brand. Brand is the Chairman of the Ohio Founders' Coalition, and he agreed to speak with Melinda about the goals and objectives of the organization."

Viewers suddenly saw a two- story wood framed house behind a neatly landscaped yard while hearing a voice over: "I'm at the home of Jim Brand near Laura, Ohio."

The scene shifted to a young woman with long dark hair shaking hands with a sixty-ish slender and balding man. "Mr. Brand... I want to thank you for agreeing to talk with me."

The man gestured for her to have a seat at a kitchen table. "Please... call me Jim."

"Jim... I could not help but notice upon our arrival... I saw a lot of security. The gate across the entrance to your driveway... security cameras along the wooded driveway and the approach to your house. Is that related to your involvement with the Ohio Founders' Coalition?"

Brand nodded slowly. "We've had some death threats. I talked my wife out of being part of this interview, because I'm concerned about her safety."

"I understand. So please, tell me about your organization."

Brand smiled. "Actually, it started out as just a few old friends sitting around having coffee in a McDonald's on Saturday mornings. You know, just a handful of grumpy old guys like me sitting around and complaining. Every Saturday, it was the same thing. We complained about taxes, government growing bigger and more intrusive…".

He closed his eyes as if trying to remember something. "I guess it was about three years ago, our conversations seemed to turn to how much we had abandoned the principles our country was founded on. A couple of the guys really got into reading books about our Founding Fathers and how the United States came about. We really got into that.

"Then some of us started talking about how our grandchildren seem to really not have a concept of how our nation came to be. So we decided that we would give our little group a name, and offered to speak to school kids. The next thing we knew, we were dressing up in character as one or the other of the Founding Fathers, and the kids just loved it.

"But that type of activity only seemed to remind us more and more as time went on just how far we had strayed from the nation America had been designed to be. So we started meeting with elected officials, sending letters and emails to our Congressman and Senators. The next thing we knew, we were having public forums…. speakers… seminars… the works.

"Friends talked to friends, and other groups around Ohio took the same name and took up the same causes. Then, when all those states seceded, we felt kind of abandoned. As conservatives, we felt like we had been stranded on an island somewhere. But when that stuff started about shelving the Constitution… oh, my gosh. We got really loud really quickly."

"Is that when the threats began?"

The host nodded slowly. "We had all that security installed just five days ago. Once we came out with a public statement in support of the Constitution and our Founding Fathers, it hit the fan. We were called racists, bigots, we were accused of supporting slaveowners... I got phone calls saying I hated gay people and even got a couple saying that I hated women."

"All because you support the founding of the United States of America?"

"Of course. I suppose you heard that speech that Senator from Pennsylvania made."

"So what does your Coalition plan to do next?"

"We're going to keep on speaking out... I want to assure teachers and school principals that we are willing to come to any school to keep educating our young people about what America is really about."

The correspondent shifted uncomfortably in her chair. "I understand that you and your organization have been lumped together in the minds of some with groups such as the Ohio Lexington Brigade and the Eastern Ohio Freedom Alliance, two militia – style organizations. Would you comment on that?"

"First of all, our hearts go out to the families of all those people killed at that meeting near Zanesville. And I must mention how senseless an act it was that killed all those innocent people in that union hall at Musgrove.

"As for those two groups, to my knowledge they have done nothing wrong or illegal. Personally, the militia thing is just not my style. But we have a lot of people who fear for the future. Sometimes people just feel the need to be ready for whatever comes along. Right now, we're sitting here in a rural area. But things can turn around in a minute. Losing the Constitution... who knows what that can bring about?"

The correspondent smiled and nodded: "One last question... is Jim Brand going to leave Ohio?"

"I plan to stay here and do everything I can to see that Ohio serves as proof that a state can remain within the United States while also ensuring freedom for its citizens, and provide an

229

atmosphere where people and businesses can enjoy economic opportunity, what we always referred to as the American Dream. And one more thing if I may... go Buckeyes."

President Calista Myers could not release her grip on the podium, the hard wood helping her to stay focused and at least slightly calm as she addressed both houses of Congress before a national television audience.

She went through her list of proposals, a list simply conveyed in more formal and diplomatic language than when her audience was only the Vice President and Attorney General at the hastily arranged daybreak meeting.

Nearly all the members of Congress sat in stone – faced silence as she delivered her message. For members of her own party, the only agreeable passage was that seizing a portion of retirement wealth. As for the Republicans, most sat in silence giving her credit for having the fortitude to voice such ideas, but they were so overwhelmed by a sense of tragedy that they were lost in virtual sorrow in seeing such a proposal, and so late in the game.

"So I say to you now, before I walk away from this podium, if you cannot vote for my proposals, then with your colleagues and all of the United States of America watching, please rise now if you can offer a better idea. Because, ladies and gentlemen, we may go over the edge before this day is done."

There was a quiet muttering throughout the chamber until Congresswoman Boyle of Ohio stood to speak: "Madam President... I know that you are very well aware of the suggestion I have made repeatedly. All Americans need to contribute anything in excess of $1 million in wealth."

There was a combination of murmurs and laughter in response as the Speaker stepped to the podium and banged the gavel to attempt to bring the chamber back in order.

Then there were catcalls as the Virginian John Perkins rose. "Madam Speaker... I stand to make a motion that the United States House of Representatives adopt President Myers' proposal. And I hope that the Senate will do so as well."

The President stepped back to the podium. "The House of Representatives has a motion on the floor. I ask the Speaker of the House and the President of the Senate to immediately convene in their respective chambers to take action."

"This is Marcia Bentley for NewsNet, and we're bringing you coverage of a most crucial and dramatic action taking place in the Capitol Building right now. Congressman John Perkins of Virginia made a motion to accept a proposal that we never would've expected from a Democrat, but President Myers did indeed make such a proposal. In fact, it was a Democrat from Illinois, Representative Carla Bigelow who seconded the motion.

"As you can see on your screen, we are now watching the electronic vote count in the House of Representatives. It appears that there may be many abstentions. And while I don't want to cast aspersions on members of Congress, voting either way on this may simply require more backbone than more than a handful of members of Congress possess.

"The time has expired... the numbers are still being calculated... I think it has passed. Yes, the House of Representatives has passed the President's proposal by a vote of 175 to 120. Now that information is already known to those in the Senate chamber. Now, all eyes will be on the Senate.

"At least in the opinion of President Myers, passage of her measures in the Senate will prevent a federal bankruptcy and default. And I'm getting word from the wizard in my earphone that Senator Marcus Gilliard of Georgia is about to make a motion. Let's listen in...".

A silver – haired man in his early 80's stepped to the microphone. "Madam President... I move that the Senate of the United States of America pass President Myers' emergency proposal as just passed by the House of Representatives in its entirety and without conference action."

Helen Corrigan, the junior senator from the State of Washington walked slowly to the microphone. "Madam President, I second the motion of my esteemed colleague from Georgia, Marcus Gilliard."

There were several outbursts of shouting, and the Senate President repeatedly banged the gavel onto her desk to bring the chamber back into order. "The emergency motion has been made and seconded. The Clerk will now call the roll."

The NewsNet pundits watched along with the viewers, not really knowing how the body of now sixty – four Senators would vote. As the results came in one by one, their speculation was fueled by wondering how history would view a Senator who made a hard choice, versus one who stood by political and philosophical principle even if it meant default and bankruptcy.

Soon even those who spent each day analyzing the minds of politicians found themselves at the point of watching in silence as the votes came in a rapid flurry as time expired.

Marcia Bentley took one last glance at her monitor, before looking at the others who had joined her at the news desk during the count, to seek their nods of assurance. "We have the total... I see that there are twenty-eight votes for the proposal, and twenty-six opposed. So the proposal put forth by President Myers has been adopted.

"Mike Silver has joined me here at the NewsNet desk in New York... I want to ask you how this measure will be absorbed by the people of the United States."

The veteran analyst shook his head. "First of all, Marcia... I want to say that I am stunned that the vote was this close. This entire scenario over the past two weeks has been a nightmare. And this may not be fair of me, but how can you reach the level of being a United States Senator, and not even be able to admit that a nightmare is a nightmare? I just find it to be staggering.

"But now it is all going to happen. An executive order will be going out within the hour telling the Internal Revenue Service to immediately set about seizing the retirement holdings that people of all ages have worked hard to set aside for their golden years. However, I really do not fault the President for taking such a step. Let's face it, a President died, and others ahead of her in the line of succession were taken out of the picture when their home states left the nation.

"No matter how any of this turns out, I think that the only person currently in the government of the United States of America who will be treated kindly by history is Calista Myers. Remember, she was the Secretary of State, a diplomat by training who was unwillingly thrust into an unimaginable situation.

"So over the next several weeks, citizens will be receiving letters from the IRS that will make them want to cry in their beer. The welfare system of this nation will be a mere shadow of itself. Foreign aid is going to stop, and only a select few embassies will be open around the world.

"In effect, virtually all non-military and safety functions of the United States government have been placed in a state of suspension. Somewhere out there, libertarians are popping champagne corks, but we really don't know how this is going to play out. And from a fiscal standpoint, the United States of America is starting from scratch."

Marcia Bentley turned toward the camera: "On that point, I want to turn to Simone Dickerson of NewsNet Business Channel who has also just joined me... Simone, we know now that the actions taken by the President and Congress are going to be referred to in all types of hyperbolic terms. I don't think it would be at all an exaggeration to refer to today's events as historic and unprecedented. But the question is, will these steps save the United States from a total financial collapse?"

"Actually, Marcia, this entire scenario is a morbidly fascinating event to financial analysts such as myself who worked for several years in the Congressional Budget Office. One thing that I observed while working there, was that our federal government became more increasingly vulnerable to threats that could have easily been avoided by simply assessing the risk possibilities.

"For example, failing to balance spending with income is a risk that every individual household understands. But refusing to keep spending in check, only to turn around and allow your major global rival, and dare I say, threat, to be the holder of your credit card was nothing short of irresponsible.

"But let's go back a little further, back to the 1960's. All of those well – intentioned poverty programs had the potential for helping the poor make great strides. The problem came when the federal government mandated the states to offer up a menu of programs designed in Washington. I understand the argument that there were states that would have otherwise implemented such concepts only while kicking and screaming. But right now, I am talking dollars.

"These federally mandated programs resulted in a web of entanglement between federal and state funds. The federal government would mandate a program, the state would have to implement it, and often the state had to provide a portion of the funding. That state matching requirement would even impact local government in some states.

"More and more of these programs were implemented, and this federal penchant for creating and imposing programs simply gained steam. When the federal government became so comfortable with spending far in excess of its income, the collective willingness to expand social programs was inevitable.

"So today, Congress found itself hanging by a thread. After turning down proposals of a similar nature, circumstances forced them to virtually wipe out much of the growth of the federal government that has taken place over the past fifty years.

"We have become so accustomed to seeing members of Congress huffing and puffing in righteous indignation over this or that little nuance of a regulation. As evening falls upon us, we're going to come to understand that most of the federal government is being dismantled by the hour.

"Our military will be preserved, along with Social Security and Medicare. But as we speak, tens of thousands of federal, state and local public employees are feeling their blood running cold. Their jobs are gone... I can't even tell you right now if there will be any jobless benefits for them.

"There will now be a mere trickle of money from Washington to the states for poverty programs and food and medical assistance. Legions of Americans who have been depending upon welfare and Food Stamp benefits are likely to have just a small portion of that income remaining."

Marcia Bentley broke in: "I know that we're talking about millions of people who have been receiving those benefits. What is going to happen with them? Can local charities and churches and such come to the rescue?"

"To a degree they will. But remember... in this package just passed by Congress, income taxes are going to go up. A healthy portion of retirement benefits put aside for the future are going to be seized. That is going to have a dramatic effect on the ability of charities and churches to help the poor. But let me go out on a limb on that matter.

"Let me be the first to say this on NewsNet... we just entered into another major Depression. But when the Great Depression occurred in the Twentieth Century, the makeup of the poor and disadvantaged was different. Families were more intact. Having children out of wedlock was hardly rare and unknown, but it was nothing like it is right now. Families were much more cohesive.

"Now we have the phenomenon of multi-generational welfare dependency. That was not the case in the prior Depression. I see this as a frightening scenario, so many Americans accustomed to having the welfare complex as either a primary or a reliably secondary source of income. And now they are going to face a loss of that complex and manifest benefits system and be thrust into the job market that is being decimated.

"So at the bottom line, we are going to see a United States government much as it used to be. It will be much smaller and simpler, and depending upon your point of view, either less intrusive or less protective."

"Welcome to NewsNet's special late-night coverage of all of those startling events taking place all around us. My name is Pamela Baxter, and I want to thank you for joining us this evening. It is now 11:00 PM in a tense New York City, and 10:00 PM in Omaha, Nebraska, capitol of the recently formed Constitutional States of America.

"And many elected officials and citizens of the United States are looking toward Omaha this evening with an emotion that can only be described as bitterness. Please watch this video of Delaware Senator Tom Mason who spoke on the Senate floor immediately after the vote was taken on President Myers' historic budget proposal:

Viewers saw a short, balding man standing at the podium in the Senate chamber: "Madam President... as we begin the long and painful process of rebuilding the nation we once knew, we are going to be walking alongside millions of United States citizens finding their lives characterized by much desperation.

"Hundreds of thousands, perhaps millions of Americans, are going to be battling the specter of starvation. There is going to be rampant homelessness and a lack of medical care.

"Depending upon one's age, we have all been regaled by parents or grandparents with sober remembrances of the Great Depression early in the Twentieth Century. We have seen the grainy black-and-white newsreels of people standing in line at soup kitchens, or standing on a street corner begging for whatever a passerby is willing to give. We are now returning to those times, if not something worse.

"As you witness these heartbreaking scenes, and as you reach into your own pocket to help those more unfortunate, I want for you to look toward Omaha. I want you to look to the capitol of the Constitutional States of America, this so – called nation formed by a secret society of greedy and self – centered individuals who put the prospects of their own wealth above their love of country.

"Bryce Hamilton and his band of robber barons can call themselves an Administration. In reality, they are nothing more than a den of traitors who were able to design an ingenious plot that succeeded in playing upon the fears of those who, unfortunately, spent too much time listening to talk radio programs.

236

"For three years, the Council for a Free America laid the groundwork for this travesty, determining how to find alluring ways to make decades of progress sound as if it were some socialist scheme.

"They made it sound as if there were some grassroots uprising that demanded secession. In reality, there was not one... single... statewide election held to determine the wishes of the general population. Not one. This entire tragedy was driven by those who had something to gain, whether it was money or power, or both.

"Madam President, I had planned to introduce a bill next week, a bill that would have for once and for all brought about the reality of a dream we had talked about for years, but always found the subject to be hammered to death.

"I had planned to introduce a bill that would finally have taken us to having a single – payer health care system in the United States. In my proposed bill, I would have introduced Americare. But that will not happen now.

"Thanks to this secession, we'll never know just how far this nation could have advanced. Rather we will be regressing by generations back to a day when the happenings in Washington D.C. were of little consequence to the average person. Some will cheer at that prospect. But Madam President, I see this as the death of a great dream. Thank you."

"Thank you and good morning. My name is Roberta Croft, and welcome to Heartland Morning, being brought to you live from a rainy Omaha. We will now get right to the news, as much is happening.

"First of all, from the other side of the globe, top Taiwanese officials met with Chinese leaders in Beijing, and in a ceremony broadcast live on television in the mainland and on the island of Taiwan, officials from both sides signed an agreement establishing the formerly independent island as a province of China.

"No mention was made of the hostilities that took place over the past three days and resulted in the deaths of several thousand sailors.

"Much changed in the United States yesterday. It appears that bankruptcy and insolvency has been averted, but at the cost of the virtual abandonment of most federal government functions, and the obliteration, for all practical purposes, of nearly all poverty programs. Throughout the night, news networks provided live coverage of these astonishing developments, compiling lists of what will no longer exist in terms of federal funding, from child care to education funding, and even public access to federal parks.

"In nearly every major city in the United States today, it is expected that there will be massive protests and demonstrations. Poverty advocates, clergy, community organizations and civil rights groups and leaders are coordinating efforts. Overnight, a national coalition named Save America blossomed on social media. Leaders of this just hours – old organization are calling for demonstrators to bring cities to a standstill.

"Large demonstrations are expected today in New York, Philadelphia, Pittsburgh, Minneapolis, Atlanta, Tampa, Cleveland, Cincinnati, Baltimore, Columbus and Denver. Many cities in the CSA are also expecting to see demonstrations expressing unity with the United States protesters. Those cities include St. Louis, Dallas,

Houston, San Antonio, also, Oklahoma City and Charleston, South Carolina.

"As for Boston, the city remains in a stranglehold of violence. Action there is so intense that we have been unable to get an update on the number of casualties, but it is assumed that now over one thousand two hundred civilians have died there.

"A growing number of Boston neighborhoods are experiencing food shortages due to the inability of trucks to reach a rapidly diminishing number of functioning stores. In addition, delivery trucks have been unable to bring drugs and medical supplies to a number of clinics in the city, and attempts to make such deliveries were suspended last night after two parcel delivery trucks carrying medications were seized and looted by rioters. The drivers of both trucks were injured in the incidents.

"Chicago is experiencing an increasing level of violence, and the downtown area is also facing food shortages. Additional Illinois National Guard troops arrived earlier this morning.

"In Los Angeles, San Francisco, San Diego, Compton, Stockton and Oakland, protesters took to the streets to demand that the government of California protect the poor from the effects of the federal cutbacks.

"Several California cities, including Los Angeles, Compton and Stockton announced that the budget crisis makes it impossible for them to call in police officers for any extra duty. Each of those cities experienced some looting and arson over the past several hours.

"In Los Angeles, police officials are refusing to confirm or deny that several sections of the city are now under virtual control of gangs. However, it was confirmed that overnight twenty-three people died from gang violence, as the gangs appear to be jockeying for influence and position.

"Business owners in many cities in the United States are said to be arming themselves out of concern for the safety of themselves and their customers. A Chicago police Captain speaking on the condition of anonymity, told one of our correspondents that he was aware of a vibrant underground trade in shotguns and large caliber handguns directed toward fearful business and shop owners in portions of the city just outside the sections under siege by rioters and protesters. He said that the city cannot even cover all the reported crimes, and he doubted that much attention was going to be paid to business owners simply trying to survive.

"And finally, we're going to get to some news from right here in the CSA. Last evening at the Great Plains Conference Center, President Bryce Hamilton announced that an unnamed oil company will make an announcement within a week that it will be constructing the largest oil refinery in the world.

"The President said that he is at liberty to say that the new refinery will be more than double the capacity of a refinery located in India, owned by Reliance Industries. The Reliance refinery handles over 600,000 barrels of oil each day.

"The new facility will be built near Port Arthur, Texas, and is expected to employ nearly ten thousand, with an additional two thousand five hundred contract workers at any given time. Estimates are that as many as two thousand additional jobs will result in the area in food service, lodging and service stations and convenience stores.

"The President explained that with so much land being opened up for drilling and fracturing, it is very possible that even more refineries will be built, and even as those that had sat inactive for several years are being brought back online.

"President Hamilton added that since the government of the United States can no longer forbid or control offshore drilling off the coasts of Texas and Louisiana, it is expected that the new Port Arthur facility will quickly reach its projected capacity of one and a half million barrels of oil per day.

"CSA Commerce Secretary Patrick Bridger announced that several large manufacturing companies are soon to announce that they will be bringing assembly productions to the CSA that had been located for many years overseas.

"He cited as an example the Iron Man Tool Company, one of the world's largest manufacturers of power tools for household and construction use. Citing a vastly more competitive environment in the CSA, company President Walter Klinger said that plans are already underway to purchase three abandoned factories in and around Charleston, West Virginia.

"Klinger says that the three factories are suitable for retrofitting, a process that should begin within sixty days and be completed within eight months. He added that around five thousand total employees will be needed for production and support positions. Iron Man plans to announce next week how prospective employees can make application.

"And when we return in a minute, CSA Treasury Secretary Tom Edelstein will join me here in the studio to talk about how the new nation will be affected by the dramatic events taking place yesterday in Washington D.C.".

Roberta Croft once again appeared on camera, but this time sitting at a small round table across from Tom Edelstein.

"Mister Edelstein, thank you for being with me today and taking time out of what I know must be an extraordinarily busy schedule right now. First of all, I would like to ask you to comment on the remarkable news taking place in the United States."

Edelstein seemed to be straining to appear alert. "First of all, I wish to express my concern and sadness over so many senseless deaths."

"And how do you respond to the comments made on the United States Senate floor by Senator Mason from Delaware?"

"Anyone with as much as an elementary level of understanding of economics should have seen that the United States of America had needlessly and carelessly put itself in a critically vulnerable position. We were just unable to say no. To blame the United States bond crisis on the formation of the CSA is nothing more than a transparent and pathetic attempt to absolve the Congress of all blame for its own nonfeasance and misfeasance in its most basic responsibility to the American people."

"And how will the bond status affect the CSA?"

"Let's start from the ground up. Countless CSA citizens own United States government bonds. Most of those individuals own them through having mutual funds. And anyone watching the market throughout the night would have seen the net asset value of those bonds plunge upon the announcement by China, only to significantly rebound early this morning after the rather gutsy move by President Myers to virtually force the Congress into taking action.

"President Myers did the right thing. A cynic may say that she had no choice, however we got to this point of crisis because Presidents and members of Congress avoided doing what had to be done for years. I will go so far as to say this: if a decade ago, a President and Congress could have summoned the courage and integrity to do what we saw take place yesterday under duress, there would have been no secession.

"But it did happen, and the actions taken yesterday prevented the situation from becoming much worse. It's not only the retirement savings accounts and family savings accounts that hold government bonds or mutual funds consisting of them.

"The pension plans hold enormous sums of government bonds. That includes nearly all retirement pension plans for public employees at any level of government, and teachers. Those government bonds had always served as a stabilizing factor to offset the more volatile corporate bonds, let alone the stock market holdings.

"That is something that I always found amusing: liberal America always liked to bash American corporations as evil and greedy. But while those public employees and teachers joined with the unions to shout out at those corporations, it was those corporate profits and dividends and growth in stock value that provided for those comfortable retirement benefits.

"But now we have seen many of those pension portfolios fall as much as 50% in net asset value over the past several days. And that happened because we mortgaged ourselves and our future to provide for immediate gratification. And because of that same budget crisis, state governments do not have any money to prop up those pension systems. That includes states in the CSA. It is possible, however, that some or all of the CSA states will be in a better position to attempt to bolster some of those pension situations. Right now, it's a little soon to tell."

The anchor leaned forward. "And what about the welfare situation?"

"I find it to be the irony of all ironies, that the CSA states are going to be more able to provide assistance to the poor over the next several months. And that is simply because most of our states have been more cautious in the promises being made. And the employment forecast for the CSA for a year from now is just that – a forecast.

"But we are expecting that a year from now we will have an actual labor shortage in the CSA collectively. I would hope that within two years from today there will be a negligible unemployment rate for our able bodied citizens. We take the stand that able-bodied individuals receiving welfare benefits are going to have a work requirement attached, so such individuals may as well take a job and have a higher standard of living in the process. There may be difficulties over the interim. We hope that local charities and churches will be of assistance."

"And what about the currency?"

"Our task force on that matter had not completed its work when the secession happened more rapidly than expected. But their preliminary report in the recommendation that will be made to our Congress suggests that we use the same denominations, and that we have a relationship with the United States much like the one that has existed for so long with Canada.

"If the government of the United States is agreeable, we would like to contract with the United States Treasury for printing of currency. Similarly, we would like to have the Denver Mint produce our coins."

"Tom Edelstein... I thank you for being here today. And when we return from this brief break, we will be speaking with Vice President Franklin Chiles about what CSA citizens may have to look forward to in our first national elections, some of which may come as a surprise, so stay tuned. This is Roberta Croft for NewsNet Heartland."

"Thank you for staying with us, and I'm pleased to have with me now Vice President Franklin Chiles. Mister Vice President, thank you for taking the time out to be here with us this morning, especially considering everything that is taking place as we speak."

"My pleasure, Roberta."

"So I understand that the CSA may be breaking the mold when it comes to the election process?"

"First of all, preliminary discussions underway by the joint election committee of House and Senate members would indicate that our elections be held over a two-week period in March. Many of our states would be suffering some rough weather at that time, but we want to be on a different election cycle from the United States. Two weeks would allow for everyone in the snowy mountainous regions to vote.

"But there are more major changes being proposed, Roberta. There appears to be a great sentiment for having a popular election of members of the House of Representatives. Those members of Congress need to stay close to and in touch with the people.

"At the same time, it appears almost certain that the committee is going to recommend that each state legislature name its two Senators."

The anchor raised her eyebrows in response. "Wow... I see that causing quite a stir."

The Vice President nodded, and then a wide grin appeared on his face. "But get this... the committee is also going to recommend that the House of Representatives choose the President and Vice President."

The anchor's expression was one of definite surprise. "And do you expect this to be accepted by both chambers?"

"I am expecting that this entire package will be adopted."

"And what about parties?"

The Vice President nodded and pursed his lips. "Right now, everyone is still operating under the old labels of Republican and Democrat. I expect that to stay the same for a while. At the same time, I think that members of those parties in the CSA are going to be found to be much more conservative than their namesakes in the United States Congress."

"Vice President Franklin Chiles... thank you for joining me this morning."

"This is Marcia Bentley for NewsNet, and I am joined in our New York studio this morning by my colleague Mike Silver. And Mike, I arrived at the studio just shortly before sunrise, but I understand that you did not have an easy time getting to our building this morning."

The visibly shaken correspondent arched his eyebrows and managed to laugh. "I don't think that we have live coverage yet of the scene outside this building, but I had a rather memorable arrival about thirty minutes ago. Just as I turned onto the street, I was greeted by a crowd that was forming, so I slowed down and the next thing I knew people were pounding on my car, and there were even a couple of them with something in their hands... ball bats... tire irons... something.

"Both windows on the passenger side of my car are gone now, and the rear window has a large chunk out of it. Maybe I shouldn't say this, but I pulled a gun out of my console and waved it at them. That made them back away far enough that I was able to turn into the parking garage. I think I may be staying here for a couple of days."

Marcia looked down at her monitor. "We are getting reports from all over the city of New York of groups of protesters... rioters... I don't know what we should call them... surrounding people in cars. Now I... wait... I have Heather Kensington on the phone. Heather is one of our camera operators... Heather... can you hear me?"

"Yes... Marcia... I'm reporting from a hospital... I won't say which one. The staff here has loaned me the use of a small meeting room, because the atmosphere here is rather loud and chaotic. I was about three blocks away from the studio when I was stopped by several people standing in the street and refusing to move.

"I tried honking my horn, but that only made the crowd grow and come closer until they had surrounded my car and began to rock it. Then one of the women pointed to my NewsNet parking permit, and all hell broke loose."

"Heather, are you hurt?"

"I have a broken arm... they're coming to get me for surgery whenever they can.... I was lucky. The crowd started rocking the car back and forth while people were screaming at me. You know, I drive a small car, so a bunch of them reached beneath the car on the passenger side and flipped the car over onto the roof. Then this great big man started screaming at the others, and then he kicked in the window next to me and reached inside and helped me unbuckle my safety belt. He pulled me out of the car and was helping me get away.

"He was a really big man, and he picked me up in his arms and was shielding me, but a couple of other guys ran up and knocked him down, and he kind of fell on me and that's how I got the broken arm. But he picked me up again and carried me to this police cruiser that was just coming onto the scene. They called for an ambulance and that's how I ended up here at the hospital. And I just want to thank you, whoever you are."

Marcia Bentley was attempting to listen as she also watched her monitor. "Heather, what can you tell us about the crowd?"

"It's hard for me to say how many... maybe three hundred... maybe five hundred. I mean there were men... women... some teenagers, even kids. White people... black people... Hispanics... the man who rescued me was an African-American, and I hope that he didn't get hurt."

The anchor appeared to be upset as she listened. "Well, Heather... I hope you heal up okay, and thanks for calling in.

"Reports of disturbing incidents are coming in from most boroughs of New York City. And as I look at my monitor, I'm being told that the situation in Boston is continuing to deteriorate, and that violence is becoming more widespread this morning in Chicago.

"Oh, my... this is going to be a long day... Philadelphia police are attempting to clear the streets in some sections of the city, as protesters and rioters have begun to spread through the downtown area breaking windows and setting buildings on fire.

"Police in Atlanta, Georgia are reporting that demonstrators have closed off most lanes of Interstate 75, and the downtown area is now largely inaccessible due to protesters sitting down on the pavement on city streets.

"I'm too flustered to calculate the time zones, but Honolulu police are asking demonstrators to refrain from any property damage.

"Police in Cleveland and Cincinnati, Newark, Milwaukee... and it's still morning... Detroit... Tampa... all of these cities are now reporting demonstrations either in progress or some level of formation.

"Our morning producer Helen is trying to sort out some of this information that is flying toward us right now... cities in which protests have turned violent include... that's nice... New York... Boston, of course, and Chicago... Cincinnati...   I don't want to forecast trouble, but to be realistic about this, there are two hours difference between us and a lot of big cities on the West Coast. And Mike, I suppose that we are free to speculate a little right now. How do you see this playing out?"

"Well, Marcia... as I sit here picking tiny pebbles of glass from my shirt collar and my eyebrows, it is safe to say that I'm not feeling very at ease right now. I can only assume at this moment that the spreading violence is a result of the decision made yesterday that is going to have the effect by my own crude calculations of reducing public assistance income to the poor by an average of 75% in most states.

"We can talk all day long about how people came to be dependent upon the government, but many of those who are on assistance but are able-bodied, do not live in areas where there is a lot of employment to be gained by the most eager of job applicants.

"There are going to be many families... I can't put a number on it... I am just assuming that a lot of families are going to be mathematically unable to pay rent and buy food. And the question of medical coverage is totally unsettled as of this morning.

"Even if families move in together to share apartments, for example, it will still be a struggle to pay the rent and buy food. And landlords will be forced to choose between taking greatly reduced rent payments for their apartments, or leaving them empty.

"Further, there are some neighborhoods in some cities so densely populated by recipients of public aid, it will be difficult if not impossible for local businesses to keep their doors open. This is going to be very bad."

In the early afternoon, President Calista Myers sat in the Situation Room of the White House, sitting next to General Byron Zeller. The man in the Marine uniform sat in silence as did the President and the Vice President next to him. They were awaiting the momentary arrival of Secretary of Defense Lawrence Spencer and Secretary of State James Florentine.

Suddenly the door to the secured room opened, and a man in the uniform of an Army Major escorted in the two final participants in the special meeting. Everyone remained in silence as the two high – ranking officials took their seats and the President cleared her throat.

"I don't know that it was ever the intention of past officials to use this room for a purpose such as this. But I certainly feel that the security of our nation has absolutely been placed in a state of grave threat during the past twenty or so hours.

"To be quite candid with all of you, I really don't know how to categorize our current situation. General Zeller... I would like to hear your thoughts."

For a moment, the General seemed to be staring at the bill of the hat he had placed on the table in front of him, while also running a hand through the thinning hair atop his head. "I suppose that when civil unrest involving such levels of violence, destruction of property and even armed resistance becomes so widespread... I would have to label it as either rebellion, insurrection or even... civil war.

"I suppose many are wondering how we could arrive so rapidly at such a state of affairs. But I suppose that the most important logistic is what we refer to as social media. We seem to be experiencing a virtual state of a form of flash mob rebellion. Now there are large sections of Los Angeles that police cannot enter because of barricades. But I'm talking about barricades set up from the other side. The rioting and looting there has become so widespread, that people are beginning to flee the area, even the suburbs.

"And right here... the Lincoln Memorial... the Washington Monument... overrun and defaced. The subways have been seized and shut down. So much track has been vandalized that the repair work will take months.

"Now, there are cities with rampant unrest, looting, arson and fatalities in virtually every one of the... I can't even remember how many states we have now."

The President sighed and rubbed her forehead as she spoke. "At this moment, the Congress of the CSA is in the process of voting on admission applications from Kentucky, Georgia, Utah, Arizona and New Mexico." Her statement was received with a stunned silence until the General resumed.

"I do understand that Georgia is a real mess right now. In spite of their own budget situation, all of their National Guard units have been called up for duty in Atlanta. The city is under a state of emergency, and everything is shut down. Several guard units are being sent in just to keep the airport open. The airport is hardly the center of the rioting, but it's going to be swarming with troops just as a precaution. That airport is critical to the flight system of the entire... America needs to keep it open.

"Now things are even getting dicey in Ohio. That guy named Jim Brand that was on television yesterday... I think he was the leader of some type of patriot group or something. I heard on the radio on the way over here that he and his wife went for a walk last evening, and when they stopped to check the mail... I understood that it was a bomb in the mailbox that killed them.

"Now some of the rival factions that used to be content with punching each other on the lawn in Columbus are getting vicious. We had that bombing at that fundraiser for that state Senate candidate, and then all those militia guys got killed in a bombing in some gun store.

"I guess all that kind of caught my interest because I spent the first ten years of my life there in a place called Bluffton, and I still have a lot of family back there. The reason I bring all this up is that we are now getting reports from the rural parts of the state. People are starting to shoot at the homes and cars of the people who don't share the same vision for the future of Ohio.

"So I am assuming that there is a potential for the same type of thing in Illinois... Iowa... Maine... Michigan. So the point is, we seem to be heading for a situation in which most of our major cities have some degree of urban warfare going on. And while state authorities are trying to stomp on the big fires, they may be stretched too thin to keep those endless regions of rural areas safe and under control.

"What I'm saying is that before the day is out, things are going to be out of control. Let alone Boston and Chicago... I understand that even in smaller cities people are starting to panic about food supplies. Groups of people are going into stores in force, stealing food while overwhelmed employees stand by unable to do anything about it. Again... I'm not just talking about large cities here. People see all the reports on television, but what sticks in their minds will be the comments about food shortages. They are savvy enough to know that we are again in a depression. They realize that the welfare programs are going away. And as every hour goes by...".

The President stood and turned away and placed her hands on her hips. After moments of an uncomfortable silence, she turned slowly to once again face the others. "I think that we all understand the unspoken conclusion that the General has come to."

She slowly scanned the faces in the room. "I must say that I am in agreement with him. Do any of you disagree?"

In the late afternoon, President Calista Myers stood in front of the main entrance at The Pentagon, as a light breeze gently tossed the carefully styled bangs that fell upon her forehead. She watched in a state of near panic as the Pentagon media coordinator counted down the seconds until she would appear on live television.

"Some of you may be familiar with the structure behind me. For decades now, the Pentagon has been the operational headquarters for the Armed Forces of the United States of America.

"During the decades since this building was constructed, tens of thousands of uniformed and civilian military staff have maintained a vigilance within the halls of this uniquely shaped building. They have evaluated threats to our security, developed ways to enhance our security, and deliberated and developed the proper responses when that security was threatened.

"Therefore, I felt that it was only fitting and proper that I stand in the shadow of the Pentagon to address the nationwide state of insurrection that now threatens that security.

"Effective immediately, and under the direction of the Chairman of the Joint Chiefs of Staff General Byron Zeller, I decree that the United States of America is under a state of martial law. I take this step reluctantly, but the order must be restored so that our citizens can be protected, our businesses protected from arson and looting, and our national infrastructure preserved.

"As I speak, General Zeller is notifying state National Guard commanders of their responsibilities in seeing to it that citizens are made aware of matters such as curfew, restricted areas and emergency services such as distribution of food and medical care. Many of those criteria will be established at the state level.

"Please understand that I have given General Zeller unrestricted authorization to federalize any National Guard units. And it must be understood, that any military forces under federal command are hereby authorized to use lethal force in the enforcement of this decree of martial law.

"Let me say once again: military forces under federal command are hereby authorized to use lethal force in the enforcement of this decree of martial law.

"One final thing: I have spoken to President Bryce Hamilton of the Constitutional States of America. President Hamilton has agreed to facilitating the safe passage of military personnel stationed at bases located within the CSA, but still functioning as part of the Armed Forces of the United States as they are transferred as needed throughout the United States of America.

"It goes without saying that this address has provided me with the most difficult moment of my life. I pray that we can come to see to the needs of each other, extinguish our anger and regain the common bond that for so long made the United States of America the greatest nation on earth. May God bless you in this time of great crisis, this time of need, and this time of fear. And above all, may God bless the United States of America.

Day two hundred eleven of the CSA – Eden's Dawn

At 6:00 AM President Bryce Hamilton sat behind the modest desk in what had been nicknamed The Red Room of the CSA Hall of Administration in downtown Omaha. He smiled as he heard a tap on the door, knowing that Nina Burton had arrived to fly with him to Arlington, Texas, and then travel with him by armored limousine to Cowboys Stadium.

She walked into the room slowly and joined him in scanning the scene. "Are you going to miss it?"

"Not really. And over the past three weeks, being interrupted by the dialysis sessions... you know."

He rose cautiously, and then walked slowly around to the side of the desk. He silently pointed to a closet door, and Nina opened it and retrieved a folded – up walker.

"Thank you for returning with us to this special joint broadcast of NewsNet and NewsNet Heartland. The Inaugural celebration really kicked into gear about two hours ago with a musical celebration of the states of the CSA. The orchestra performed abbreviated versions of so many songs symbolizing not only individual states, but The South and the Great American West, the two regions that are most prominent in the new nation.

"Of course as time has drawn near to the swearing-in ceremonies, the approximately 80,000 people on hand have grown more energetic and boisterous. Needless to say, when the next to last song was played, that being The Eyes of Texas Are Upon You, the crowd, much of it from here in the Lone Star State, cheered loudly.

"But what brought the house down was the final musical item, a rousing rendition of They Call the Wind Mariah, sung by Samuel Addisson of the Dallas Opera. The Lerner and Loewe song, from the musical Paint Your Wagon, expresses the hardship and wonder encountered by those who settled the American West.

"And I hope that all of you were with us earlier today for the swearing in of the new Vice President of the CSA, Representative Walter Cortez. Those of you watching in the United States are likely not as familiar with Cortez as the rest of our viewers. However, then Representative Cortez made his mark quickly after the formation of the CSA, finding common ground between members of the Congress who want to exercise more control over illegal immigration while dealing with those already here.

"Vice President Cortez soon became the master of negotiation and compromise, and his star rose quickly. And now is the moment we have been waiting for... The Chief Justice of the Supreme Court of the Constitutional States of America is approaching the podium.

"Judge Emory Langley will now conduct the swearing-in...".

The Judge held out a Bible. "The President – elect will now recite the oath of office." There was a brief burst of cheering throughout the large stadium, and then the large venue became suddenly and respectfully silent as the new President stepped forward.

"I, Colleen McBride, do solemnly swear to uphold and defend the Constitution of the Constitutional States of America, to defend it from all enemies, foreign and domestic, and to adhere to the principles of America's founders. So help me God."

"So there you have it... Colleen McBride has been duly sworn in to serve the first full Presidential term for the Constitutional States of America. As you can see, she is waving to a cheering crowd, decked out in a dark gray pantsuit with a noticeably Western flair, a fashionable tan Stetson hat, and even a pair of Western boots.

"She is now trying to quiet the crowd, but having only marginal success as this large stadium full of people continues to cheer. You can only speculate that, perhaps in the back of everyone's mind there is a collective sense of relief that the new nation made it to this day... President Colleen McBride is now about to begin her Inaugural address...".

"My fellow citizens... I stand before you honored but humbled for the great privilege that has been bestowed upon me. I hope that I will justify the decision to make me your President.

"It is my hope that a year from now, when one of you is asked to name your President, you will have to think for a moment to remember my name. For if that is the case, we will have been successful in our quest to make your national government less relevant to your every day life.

"From this day on, however, we must not grow complacent in our duty to prevent government from being an intrusive element in our personal lives and businesses. Too many people have sacrificed too much.

"The easiest thing to do in life is to accept the re-creation of what you have previously known. But no matter how many years pass, no matter how many generations slip into our history, we can never again tolerate the mistakes that brought about the momentous events of the past two years.

"Before I conclude, I wish to thank those who served as interim officials in the government of the Constitutional States of America. But most of all, I wish to thank the man who suddenly became my mentor – President Bryce Hamilton."

The new President turned to face the man sitting several feet behind her, and joined in the applause and standing ovation that lasted for several minutes. Partway through, she leaned down to the elderly man and his wife, and he slowly rose to his feet with the help of a cane handed to him by one of his guards. He waved to the crowd, and then slowly sat back down.

The ovation finally subsiding, the new President once again turned to the microphone. "I cannot replace a person of the stature of Bryce Hamilton. I can only assume the same office, and keep in mind his goals, his hopes for...". The President's voice began to tremble: "... his...... his hopes for the... the future of our nation...uhm...oh, my.... the example he set... of courage...... of integrity......... of love of ... America...... will be ever present in my thoughts...... and prayers.

"I ask for God's special blessing on President and Cynthia Hamilton in this difficult time in their lives. May God bless all of you... may God bless the Constitutional States of America... May God bless all of America."

"Now, the cheering begins again as the orchestra strikes up a fast – paced version of 'Oklahoma' in honor of President McBride's home state. As you can see, she's leaning down and embracing Bryce and Cynthia Hamilton. They really have not known each other that long, but they rapidly developed a close relationship.

"In a recent interview, Cynthia Hamilton went so far as to say that Colleen McBride had become the daughter she never had. So while the new President learns to cope with being in her new position, she will be distracted to some degree by seeing someone who had so impacted her life deal with faltering health."

"This is Megan Howard for NewsNet Heartland, and I want to thank you for joining us this evening for this exclusive interview with President Colleen McBride." Viewers saw the two women sitting in a set of lawn chairs in the rear of Prairie Manner, the old and stately Omaha home that had been purchased by Bryce and Cynthia Hamilton, and donated to the CSA for use as a Presidential residence.

"Madam President... I think that by now everyone understands that Bryce and Cynthia Hamilton are still living here. And of course, everyone wants to know about their health."

"Yes Megan... I know that we get a lot of inquiries. As for the President, he attempts to be very candid with everyone that he talks to, and he makes it clear that he probably has no more than a year to live. As for Mrs. Hamilton, she is frail but holding her own.

"Our children spend a lot of time with them. They have somewhat bonded as you may expect. But I make sure that our children have a clear understanding about their conditions. And as for me, I am blessed to have such wonderful advisers and friends in my home."

"I know that it is difficult to speak of the ongoing development of the CSA when virtual depression conditions are rampant in the United States. But how pleased are you with the results of the CSA business environment?"

"I have to emphasize, Megan, that the business environment and our emphasis on personal freedom go hand in hand. The CSA quickly became a nation in which individuals and families could start a business, confident of dealing with a bare minimum of regulations. At the same time, our citizens can go to work for an employer, knowing that if that employer goes out of business, it will not be because of government meddling and irrational levels of taxation.

"I must admit that I was stunned by how quickly we faced labor shortages in some of the states. Overall, we are finding ourselves statistically in a state of what is referred to as full employment.

"There have been a variety of segments of our economy that have simply blossomed. The new auto plants are being hindered in production because of the dire economic situation in the United States, but they are still doing a lot of exporting to Europe. In addition the new plant making those miniature commuter cars for some of the Third World nations are exceeding initial sales expectations. Of course, anything to do with the firearms industry is flourishing, and that includes a healthy export market.

"But the star of our economic show is the energy production boom. Fortunately, many thousands of people from the United States have been able to come here to find employment in the oil and gas production complexes. And many thousands more have moved here to find work in building new homes and working in service industries."

"President McBride... I know that there has been some criticism of the CSA for the decision to quickly implement more rigid immigration rules, including for United States citizens. Would you please comment on that?"

"We had hoped to maintain what would have been virtually open borders between the two Americas. That still works for travel and business. But as times became more desperate in the United States, and we found ourselves dealing with people who wanted to reside here without contributing to our society or our economy, we were forced to make potential new citizens apply for the right."

"And I understand that the CSA has actually deported some people back to the United States?"

"That is correct. We did not want to establish a bureaucracy to deal with immigration from the United States, but some came here for the wrong reasons. We make it clear... we do not give out welfare benefits like candy, and to be hired you must now have a work permit. We also have a citizenship program similar to that we were all long familiar with in the United States."

"None of us can forget the uproar and outrage that took place when you had various state National Guard units clear out those immigrant camps."

"I want everyone to understand, Megan... everyone was given the choice to apply for work permits or to be taken back to the border of the state from which they had crossed over. It was one of the hardest decisions I ever had to make.

"But I did not want to repeat the mistake we made for so many years along our border with Mexico. People were leaving a chaotic environment... I understand that. But their environment was chaotic because their federal government brought chaos upon itself, and their states chose not to join the CSA.

"President Hamilton reinforced to me in his wise counsel what my parents had taught me, and life's experience has reinforced... decisions have consequences. I feel sorry for innocent citizens caught up in that reality. But the CSA collectively continues to send trainloads and truckloads of food relief to the United States.

"The states that formed the CSA took a great risk. Fortunately, our success allows us to do what we can to mitigate the crisis. But we cannot be all things to all people, and as I said before, we are not going to bring that same crisis upon ourselves.

"Because the United States became reckless and order broke down, we are having to spend resources on security that should not be required. We have to fight increasing gang infiltration in several areas, and we have to make sure that our state and local law enforcement and National Guard personnel have the necessary resources to protect legitimate CSA residents from intruding, marauding thugs."

"Earlier you referenced how vibrant the energy production sector of the economy has become. Would you address the dispute between the energy companies that are still required by previously established contracts to place their oil and natural gas on the global commodities markets, and the newly formed companies that refuse to do so?"

"Certainly... I want to say first that I will not be pleased to see companies located in the CSA not fulfilling obligations entered ɔ previous to our nationhood. Of course, we have tried to minimize our regulatory interference. I can only speculate that our Supreme Court may have to resolve that.

"But every contract has an expiration date. Part of freedom is having the right to sell a product to whomever you so choose. If you have an oil company, and you want to sell it to a refining company in Texas, or a plastics factory in New Jersey, that should be your choice. Just because there is a global oil market, that does not mean that you have to submit to some artificial pricing structure.

"We are the Constitutional States of America. We have a carefully stipulated defense pact with the United States. Aside from that, we have so far managed to avoid what used to be called foreign entanglements. We have signed no treaties or international trade agreements. We have not joined the United Nations. Some of those things may change through time, but those changes will come by way of very careful and cautious deliberation. After all, if we wanted to operate by peer pressure, we could have all just stayed at home."

"This is Megan Howard for NewsNet Heartland, reporting to you from the CenturyLink Center, the home court of the Creighton University Bluejays mens' basketball team. It was another era when President Bryce Hamilton was a powerful force for the team, but as he neared death, he joked to wife Cynthia that he wanted to appear at center court one more time, but promised that he would not startle the mourners by suddenly leaping upward this time.

"As our cameras zoom in, you can see his wife of more than five decades sitting next to the coffin and receiving words of sympathy and comfort from the line of visitors that is stretching far beyond our sight. And you may be surprised, but that is indeed President Colleen McBride standing behind her with her hands on her close friend's shoulders.

"Just ten days ago, President Hamilton agreed to a final interview, under the condition that it not be broadcast until after his death. We will bring that to you in a moment. As you watch, you can see that he labored to speak as he struggled with the last stages of kidney failure and leukemia.

"Still, as you will see now, Bryce Hamilton was his direct, candid and confident self right up to the end. And now we bring you that interview...".

Viewers suddenly saw the correspondent sitting in a room dominated by a fireplace in the background. Several feet from her sat the former President.

"Mister President... I want to thank you for granting this interview."

"It's my pleasure."

"I would like to ask you first of all, how you think history will treat your actions over the past three years?"

"That would all depend upon the point of view of the historian doing said writing. An historian with a bias toward a socialistic form of government will denigrate my actions. One with a free - market or libertarian slant will be much more kind."

"I was wondering if you would talk about some of the things ιnat happened as a result of your movement that you simply did not expect."

"Every action you take is going to generate some affect you could not have predicted. You simply cannot predict the reactions of everyone affected by a certain scenario. But that does not mean that you do not do what you think is right and necessary out of fear of unknown consequences.

"I always have felt that you should not ask a question if you are not certain that you can handle hearing every conceivable answer. I just know that everything worthwhile in life involves risks. The only way you can avoid the consequences of your actions, is to take no actions."

"But do you have regrets about the course of action you took?"

"Give me…… just a moment………… my only regret is that I did not become involved sooner in that movement."

"What are the best things, in your opinion, that resulted from the secession of states and the establishment of the Constitutional States of America?"

"First of all, tens of millions of Americans are now living with more personal and economic freedom. There are areas, St. Louis in particular, that have seen prosperity unlike had been known in a couple of generations.

"A new nation came about that has virtual full employment, a minimum of government interference in business, and the chance for any person to take part in this environment of opportunity. And in the process, they are seeing their government actively seek ways in which to reduce or even avoid taxes.

"We have also established a nation where people are free to protect themselves and their families and businesses, and those who are adjudged to be a threat to those freedoms are dealt with firmly.

"We have a nation in which our laws and our judicial system deal with facts, not emotions and feelings. And our Constitution means what our Constitution says. Documents do not evolve."

"If you don't mind, Mister President... I would like to ask you if there are results of the secession and establishment of the CSA that bother you."

"Many. I think I established earlier in this interview that I find that unintended consequences are an unfortunate reality in the making of a decision on any matter of importance.

"As for those who blamed the bond crisis on our decision to withdraw from the United States, I can only shake my head in disappointment at such cowardice of principle. The bonds were vulnerable because the bonds had been rendered vulnerable by the actions and inactions of a Congress of the United States that had proved itself unworthy of holding the federal checkbook in its hands.

"Let me correct that, and replace checkbook with credit card. You can only write so many checks before they bounce, but you can keep on charging goodies on a credit card until you hit the limit, and then you can call the bank and ask for them to approve a bigger limit.

"That is how we operated as a nation. To try to place the blame on those who demanded the spending stopped is an absurdity.

"At the same time, many things happened that I wish would not have happened. The establishment of the CSA is not responsible for the people who died in violence in so many cities, small towns and even rural areas.

"The CSA did not cause the shortages of food, shelter and medicines. Those shortages came about through the violence of those who could not fathom that they were not born to be provided for by taking away what others had worked for.

"When the Council for a Free America was founded, it came about through the efforts of many individuals who had tried to convince our national leaders that our society was promoting practices and lifestyles that would prove to be self- destructive at the point of any significant economic downturn. To my dying day, perhaps next week, I will be struggling to understand how someone can reach a state wide office, or be elected to the House of

ntatives or the Senate, and not understand the simple
_iple that what you subsidize, you get more of.

"I feel badly that the United States finds itself in a new Great Depression. It sickens me to see the rampant poverty, the overwhelming homelessness and the lack of food that states in the CSA are trying to help alleviate by the donations and shipments.

"Hopefully, our decision to relinquish any claims to a portion of the gold bullion at Fort Knox will allow the United States to put that gold up for sale on the world market to help alleviate some of those critical problems it is facing. We are working our way back to a gold standard for our economy, and that gold will be mined and produced in the CSA.

"Perhaps I have not properly answered one of your questions... I feel very badly that Southern California has been so savaged by the turn of events. I feel badly for those who fled, and I understand that Southern California had always held a special place in our national identity before the withdrawal.

"I can only hope and pray that some type of order can be restored, rather than the current situation that leaves so many millions without a certainty of their nationhood. It is my hope that martial law can soon end in the United States, but I know that the United States military will need more time to gain full control of Los Angeles and the surrounding counties."

The reporter began to speak, and then hesitated. "Do you have any regrets in what has been a long and memorable life?"

"I regret...... that I...... I never agreed to Cynthia's wish to...... adopt children. It was unfortunate for us.........uhm...... it was unfortunate for some children who missed out on having an undoubtedly wonderful mother and a cranky and grumpy father."

Hamilton seemed to struggle for a moment to catch his breath. "I also wish that I would have gone back to Creighton to teach for at least a few years."

"Mister President...... is there anything else you would like to say to our viewers?"

"Just always remember that...... a baby is born free. Any restrictions on his or her freedom are......... are imposed by society, whether.......... justifiably or unjustifiably. As we grow up, we must decide for ourselves which is which.

"If you decide that a restriction is unjust, and you do not protest, you are betraying that freedom that was given you at birth. And when you protest, know that there will be consequences to your protest. But in any case, know that someday, in your last days, before you face God's judgment, you will determine for yourself how well you...... nurtured that initial and...... precious gift."

The End

Made in the USA
Lexington, KY
08 November 2019